SERPENTINE

CINDY PON

Month9Books

Published by Month9Books
Cover illustration by Zachary Schoenbaum
Title design and book jacket by Najla Qamber Designs
Cover Copyright © 2015 Month9Books

Month9Books

PRAISE FOR SERPENTINE

"*Serpentine* is unique and surprising, with a beautifully-drawn fantasy world that sucked me right in! I love Skybright's transformative power, and how she learns to take charge of it." -- Kristin Cashore, *New York Times* bestselling author of the Graceling Realm Series

"Vivid worldbuilding, incendiary romance, heart-pounding action, and characters that will win you over--I highly recommend *Serpentine*." -- Cinda Williams Chima, bestselling author of the Seven Realms and Heir Chronicles

"*Serpentine*'s world oozes with lush details and rich lore, and the characters crackle with life. This is one story that you'll want to lose yourself in." -- Marie Lu, *New York Times* bestselling author of *Legend* and *The Young Elites*

Dedicated to Juliet Grames, the best editor I never had.
This sister friendship story is for you.

SERPENTINE

CINDY PON

CHAPTER ONE

The mountain was still shrouded in mist.

Skybright felt its cold tendrils against her nape as she climbed the giant cypress tree. She could almost believe she was in the heavens and the immortals themselves lived beyond the high monastery walls. A strange quiet had settled over Tian Kuan mountain, as if the mist had turned into something solid, blanketing their surroundings in silence. Skybright loved mornings like these. She scooted further up the thick gnarled branch, clinging with her legs, not daring to look down. Rough bark scraped her palms, and she held her breath as she grabbed a branch above her with both hands and eased herself onto her feet, crouching low, like a cat about to spring. She glimpsed the far edge of a square; dense fog hovered just above the green stone tiles of curved rooflines.

Zhen Ni gasped from below.

Skybright glanced down at her mistress. Zhen Ni's pale face was turned upward, her eyes wide. Skybright quickly looked away and gulped. She had never been this high up before--if she fell she'd surely break her neck.

"Take care," her mistress said.

Take care! Zhen Ni was the one who had concocted this mad plan to begin with, convincing Skybright the monastery wall truly wasn't *that* high, and that she could climb the cypress tree with ease. Curiosity was her mistress's weakness, and she simply had to know what went on within the monastery, behind its grand facade. Of course, Skybright would have to do the climbing. She couldn't glare at her mistress, as it meant risking a glance downward again. Instead, Skybright rose slowly, willing her legs to keep steady, until she finally stood, her cloth shoes digging into the wood. She hugged the higher branch to her chest and murmured a prayer to the Goddess of Mercy.

Standing, she had a full view of the immense square hidden behind the walls, flanked by two red rectangular temples. A pair of fierce stone lions guarded each temple, and tall cypress trees dotted the edges of the square. Hundreds of monks, dressed in slate blue sleeveless tunics and trousers, sat cross-legged on the gray stone floor. While Zhen Ni and Skybright had been ascending the mountain, the monks' strong voices had reverberated across the tall peak, counting as they practiced their forms. Now, they were so still and silent that Skybright blinked, wondering if they were statues as well—or an illusion. Each monk's head was closely shaved, and they sat with their elbows resting against their knees, exact replicas of one another.

Not even the wind stirred.

"What can you see?" Zhen Ni asked, her impatient voice too loud to be a whisper.

Skybright ignored her. She scanned the endless rows of monks, each offering a three-quarter profile, when her eyes rested on one that did not appear like the rest. His hair wasn't shorn, but shoulder length, and tied back. His tunic and trousers were tan. He sat in the very back, near the edge. As if he sensed her watching, he tilted his chin until their eyes met across the great distance.

She froze, feeling caught. And in those few quick moments, his gaze swept across her, seeming to take in every detail, before he turned his head back toward the magnificent temples, his expression never changing. Heart thudding, Skybright maneuvered until she was straddling the branch again, then scrambled as fast as she could down the giant cypress.

Her legs trembled when she finally reached the ground.

"Well, what did you see?" Zhen Ni tugged at her sleeve, her face shining with curiosity.

"Monks. So many of them." She began walking back toward town, not waiting for her mistress as proper decorum dictated.

Surprised, Zhen Ni picked up her skirt so she wouldn't trip on the embroidered hem and followed. "Could you see their faces?"

She shook her head, even as she recalled the slender eyes of the boy who had seen her. "They were meditating."

The two girls hurried now through the trees. The fog had begun to lift, allowing glimmers of sunlight, and the earth was soft and damp beneath their feet. Skybright and Zhen Ni clasped hands and ran—they would be in trouble if their absence were noticed.

Skybright brought a late morning meal of rice porridge to Zhen Ni's spacious reception hall and dined with her mistress. The two girls were now draped across Zhen Ni's expansive bed, playing a game of Go. Her mistress was the better player, yet Skybright still had to keep an eye on the game, to be sure she never won by chance or from carelessness on Zhen Ni's part. The last time she had won, Zhen Ni had pounded the bed so hard with her fists, the black and white stones scattered and bounced to the floor. Skybright never did find all of the pieces.

Morning light filled the bedchamber through lattice windows cast wide open. The walls were papered in the palest green, and Zhen Ni had decorated them with several magnificent lotus paintings—her favorite flower. Despite the open windows, the bedchamber was warm, and Skybright felt her chin dip, her lids growing heavy. Zhen Ni gave a languid yawn and stretched like a cat onto her side, leaning her head against her arm. A sharp tap on the reception hall's door startled both girls. Skybright jumped from the tall platform bed as Zhen Ni swung her legs down the side, patting the gold ornaments woven in her hair.

"Your mother's bringing a guest to visit, mistress," Rose, another handmaid, said from outside.

"Now?" Zhen Ni asked as Skybright smoothed her mistress's peach tunic and skirt.

"She's on her way, mistress," replied Rose's muffled voice.

Zhen Ni sighed and gave Skybright an exasperated look before saying, "Thank you, Rose."

Lady Yuan entered the quarters soon after, trailed by a woman in her forties, but dressed much more plainly, with her hair pulled into a tight bun. If Lady Yuan was an iridescent king fisher, then this woman clad in brown and gray was a dull hen. Yet there was a keen sharpness to the woman's eyes as she took in the opulent reception hall, decorated in pale gold and pink, before her gaze glided to Zhen Ni's face.

"I've brought a special surprise for you today, Daughter. Madame Lo is the best-regarded seer of our time. We're fortunate to have her visiting so far from the Capital." Lady Yuan smiled at both girls, her excitement obvious. She had grown plumper in these past few years; it had softened her features and rounded her chin.

Madame Lo inclined her head. "You honor me, Lady Yuan. It's been too long since I've visited the mountains. I consider it a retreat."

Zhen Ni bowed to the woman. "The honor is mine." A

flush colored her cheeks as she turned to her mother. "Why didn't you tell me?"

"I wasn't certain if Madame Lo could make it until she actually arrived at our door," Lady Yuan said.

Zhen Ni swept an arm toward the curved-back chairs. "Please sit."

"You've not yet started your monthly letting," the seer stated, and everyone froze as if she had picked up a vase and smashed it to the floor.

"Mother?" Zhen Ni's voice was barely a whisper.

Lady Yuan sat down, arranging her silk skirt with nervous fingers.

"Dear girl, the fact that you've not reached womanhood shines as bright on your face as the moon in full bloom. I'm a seer, after all." Instead of following her hostess' lead and sitting, Madame Lo stood before them and scrutinized Zhen Ni. Despite her plain dress, two stunning jade bracelets encircled the fortuneteller's fine-boned wrist. One in a clear crisp green, and the other a deep lavender, both wrought with delicate gold details. They flashed and gleamed under the bright lantern lights, mesmerizing Skybright. Madame Lo lifted a hand to her chin, and her dark, piercing eyes slid to Skybright's own face for a breath before she said, "But don't fret, Mistress Yuan, your monthly letting will start soon enough."

A chill slithered down Skybright's spine when her eyes had met the seer's, and she retreated a step to leave when Zhen Ni grabbed her hand and pulled her to the plush chair beside her own. "So, Madame Lo, how do you tell your fortunes?" Her mistress wore a faint smile, but Skybright heard the hesitancy in her voice.

The seer gathered her brown skirt and finally seated herself. "I use your birth date and time, and study your facial features as well."

Zhen Ni ducked her head, staring at her folded hands. "I see," she murmured.

"Tell us what you've divined," Lady Yuan said, turning to the other woman across the enameled table. "Will she have a good husband? And many children?"

Zhen Ni caught her lower lip between her teeth, something she did when she was anxious. The familiar clatter of china against lacquered trays, a pleasant sound, carried from the covered corridor outside, along with the barely perceptible whisper of slippered feet. Rose entered, followed by another handmaid, Oriole, who set small dishes of lychees and sweets on the tables beside them. The delicate aroma of jasmine tea filled the reception hall. Pouring the brew into celadon cups, Rose then offered one to each of the women with both hands. Her dark eyes flickered to Lady Yuan, and the lady gave the barest nod before Rose gave a steaming cup to Skybright as well.

The two handmaids then slipped out, after bowing their heads.

They took time to sip their tea, quiet for a long moment, before Zhen Ni, with a raised chin, finally met Madame Lo's knowing eyes and asked, "Will I fall in love?"

"Love!" Lady Yuan cut in. "Love comes later, Daughter."

"When did you fall in love with Father?" Zhen Ni plucked at the delicate beading on her sleeve edge.

"Not until ten years after we were wed," Lady Yuan said. "Love takes time." She nodded at Zhen Ni, as if in encouragement. But Zhen Ni wouldn't look at her mother.

"I've composed and read her star chart according to her birth date and time. And what they tell me confirms what I see in your features, Mistress Yuan."

They all leaned forward while the seer pressed the tips of her long fingers together, her wide mouth drawn tense. Skybright wondered if the pause was for theatrics. But when Madame Lo spoke, it was with such care and authority that the thought disappeared from her mind.

"You're a willful girl."

Zhen Ni crossed her arms and reclined into the cushion. Skybright struggled to keep her face straight.

"This will pose challenges for you. Cause grief for you and your family. The shape and set of your chin only emphasize what your star chart indicates. You will love. Truly and deeply. The slight tilt of your eyes, the sheen to them, say as much. You're a romantic, and sensual—see the shape of your upper lip, and the curve of your lower. You will suffer heartache."

Zhen Ni's dark brows had drawn together, and she gripped her hands so tightly that the nails bit into her skin.

Madame Lo rose from her seat. She was a slight woman and moved with an assurance that lent her grace. Her brown tunic and skirt were loose and edged with gray, worn only for function. Skybright tried to imagine the woman in turquoise or lavender—any bright color—but was unable. The seer didn't need any extravagance but the glittering bracelets at her wrist, and the sharp light of her dark eyes. Madame Lo kneeled beside Zhen Ni's chair and extended a hand to her face. Her mistress shrank from the older woman, as if her fingertips were barbed.

"Her ears are beautifully shaped. See how thick the lobes are? This coupled with the wideness of her nose all point to her fortune in having been born into such an illustrious family. You'll find a very wealthy husband for her to marry, Lady Yuan." Madame Lo stood and returned to her chair, before taking another sip of tea. "She'll have at least two children. More, I cannot say."

"Will she marry an eldest son?" Lady Yuan asked. "Will she bear a boy herself?"

"I fear I have nothing more specific, Lady Yuan."

Zhen Ni had not relaxed beside her, but was still sitting rigid as a bamboo stalk, and leaning toward Skybright as if for shelter. "How can I marry well yet suffer heartache?" asked Zhen Ni.

"One does not exclude the other," said the seer.

"We all suffer from the pangs of love at least once in our lives, Daughter. It's nothing to worry over. The important thing is that you'll marry well and have children!" Lady Yuan smiled, her face glowing with pleasure.

"I think I've heard enough, Madame Lo," Zhen Ni said briskly, and her mother cleared her throat before taking a sip of tea. Zhen Ni blushed. "You honor me with a personal reading."

"It was a pleasure," Madame Lo replied. "I hope it has

helped to ease your mother's mind."

"My gratitude, Madame Lo," said Lady Yuan.

Skybright eyed the ginger candy on a plate beside her. It was Zhen Ni's favorite, but she hadn't touched any of the sweets since they had been brought. Skybright would have liked some lychees, but decorum didn't allow her to eat until everyone else had taken something for herself first. Instead, she stood and refilled the teacups. The fragrant scent of jasmine rose with the steam.

"What about a reading for Skybright?" Zhen Ni asked after a long pause.

Skybright almost exclaimed aloud, but bit her tongue.

"Skybright? Of course." Lady Yuan said. "But what's there to tell?"

Madame Lo turned her attention to Skybright fully for the first time, and Skybright sank deeper into her seat, feeling exposed. "I would need her birth date and time. A star chart takes at least three days to prepare."

"We don't know when Skybright was born, exactly," Zhen Ni said.

Madame Lo studied her face as if she were a painting. Skybright willed herself to keep her head raised. "You're Zhen Ni's handmaid?"

"Yes. And my companion since we were babes."

"Let the girl speak for herself," the seer said.

All three looked to Skybright, and she swallowed, feeling the heat rise to her cheeks. She wasn't used to being noticed, much less being the center of attention. "I'm an orphan."

"I see," Madame Lo replied. "And you were taken in by the Yuans?"

"She was left on our doorstep in a basket--"

"She wasn't more than a few days' old--"

Lady Yuan and Zhen Ni spoke over each other but both stopped abruptly when Madame Lo slapped her palm against the carved armrest. Lady Yuan jolted in her chair and Zhen Ni attempted to appear contrite.

"It's as they say, Madame Lo," Skybright said. "I know nothing more beyond that."

The seer beckoned with a curl of her fingers. "Come here, girl."

Skybright rose and stood before Madame Lo, feeling the damp of her palms. She had spent very little time wondering about her past, her parents, where she came from. It seemed pointless and impractical. Her life was full with daily responsibilities and rituals, with being a handmaid and companion to Zhen Ni. Now, this stranger might tell her more about her future or her past—probably useless or false knowledge, as far as Skybright was concerned. If she had a family, if her parents were still alive and wanted her, wouldn't they have come back for her by now?

"Kneel," Madame Lo said.

Skybright lowered herself onto the cold stone floor. The seer took her chin in one hand, turning her face this way and that, as a merchant would study cattle before purchasing. Skybright held her arms still at her sides, her hands fisted.

"There's an unusual symmetry to your face." Madame Lo

tilted Skybright's head to examine her ears. "Your features reveal little to me." Skybright wanted to jerk away, but steadied herself. "She's no classic beauty," Madame Lo went on, speaking to Zhen Ni and Lady Yuan directly. "See how the mouth is too full, the eyes set slightly far apart. The nose is narrow, the bridge too tall—there is no wealth there. No fortune. Yet the face as a whole—"

"I've always thought Skybright quite pretty," Zhen Ni said.

"Yes. Not a classic beauty, but the features come together to create something quite alluring. Almost unearthly."

"But this tells us so little, Madame Lo," Lady Yuan said, choosing a candied persimmon from the tray.

"Will she meet a good man?" Zhen Ni asked.

"Daughter!" Lady Yuan reprimanded.

Because they all knew Skybright would be a handmaid to Zhen Ni for life, and never marry.

"She could take a lover," Zhen Ni retorted.

Skybright bowed her head, and Madame Lo patted her hot cheek, as if in sympathy. Then the seer's grip tightened, her long nails digging into Skybright's face, and Skybright gasped in surprise and pain. Grimacing, Madame Lo dropped her hand, then pressed her knuckles against her eyes. "I'm sorry, Skybright," she murmured. "This has never happened to me before."

The seer's complexion had turned ashen, and Skybright could see she was unsettled. Alarmed, she sensed that Madame Lo was rarely fazed, much less showing it as she did now. She jumped to her feet, lifting the ceramic pot so she could pour the seer more tea.

"What's the matter?" Lady Yuan exclaimed.

"When I touched Skybright, her image changed. It was as if her true self was veiled, and I was unable to see her clearly. I've never encountered the like before in any of my readings, and I've done hundreds." Madame Lo reached for her teacup and took a long sip. Her hand trembled. The seer drew a breath before saying, "But she's strong. That much comes across."

Zhen Ni nibbled on a ginger candy and watched Skybright with interest. "Have you ever thought of yourself as alluring, Sky? As strong?"

"Never, mistress," Skybright replied. Madame Lo's revelations meant little to her—they were only frivolous nonsense.

"I can see it," Zhen Ni said, her dark eyes gleaming as she nodded to the seer. "I never noticed before, but now I can see it."

Zhen Ni fiddled with the jars and bottles on her vanity as Skybright brushed her black hair then plaited it, weaving luminous pearls into the single braid. Her mistress had been quiet since Madame Lo's visit earlier in the day, her usually animated face appearing pensive for much of the afternoon. In an attempt to coax her into a better mood, Skybright had suggested a new hairstyle and outfit in time for Zhen Ni's evening meal with her mother in the main hall. Her mistress had agreed with a distracted wave of her hand.

"Mama said a family friend's daughter will be staying with us through the summer," Zhen Ni said and began chewing on her nail. "She's our age."

Skybright swatted at her mistress's hand.

The smile Zhen Ni gave her lacked its usual mischievousness. "I hate waiting. I wish it would never happen." Their eyes met in the bronzed mirror, and Skybright took the opportunity to adjust the jade lotus pendant encircling her mistress's neck.

Skybright knew she wasn't talking about the girl who would be visiting.

"I know Mama's eager to show me that book as soon as my monthly letting begins."

Zhen Ni's older sister, Min, had sneaked *The Book of Making* to share with them when they were just fourteen years. All three had gawked at the dozens of illustrations depicted, teaching a bride how to best please her future husband in the bedchamber and become with child quickly. Now, two years later, Min was wed and living with her husband's family, already expecting her first babe.

"To think Mama's so desperate to marry me off, she hired that seer!" Zhen Ni said. "You're so fortunate not to have to … suffer through any of it."

Skybright began making Zhen Ni's expansive platform bed, straightening the silk sheets and plumping the brocaded cushions. Her mistress had lain in it for much of the afternoon, without ever falling asleep. "I'll go with you when you marry, and have to leave the Yuan manor too."

"You would come with me, Sky?" Zhen Ni grabbed her hand and smiled coyly, knowing Skybright had no choice.

Skybright rolled her eyes. "Of course."

"It would be a great comfort to me to have you by my side." Zhen Ni sighed, her shoulders drooping.

Skybright laughed and, because she looked so pitiful, gripped her mistress's hand. Zhen Ni's most beautiful feature was her eyes, almond shaped and a deep honeyed brown. They often appeared to have sheen to them, as if she were on the verge of uproarious laughter or dramatic tears. She was half a head taller than Skybright, and more slender of build.

And as Zhen Ni considered her, her mouth twisted into a scheming smile, one that Skybright knew all too well. Wary, she dropped her mistress's hand.

"You know you're supposed to help me. Teach me to be a better wife to my future husband."

"Teach you?"

Zhen Ni nodded. "A good handmaid … practices with her mistress."

Skybright blushed, finally realizing what she was implying. The illustrations from *The Book of Making* had always featured a man and a woman. It had never crossed her mind that … Skybright swallowed, before saying, "I've never heard of such a thing."

"You wouldn't have. But Min told me some households require it of their daughters before they marry, to make them better wives. It's called mirroring." Zhen Ni grinned wider, the same wicked grin as when she had plucked the eyeballs from the steamed fish when they were eight years and convinced Skybright to eat one, telling her it was a delicacy and would make her smarter. She would never forget the wet, gristly texture of it, the hard marble in the middle. How it had burst in her mouth. Zhen Ni had cackled when she spat it out, almost retching.

"Don't worry, Sky." Zhen Ni drew closer, then leaned forward and pressed her mouth against Skybright's.

Skybright startled but didn't pull back. Her mistress's eyes were closed, and the delicate scent of peach cream enveloped her senses—the cream she had rubbed into Zhen Ni's face and throat earlier. Her lips were soft, supple, making Skybright suddenly aware of how rough her own were.

Zhen Ni put her hand on one shoulder and squeezed, before she spun away and collapsed onto the bed, giggling. "Oh!" She rolled, quite unladylike, twisting the sheets. "Oh," she snorted, "We just had our first kiss!"

After a few moments, she sat up and rubbed the tears from her eyes. "How was it?"

Skybright hadn't moved, not knowing how to respond, afraid of what her mistress might suggest next. "Your lips … were soft."

Zhen Ni covered her mouth with both hands and began laughing uncontrollably again. "Dear darling Skybright." She shook her head. "There is no guile to you. It's why I adore you."

"How did it feel to you?" Skybright was too curious not

to ask.

Zhen Ni scrubbed at her mouth with the back of her hand with exaggerated disgust. "It was like kissing my own sister!"

Skybright pitched a fat cushion at her, and Zhen Ni squealed, barely dodging it in time. She then fell into bed and laughed with her.

Skybright couldn't fall asleep that night.

It was near the end of the sixth moon, and the summer air was heavy and hot. She kicked the thin sheet aside and wound her thick hair away from her damp neck, trying to find a cool spot on the narrow bed. Her mind kept returning to the kiss she had exchanged with Zhen Ni. The kiss itself had been chaste, like she had shared with Zhen Ni before on the cheek. But there was an undercurrent there, an expectation, a bated breath. It seemed to have stoked something deep inside of her, as if touching her mouth to someone else's had kindled a hidden desire, dormant until now.

She let out a long sigh, feeling the back of her arms stick to the bamboo mat. The face of the young monk who had glimpsed her clinging to a branch bloomed beneath her eyelids, how his expression never changed as he assessed her, as if they stood in front of each other at arm's length. Who was he? And why wasn't his hair cut like all the others?

Her dreams, when she finally fell asleep, were scattered and warm.

Then insistent.

Skybright woke in a fevered haze, feeling as if she were drunk. It was still night, so dark that she couldn't see. Heat radiated from her groin downward, pulsing through her legs, tingling her feet, then ricocheting back again. Her thighs and calves ached of it, of melding and severing.

She gasped, trying to rise. She clutched at her legs, and her hands sprang back as she cried out. No sound came and she whimpered, rubbing her ears. Had she gone deaf as well? Skybright touched her legs again, but they were no longer there, replaced by something sleek and supple that wasn't her skin, wasn't her flesh.

This must be a dream.

A nightmare.

She tried to swing her lower half off the bedside, but instead thrashed and thumped to the stone floor below. Its rough coldness scraped her torso and elbows. Unable to stand, she dragged herself across the ground toward the lantern resting on her small cherry wood dresser. Something knocked over and hit her back. She hissed. Pulling herself up, she grabbed the lantern and a match. Her hands shook as she lit the wick.

The light's warmth was familiar, comforting. Skybright twisted, held the lantern over her lower half, and nearly dropped it. A thick serpent coil snaked behind her, where her legs should have been, the ruby red scales glittering even in the wan light. She glided her hand along its smooth length, and felt it as her own flesh. The serpent length began at her waist, but the scales covered her abdomen, rising to just beneath her breasts. She was naked. Where had her sleep clothes gone?

The lantern jangled in her grasp, and she set it on the ground, running her hands over her face, now in a panic. Her features felt the same. She pushed herself, slid back to the dresser, and grabbed the pearl hand mirror that had been a birthday gift from Zhen Ni. Her familiar face reflected back at her, although her eyes were dark and wild, and her long hair seemed alive, floating about her shoulders.

A silent sob shook her, tremored from her chest through to the tip of her grotesque tail. Then she glimpsed something that caused her heartbeat to stutter. Slowly, she opened her mouth, and a long forked tongue escaped from it, waggling, as if taunting her.

The hand mirror crashed to the ground, and Skybright clawed at her neck with both hands, unable to speak, to scream. Her serpent coil jerked, swept the lantern on its side, and the flame was doused, casting her into darkness.

Quiet knocking stirred her awake.

The door panel slid aside and Zhen Ni poked her head through, then tiptoed inside, closing the panel behind her.

"You're late. Of all the days!"

Sunshine flooded the small chamber when Zhen Ni opened the lattice window and Skybright struggled to rise, hysteria smothering her chest.

"What happened in here?" Her mistress stared at the toppled stool and broken lantern with oil seeping out beneath, then looked at her and gaped. "Why are you naked?"

Skybright glanced down and saw her legs, stuck her tongue to the roof of her mouth. "I'm—" She choked with relief when she could speak, "I was hot. Last night." It must have been a nightmare. She had a fever and was hallucinating.

Zhen Ni drew to her bedside and waved her hands at her torso. "When did you get *those*?" she exclaimed.

Skybright peered down again, momentarily terrified, to realize that Zhen Ni had been pointing at her breasts. She crossed her arms, flushing.

"You've become a woman," her mistress said in a quiet voice, her expression serious and thoughtful.

She wrapped the thin sheet around herself, laughing from a mixture of embarrassment and disorientation. "We're the same age!"

"I certainly don't look like *that*."

Skybright was familiar with her mistress's physique, being the one to help her bathe, and Zhen Ni was willowy, lacking the curves that Skybright had. Curves hidden beneath loose tunics that, until now, Skybright had never given a second thought.

Zhen Ni stooped down so that they were eye level. "It's happened, Sky," she whispered. "My monthly letting came."

Skybright clapped her hand over her mouth. "Mistress—" But something in Zhen Ni's measured gaze stopped her short.

"I've bled onto the sheet. You must strip and wash them. Hide the evidence." Zhen Ni paused. Skybright had known her a lifetime and had never seen this look of fierce determination in her mistress's eyes. "Mama can never know."

CHAPTER TWO

Skybright cradled the woven basket to her side. She had left under the pretense of going into town to buy a new silk handkerchief and pears for Zhen Ni. In truth, she had her mistress's bed sheet, hoping to wash it at the creek.

She and Zhen Ni had shared their morning meal of rice porridge and pickles in silence. When they spoke after, it was in hushed tones. She had fetched a medicinal tea to ease her mistress's cramps, and told everyone in the household that Zhen Ni was suffering from a headache and needed quiet and rest.

The forest towered, seemed to lean forward in greeting. Soon, she was lost in its depths, making her way down a familiar yet barely marked path to the creek. It felt good to be outside the manor, today of all days. When she had asked, Zhen

Ni had described the cramps feeling as if someone squeezed her womb in a tight fist, bringing waves of aching pain like she'd never experienced. Skybright remembered the heat she had suffered the night before in her fevered dreams, as if her lower half were fracturing then melding together again.

She placed the basket on a rock and shook out the sheet, picking up the chunk of square soap. Skybright sang as she worked, enjoying the feel of sunlight on her bare neck, where her hair had been wound into two tight buns low against her nape. She scrubbed the stain out and wondered how Zhen Ni was faring right now without her, wondered when she, too, would begin her own monthly letting. A lucid image of a serpentine coil flashed in her mind—a forked tongue darting—and she winced. Skybright scoured the sheet harder, until it was spotless, her arms sore from the task.

"It's a nice morning for song," a soft voice said behind her—a male voice—and Skybright leaped to her feet, turning to thrust the lathered soap in front of her like a weapon.

The young man smiled. "You're quick." He carried a wooden staff that was taller than he was, long enough that he could whack her in the head without taking a step.

She grimaced at her soap. "You frightened me."

"I apologize." He inclined his head.

He wasn't more than seventeen years, dressed in a tan sleeveless tunic that revealed wiry arms. His slender eyes were near black in color. Skybright took a small step forward. He lifted his chin, as if in challenge, and she saw the angry red mark covering his neck, like a hand had seized him by the throat, burning an imprint into his flesh.

"You're … him," she said.

"And you are her. The girl spying in the tree." He laughed, and it was warm and unguarded.

"I wasn't—" She stuttered. "I was—"

"Chasing after a lost cat?" he offered.

She smiled despite herself. Skybright had never spoken to a boy so near her own age before, other than to haggle over the price of vegetables at the market.

"I'm Kai Sen." He half bowed, gripping his staff with both hands so it was parallel to the ground.

"Skybright." She nodded shyly.

He pointed at her washing. "I didn't mean to interrupt. Do you mind if I rest here a few moments?"

Skybright returned to wringing the sheet, and he sat near her by the creek's bank. Feeling self-conscious, she was relieved that he was gazing at the water. The thick trees surrounding them made it seem as if they were the only people for several leagues. He closed his eyes and tilted his face toward the sky, seeming content. She submerged the sheet, splashing the water just to make some noise.

"So truthfully, were you spying?" Kai Sen asked, breaking the silence.

She tucked a stray strand of hair behind her ear. "My mistress talked me into it. She's always full of wild notions."

"Was it worth the climb?"

"I saw you." She wrung the sheet, then realized her simple statement could be construed another way. She wasn't normally so coy, but he truly was the most interesting thing she had seen during her tree-climbing escapade. Mortified, she considered putting the wet sheet over her head.

His dark brows lifted, then he laughed again. She liked his laugh—so full and unrestrained.

"I hope it was an easy climb then." He grinned at her, his fingers searching for stones near the water's edge. His hands were broad, darkened by the sun. She shook the sheet out, draped it over a rock, and sat down beside him, the staff resting across his lap a buffer between them.

"Why do you not look like the others?" she asked.

He cast a pebble into the water, and it bounced once before sinking. "You don't mince words."

How was she supposed to talk to a boy? Differently somehow? She hadn't an inkling. All Skybright knew was that his nearness unsettled her in a way that she wasn't able to explain. "My mistress says I'm too forthright."

He flicked a glance at her, and she remembered how he had studied her from that great distance in the immense temple square, as if he could see within her. "There's an openness in your face, yes." The corners of his mouth quirked upwards as he pitched another stone into the creek. "I don't look like the others because I'm not truly a monk."

"Ah." She furrowed her brows, but he didn't look at her.

"I study and train at the monastery as a monk would. But officially, the abbot won't allow me to take my vow because of this." He lifted his chin. The birthmark was a deep red, like nothing she had ever seen, making the parts of his throat that were flesh-colored appear exposed and vulnerable.

"It's only a birthmark," she said.

His smile was rueful. "My parents gave me to the monastery when I was six years because of this birthmark. They were superstitious people from a rural village and believed I was dragged by the throat into this life by the hell lord himself."

It seemed a cruel fate, to have had parents then to lose them because of something so superficial. For the briefest moment, she wondered about her own parents, where she had come from. "But what does the abbot think?"

"I don't know." His head dropped, and some of his hair escaped the twine and fell across his brow. "The abbot took me in, raised me for eleven years. I've never asked what he truly thought."

They sat in silence for some time, listening to the rustle of the forest, the soft stir and hum of hidden birds and creatures. She found a stone and tried to bounce it off the water, but it plopped and sank. Kai Sen's rock followed, skipping three times before vanishing below the surface.

"And you? You're a tree-climbing handmaid spy?"

Skybright burst into laughter, sending a bird from a nearby tree spiraling into the clear sky. She'd never laughed like that with anyone except Zhen Ni. "Something like that."

"To be truthful, I haven't been able to stop wondering about you. Every time I meditated, I saw an image of you perched high in that cypress tree gaping down at us." He chuckled. "It was the most unexpected and absurd thing I'd ever seen."

"I wasn't gaping," she said, indignant.

"Oh, you were gaping. Fortunate thing, too, otherwise I would have thought some goddess or nymph had descended upon—"

"There you are! I wondered where you disappeared to." A lanky boy the same age as Kai Sen ran up to them. "You'll get me in trouble if we don't head back now!" The boy's head was shaved, and he was dressed in slate blue, like all the monks she had seen the other day.

Kai Sen stood, rolling the tall staff easily from one palm to the other. "I forgot the time, talking here with Skybright."

She scrambled to her feet, embarrassed, and the new boy gawked at her as if he'd never seen a girl before. She picked up the sheet and shook it as a distraction, enjoying the crisp snapping sound.

"Close your mouth, Han," Kai Sen prodded him in the chest with his staff.

Han clamped his mouth shut, then grinned boyishly. "Kai has the heart of a wandering monk," he told Skybright. "I'm always herding him back to the monastery. First time I've found him with a girl, though."

Skybright suppressed a smile as she folded the sheet.

"Brother, let's go." Kai Sen clasped the taller boy by the shoulder. "Before you embarrass me even more." He turned and gave her a nod. "Maybe we'll meet again? I'll look for you in the trees?"

She laughed, shaking her head. "I don't think I'll do that again."

"That's a pity," Kai Sen replied, and Han tugged him

by the tunic edge to go. He grinned and waved once, before disappearing into the thicket.

Skybright had taken so long that she'd missed the midday meal. Surprised not to find Zhen Ni in her quarters, she wandered through the manor until she saw everyone gathered in the main hall. The two paneled doors had been folded open, letting in the summer breeze and light. Lilies in bright yellow and orange adorned each table, scenting the air with their strong musk. The red five-sided lanterns were already lit overhead. Lady Yuan sat with Zhen Ni beside her, chatting to another woman and girl across from them.

Someone had dressed Zhen Ni in a pale pink tunic and skirt. As with all her mistress's clothes, they were intricately beaded, befitting the family's status and wealth as successful merchants. Skybright noticed, with annoyance, that the jewels pinned in Zhen Ni's hair didn't match her outfit. It must have been her stand in, Rose's, mistake.

"There you are, Skybright," Lady Yuan exclaimed.

The guests half-turned to glance at her. Skybright bowed her head, but not before sneaking a long look. The girl was petite, with large eyes set beneath delicate eyebrows, and a round nose over a rosebud mouth. She was not dressed as resplendently as Zhen Ni, her outfit not even rivaling

Skybright's own. Her family obviously didn't enjoy the same stature as the Yuans.

"Lady Fei and her daughter Lan have just arrived after a long journey. Oriole is fetching us some tea. Could you go to the kitchen and ask for the custard buns and nut cakes Cook made this morning?"

Skybright retreated, and hurried toward the kitchen, weaving past the fragrant honeysuckle and quiet pavilions in the courtyards. When she arrived, she helped Cook arrange the freshly made treats on a lacquered tray inlaid with pearl, before tucking a lotus from the pond among the desserts. It would please Zhen Ni. Her trip back was at a brisk, yet careful pace.

When Skybright set the beautiful display of desserts in front of the women, Zhen Ni caught her eye and smiled, having seen the blushing pink lotus. "It matches my dress perfectly," she said.

"Thank you, Skybright," Lady Yuan said. "You may go now."

But Zhen Ni grabbed Skybright's sleeve. "Do let her stay, Mama." She flashed her most winning smile. "Skybright should get to know Lan as well."

"Of course." Lady Yuan indicated the carved stool in the corner. "Join us." She passed the desserts on cerulean plates to the guests. "Zhen Ni and Skybright are almost sisters. The goddess left Skybright at our doorstep right before Zhen Ni was born, like a gift for our youngest daughter."

"Mama, don't speak of Skybright as if she were a pet Chow!"

Skybright managed to smother her smile, but Lan laughed, a surprisingly rich sound coming from such a small frame, and clapped a hand over her mouth like she had surprised herself.

Lady Yuan took a long sip of tea, her bejeweled fingers holding the porcelain cup just so, before setting it down with artful grace. "It's my fault," she said to Lady Fei, flashing a smile at Zhen Ni. "I've spoiled her, even Master Yuan says so—and then he does the same!" Master Yuan was a merchant and away traveling many months out of the year, but whenever he returned, his carriage was always piled high with heaps of gifts for Zhen Ni.

"You're truly fortunate to have four children, and three already wed." Lady Fei nibbled on a nut cake. Lan had inherited her mother's small, full mouth. "We're still searching for a suitable match for our Lan."

Skybright and Zhen Ni pointedly avoided each other's gaze. As the women discussed betrothal gifts and the best dates to wed for their daughters, Skybright's mind wandered back to thoughts of the stream. Of the warmth of sunlight against her skin, and Kai Sen's laughter. Of the way he had studied her with those dark brown eyes.

The next few days passed quickly as Lan settled into her new quarters, near Zhen Ni's. She had not come accompanied by her own handmaid, so Lady Yuan assigned a girl of fourteen years called Pearl to help her. And all the while, Skybright and Zhen Ni were on edge, frightened that their secret would be discovered somehow. Skybright went to her mistress even earlier each morning, soon after the rooster's crow. Zhen Ni was more pale than usual, and they took great care to add color to her cheeks before she greeted anyone.

Lan's arrival proved to be a good distraction. Zhen Ni and Lan spent their mornings gossiping and embroidering before taking a midday meal, then scattering into the gardens to sip chilled honeyed tea. Lan was better at embroidering than Zhen Ni, but Skybright's mistress proved to be the best with composing lyrics and playing the lute. Skybright couldn't do either very well, but had the prettiest singing voice, and was often asked to accompany Zhen Ni as she plucked at the lute strings. Rose and Pearl stayed near, fanning their mistresses, as the summer days were becoming unbearably hot.

Skybright retired exhausted in the evenings, not having given further thought to her feverish dreams from the previous week. But tonight, a familiar tingling below her waist woke her. Terrified, she reared up and grabbed at her legs. They were still there, still the same. She gave a loud sigh of relief, but even before the full exhale, her flesh began to undulate and change beneath her fingers. Bones, ligaments, and joints warped and crackled, melted away, striking with that unbearable heat.

Smooth scales rippled over her human flesh, like dragonfly wings fluttering their way from her feet to cover her abdomen. She swept both hands across her torso, the clothes having evaporated from her, and gasped. Her snake tongue darted out, oppressing her voice, and she could taste the air with it; the whiff of smoke from the snuffed lantern, the bitterness of the gardenia musk Zhen Ni had rubbed into her wrists in the morning, all tinged by the scent of her own sweat and fear.

She fell out of bed, her long serpent body slapping the ground with a loud thwack. Crawling with her hands, she pulled herself up by the window ledge and lit the lantern. She saw the thick coil that began at her waist, just as the last time— but this was no nightmare. Skybright pinched the flesh of her upper arms, her cheeks, then where her hip should be, and the end of her tail flipped, like it had a mind of its own.

"No," she tried to say. But all that came out was a guttural rasp.

How could this be real?

To her horror, a rooster began to crow. Skybright scrambled on her hands and slid the door aside, hefting her long serpent body, which was at least four times the length of her legs, behind her. She shut the door, fighting panic. She must leave the manor. No one could see her like this—a monstrosity. What if she never changed back?

She crawled awkwardly, using her arms but beginning to push herself a little with her muscular coils. Fumbling too long with the key Zhen Ni had stolen for their escapades, Skybright thrust her way through a narrow side door used by servants and into a dark alley. She had enough wits about her to tie the string the key dangled from around her wrist. More than one rooster was now crying at the morning light in greeting, and some neighborhood dogs responded to the cacophony. In desperation, she tried to quicken her pace as she slithered toward the forest, propelling herself more and more with her serpent length. Her lungs felt as if they would burst from exertion and terror, and a sense of overwhelming grief. She sobbed, but what came out was a long hiss. The mutt that had been barking ferociously behind the neighbor's wall quieted with a yip, then whimpered.

She had never liked that mean mutt.

The jagged line of trees was a familiar and welcome sight, and Skybright snaked toward it, unused to her lower vantage point. Her serpentine body met the ground where her hips used to be, although she found she could rise higher on her coil if she wanted to. Swallowed by darkness, she made her way between the trees, tasting the earthy tang of the forest on her tongue. The ground vibrated with life, telling her how many nocturnal creatures were still scampering to their nests, even as others were just rising for the day. No humans were nearby.

Skybright navigated with only her coils now. Each powerful thrust propelled her forward, and her speed increased as she pushed her way deeper and deeper, going further than she had ever strolled before with Zhen Ni in their explorations. It wasn't until morning sunshine glimmered through the thick branches of the trees that she collapsed beneath one, exhausted, unable to shed the tears that weighed heavy against her heart. Why was this happening to her? Curling herself up, her serpent length wound in tight circles, the sight turning her stomach. She shut her eyes so she could no longer see it.

৩৩৩

Skybright woke from the feel of a hand pressed against her upper arm, warm and reassuring. Groggy, she opened her eyes and squinted. Kai Sen's concerned face filled her vision, and she bolted to a sitting position, clutching a tan tunic to herself. It was long sleeved, thank the goddess, and she tucked herself as small as she could beneath it.

He sat down across from her, allowing some distance, folding those lean arms over his knees. The tall staff he had carried before rested beside him. His chest was bare, as he had given her his tunic. "Are you all right?" he asked.

She blinked, feeling woozy. "What time is it?" Her voice sounded thick in her own ears, odd.

"A few gongs before the midday meal yet." The gongs set the schedule at the monastery, and could often be heard as far as their manor, if she paused to listen for them.

Skybright thrust her face against her knees, which were pulled tight to her chest. Kai Sen's tunic smelled faintly of camphor wood. The wind stirred, lifting a corner of the cloth, and she clutched her legs harder, acutely aware of her nakedness beneath. Although Skybright was glad to see Kai Sen, she wished he hadn't discovered her, like some wild animal, naked and disoriented in the forest.

"What happened?" he asked in a quiet voice.

How could she explain this away? It was impossible. Zhen Ni would be hysterical with worry. She had never disappeared like that before. The entire staff would be out searching for her. Skybright took a deep breath that shuddered into a silent sob.

"I can't say." She raised her eyes and swallowed the sour taste in her mouth. "I must have wandered in my sleep."

"I've sent Han back for a robe. He ... didn't see you." Kai Sen's gaze held steady, and she was grateful for it. "When I found you, I thought you were injured or—" he cleared his throat. "Has this happened before?"

"No," she lied, hating the way her scalp tingled from it.

"We're leagues from town." He lowered his chin. "I'm only glad that I was the one to find you."

His concern warmed her, even as she shivered beneath the thin fabric of his tunic.

"I wish I had more to offer." He smiled, and Skybright realized with shock that she wanted to flick her tongue out, to taste the scent of him.

In that moment, someone shouted from beyond the trees, and Kai Sen leaped to his feet. "It's Han." He ran, faster than Skybright had seen anyone run, and disappeared among the thickets.

Skybright suddenly remembered the stories of serpent demons, always women, who would shape shift after luring victims with their beautiful faces. Zhen Ni's sister, Min, had spoken of them. Skybright recalled how Min had widened her eyes and said in a hushed voice, "She acts the helpless maiden, but when she has you alone in the dark of night, that's when she attacks!" Min had leaped at them, baring her teeth and hissing. "The beautiful woman changes into a giant serpent." Min threw her arms out wide to emphasize her length. "She'll sink her long fangs into your flesh to poison you, then swallow you whole. And the worst part? You'll still be alive when she does it!" Min gnashed her teeth and smacked her lips. Skybright and Zhen Ni had clutched each other during the tale, squealing and giggling.

Was this what she was—a monster of folklore? How could it be possible? She tightened her arms around her knees.

Kai Sen returned with a wheat-colored monk's robe. "It was the best Han could find," he said apologetically. "Here." He stuck his hand out and turned his face away to show he wasn't looking.

But Skybright took the opportunity to do just that. His chest and torso were as muscular and lithe as his arms. She marveled at how different his body appeared compared to hers, all hard lines and angles. He was as tan as she was pale, letting her know that he often went shirtless in the sun. Kai Sen's stance exposed his throat to her, and that strange birthmark, which seemed to have deepened to the color of plum wine this morning. Skybright resisted the urge to press her hand over it, to see if it was indeed in the exact shape of a palm. She reached for the robe instead and wrapped it around herself, tying it securely at the waist. The sleeves were too long, and the hem dragged against the ground, but she was relieved to feel the soft cotton against her skin.

"Thank you, truly. To you and Han both."

He turned to assess her, unable to keep from grinning. "I've never seen a monk's robe on someone so—" He stopped mid-sentence, and appeared flustered for the first time since they'd met. "Never on a girl before." His smile turned lop-sided, and she wondered what he had been about to say.

"I should return to my mistress." Skybright drew the robe tighter around herself. "She must be so worried."

Kai Sen nodded. "Let me walk you back—"

"No, you've done more than enough, I couldn't ask—"

"It would ease my own mind, Skybright. Please."

Taking note of the unfamiliar surroundings, she said, "Then I would be grateful for your company."

Kai Sen drew his own tunic on and tied the sash, smiling. "I promised Han I would return as soon as I took you back."

He led the way through the trees with dexterity, knowing exactly which way to go. She followed, feeling the soft earth and pebbles beneath her bare feet. What must he think of her? The strange girl who climbed trees and wandered naked in the forest at night. Her ears burned at the thought, and she was glad he didn't see. Some time later, he slowed and glanced her way. "You are certain you're all right?" He paused. "Your mistress … she treats you well?"

Humiliated, she colored even more. "They're so kind to me. Zhen Ni treats me like her own sister."

"Good. I'm glad," he said. "It's just, I don't often find beautiful girls sleeping naked in the forest."

Her mouth dropped, then she burst into laughter when she

saw the teasing slant of his gaze.

"Not that I'm complaining," Kai Sen went on. "But the last time I was caught undressed in the forest, it was because Han had stolen my clothes from the river bank and I had to return to the monastery plastered in cypress leaves. They were prickly. And didn't do the job well." He cleared his throat and grinned at her.

She laughed harder. "Han didn't!"

"Han did. Don't worry, I got him back." Kai Sen laughed with her, and it eased Skybright's heart. His laughter made everything feel normal and right again. She reached overhead to grab a sprig of cypress, sweeping her palm across the needle-like leaves, trying to picture Kai Sen returning to the monastery covered in them, and chuckled again.

They strolled beneath the cool shadow of the majestic forest, and Skybright remembered how the earth vibrated and hummed with life the previous night, when it seemed she could detect every small movement and animal near her within leagues, smell and taste them on her tongue.

"Do you practice forms with the staff?" she asked.

"I do. We're taught to use an array of weapons, but I'm most comfortable with the staff." He spun it from one hand to the other, without thought, by reflex. He wielded it as if it were an extension of him.

"But I thought monks were against violence?"

"Fair point. The techniques and forms help strengthen us not only physically, but mentally and spiritually. And we've been known to take to arms and go to war to defend our kingdom in the past. Then, there are always the demons." He said the last part with a mischievous wink, but she felt both arms prickling. "We must always be prepared."

"Demons?" she whispered.

"From the ancient texts. The ones that roam the underworld, the ones that roam our own world."

"Do they exist?" She shivered despite herself. Kai Sen noticed and drew closer, but she wasn't shivering for the reasons he thought.

"I've not seen the like myself. But the abbot believes what the books say."

They were now by the creek where they had met the first time, not too far from the Yuan manor. "You've read these books?" Skybright tried to keep her voice even.

"We study them, yes. Why?"

"I need to—" She rubbed at her throbbing temples in frustration. "Could you research something for me?"

He peered at her, his handsome face curious. "If I can. On what?"

"The serpent demon."

Kai Sen's eyebrows lifted.

"Do you know anything about them?" she asked.

"Not beyond the usual old wives' tales of warning."

They heard the distant gong from the monastery and Kai Sen whipped toward the sound, his stance as taut as a tiger about to leap. "Han's going to kill me."

"I can find my way back. I know where I am."

"It's my fault. I took my time on purpose." He grinned.

"I'll see what I can find. When can I meet you again?"

"Back here, in three days' time? In the morning."

"I'll look for you, Skybright." Kai Sen jogged back in the direction of the still reverberating gong. "Keep safe until then."

She waved, sorry to see him go. Skybright wasn't certain that she could keep safe. She wasn't certain about anything any longer.

CHAPTER THREE

Skybright sneaked back into the Yuan manor through the unguarded side entrance, relieved that no one saw her along the way in the dim alley. Like all matriarchs, Lady Yuan was unconcerned with the goings on of her servants—as long as they performed their duties and kept out of trouble. Skybright always had, until today. The door panels to her small quarters were wide open, but the room was empty. She quickly changed into a silk tunic and trousers in sky blue, beaded at the collar and along the sleeve edges in silver, a mark of her mistress's favor. She plaited her thick hair into two braids and wound them tight against her neck. She hadn't even realized that Kai Sen had seen her hair unbound until now—something saved only for a husband. Skybright snorted, and had to suppress the hysterical laughter that was rising within her. What did it matter if he had seen her hair unbound when he had already seen her unclothed? She pressed a hand to her mouth and bit the flesh of her index finger to calm herself.

Hurried footsteps and excited conversation carried to her from across the courtyard, and she ran to Zhen Ni's quarters, pushing the panel aside without knocking. Stepping through the reception hall, she found her mistress hunched over on the platform bed, her hair in disarray. Lan had her arm wrapped around Zhen Ni and dabbed at her wet cheeks with an emerald handkerchief, a gesture both intimate and tender. Whispering soft words into Zhen Ni's ear, Lan leaned closer till their faces were nearly touching.

"Mistress!" Skybright threw herself at Zhen Ni's feet and knocked her forehead against the floor. "Forgive me, I didn't mean to worry you."

Her mistress uttered a strangled cry.

"Worry me!" Zhen Ni pressed her hands beneath Skybright's chin and lifted it. Her mistress's hair had been haphazardly arranged that morning, and most of it had escaped in wild wisps around her face. She hadn't bothered with any cosmetics or accessories.

"I thought you'd been kidnapped, or ran away, or were murdered—"

"None of those." Skybright squeezed Zhen Ni's wrists. "I'm here. I'm well."

Zhen Ni allowed herself one more sob and snatched the handkerchief from Lan, blowing her nose noisily. The other girl folded her hands in her lap, eyes downcast. She sat with her thigh pressed against Zhen Ni's, and Skybright felt a sharp pang of jealousy, that Lan felt so close and comfortable with her mistress in the short time they'd known each other. Distracted, she didn't sense Zhen Ni's wrath until she shook Skybright hard by the shoulders.

"Where were you?" Her mistress's porcelain complexion was mottled. "Where did you go?"

"I—" Skybright had never lied to her mistress before. "I must have wandered away in my sleep."

Zhen Ni wrung the silk handkerchief, twisting it mercilessly. "You sleep walked? But you've never done that before. You don't even talk in your sleep."

Skybright bowed her head. It still ached, and she couldn't bear seeing her mistress's face any longer. She had to lie. A rush of dizziness seized her, and she crouched low again. The bedchamber spun in lazy circles. "I don't feel well."

"Skybright!" Zhen Ni slid from the edge of the bed, folding her arm around Skybright's shoulders. "Lan, could you ask my mother to fetch Nanny Bai? Please hurry."

She heard Lan's retreating footsteps. Zhen Ni stroked Skybright's hair and held her. Skybright clutched at her own tunic and leaned into her mistress, refusing to cry. Zhen Ni hadn't put on any perfume that morning, she noticed. The jasmine would do for today, Skybright thought, once she had the chance to rearrange her mistress's hair and pin the kingfisher hair sticks into her locks.

Yes.

The jasmine perfume would be perfect.

Skybright drifted in and out of consciousness after Zhen Ni helped her into her own bed, plumping the cushions behind her as if she were the handmaid and Skybright her mistress. Unused to being fussed over, she tried to wave her mistress away and rise, only to be pushed back against the cushions.

"Don't be a fool, Sky. I command that you lie back and rest!"

Skybright smiled weakly at that. Zhen Ni was used to getting her way. She leaned back and closed her eyes while her mistress sat beside her.

"You like Lan," Skybright said after a while.

There was such a long pause, she opened her eyes, wondering if Zhen Ni had not heard her. Her mistress was studying her with an unreadable expression, and Skybright had always been able to read her mistress as easily as a deck of cards. "She makes a good friend. I enjoy her company." Zhen Ni arched her graceful neck and examined a lotus painting, avoiding eye contact in that way she did when she was being evasive. "Don't you like her?"

"She's nice," Skybright said. But in truth, Skybright wasn't used to sharing Zhen Ni's attentions, not used to seeing her laugh and chatter so easily with another girl their age. They sat without looking at each other, and listened to the soft trickle of the waterfall from the courtyard. "I can never be a true friend to you," Skybright whispered after a long silence. "I can only ever be your handmaid."

"Sky!" Zhen Ni grabbed her hand. "You're my sister, my better and kinder half." She gripped her fingers. "How can you say such a thing? You're delirious!"

Lady Yuan swished in with a bustle of flowing silk panels on her beautiful dress, followed by Nanny Bai and Lan. "Skybright! You've sent the household in an uproar. We've had servants scouring the entire village and had others going into town to search for you, twice."

"Three times," Zhen Ni said.

"I'm sorry, Lady Yuan. I must have wandered off in my sleep." Skybright stared at the silk sheet embroidered with chrysanthemums.

Lady Yuan stood beside the bed and touched the back of her hand to Skybright's brow. "Zhen Ni said you weren't feeling well?"

"I think … I'm just overtired, Lady."

"It isn't—?"

"No, Lady. It isn't that." Skybright had a feeling that her monthly letting would never come.

Lady Yuan nodded and smoothed the stray strands of hair from Skybright's brow. It was such an intimate, maternal gesture, one that they had never shared before, that Skybright almost cringed. Lady Yuan clapped her hands. "Come girls, let's leave Skybright with Nanny Bai."

Zhen Ni gave her a hug before following her mother and

Lan out into the courtyard.

Skybright breathed a sigh of relief and sank into the cushions.

"What happened, child?" Nanny Bai asked. What had once been a husky voice was now coarse with age. The same voice that used to sing her to sleep on rare occasions. Nanny Bai was the closest thing she ever had to a mother.

"It's as I said. I think I wandered off in my sleep."

The older woman felt the pulse at her wrist and her throat, leaned closer to listen to her breathing. "You never sleep walked as a child. It's … unusual to start so late in age."

"Am I that old?" Skybright asked without thinking.

Nanny Bai laughed, the sound like the wind stirring brittle leaves. "Where did you go?"

"Into the forest."

The older woman made a strange noise in her throat, catching Skybright's attention. The lines around her old nursemaid's eyes and along her mouth had deepened in these passing years, but her brown eyes were still as sharp as ever. She smelled of pungent herbs, as she always did—a rich, earthy bitterness.

"What is it?" Skybright whispered.

"I've never told anyone this, because it was *your* story." Nanny Bai glanced down at her strong, able hands, though the knuckles were beginning to thicken with age. "I was the one to find you, yes. But it wasn't at our front doorstep."

Skybright pushed herself up. "What do you mean?"

"I found you abandoned in the forest, child."

She shook her head in disbelief, and her old nursemaid clucked her tongue in sympathy. "It was the beginning of summer, and the weather was fine that day. I decided to go into town to pick up some medicinal herbs—Lady Yuan was so near to giving birth to our Zhen Ni. For some reason, I was drawn to the forest, and taking my way through there." Nanny Bai paused, lost in the past. "It was unusual, as I never walked through the forest. Not alone."

Skybright knew it was true. Her old nursemaid seemed to avoid it, often sending Skybright into the thickets to gather wild mushrooms and plants for her, never saying why she disliked entering its cool depths.

"But that morning, something drew me." She said again, nodding for emphasis. "And I followed the creek, not wanting to lose my way, but I heard something deep within the forest. A baby's cry." She closed her eyes. "I thought it was some sort of trickery—strange things can lurk among the trees—or that I had imagined it. But it didn't cease. I tracked the sound, until I was lost in the thickets. And there you were."

Abandoned in the forest … left to die.

"You weren't a day old, child. And it was as if your mother had given birth to you in the wild and left you there, with your cord still attached. You weren't covered or swaddled. It's a wonder some wild animal didn't come along—"

Skybright's tears finally came, held in since the previous night, when she had slithered her way back into the forest as a monstrosity—the same forest where she had been cast aside by a mother who didn't care if she lived.

"Dear." Nanny Bai touched her arm. "I'm sorry to be so blunt. But I thought you should know. You understand now why I never before spoke the truth? I feared that Lady Yuan would not have wanted you if I did." She smiled a gentle smile. "I took you home wrapped in the cloth I had intended for my herbs, and bathed you, then presented you swaddled in red satin in a pretty woven basket to the Lady."

Skybright rubbed her face, furious with herself for crying. What was the point of wasted tears?

"You know how Lady Yuan always loves a gift well presented," Nanny Bai said.

She laughed, even though it sounded bitter to her ears. "Thank you, dear nanny. You saved my life."

"Look at the lovely, capable young woman you've grown into, Skybright." She patted her arm again. "You would have made any mother proud. It's a pity you can never wed, but Zhen Ni loves you as her own sister. Your lot in life could have been much worse."

The older woman rose, still agile despite her age. "You're weak from exhaustion and overexcitement. I'll bring something to help you sleep."

Skybright nodded. "Thank you again, Nanny Bai. And— and my mother left nothing behind at all? No memento for me?"

Her old nursemaid shook her head in regret. "Nothing. It was clear you were a newborn babe. Although … " Hesitant, Nanny Bai tugged at her tunic edge.

"What?" Skybright's hands tingled, as if in warning or anticipation.

"When I washed you that first time, there were flakes stuck to you. Like scales from a fish. They were quite beautiful but … strange."

"Like scales from a fish," Skybright repeated dumbly. "What color were they?"

"Crimson," Nanny Bai said. "They glittered like jewels in the light."

Skybright dozed through to the next morning after taking the bitter draught Nanny Bai offered her. Zhen Ni had refused to let her return to her own quarters. In the evening, Skybright was vaguely aware of her mistress slipping into the large bed beside her. She woke with a start before dawn, her forehead covered in sweat. Terrified, she kicked her legs beneath the thin sheet, feeling her toes and her knees. What would happen if she changed with her mistress beside her? Skybright's throat closed at the thought. She heard Zhen Ni's steady breathing, and slipped out of bed and into a courtyard dimly lit by starlight.

When she had shifted, it was always at nighttime—she only wished she knew what triggered it, so she could anticipate it. Could she control it somehow? Will it away when it happened? Skybright sat on the stone bench beneath a peach tree, digging her toes into the earth and enjoying its coolness.

Miiissssstress …

The hairs on Skybright's neck rose and sharp needles danced across her scalp. The word was carried on a soft summer breeze, barely audible. Her imagination, after the past week, was getting the better of her.

Huuuuungry!

Skybright leaped from the bench and whirled, turning in a circle, heart in her throat. That word had been as loud as a stone falling from the sky.

"Who is it?" she said into the night.

Another breeze rustled the leaves overhead, seeming to hold and then disperse a multitude of pleading voices.

Pleeeease...

Coooome...

A single firefly materialized in front of her, hovering before her nose. It looped three times and flew a few steps ahead. She followed the insect, past the dark quarters, along winding stone paths. If she concentrated enough, Skybright thought she could hear the murmur of a hundred voices upon the wind.

Finally, the firefly paused in front of the main gate into the manor, with its grand double doors. She unlatched the lock and pulled one door open. It groaned like a dragon disturbed in its sleep, and Skybright stepped across the threshold. The heavy door slammed shut by itself; an empty street greeted her. Their manor was not near the main road, but their street was broad enough for horses and carriages to travel through. Plum trees dotted the wide path, and she could see the neighbor's red gate and main entrance across the way.

The firefly had vanished, and Skybright stood with her

head tilted, listening.

Miiiiistress Skkkky …

Shadows darted around her, an icy wind. She clutched her bare arms with her hands. "Who are you?" she whispered into the night. The air stilled, then wavered. Images coalesced, and a group of people suddenly surrounded her. There were men and women, girls and boys, dressed in shabby clothing with dirt-smudged faces. She knew she should have been afraid, but instead, she was only curious.

They gaped at her with mournful faces, but when she tried to look at one straight on, the spirit would melt into shadow again, absorbed by moonlight. So she observed them from the corners of her eyes. At least a hundred ghosts surrounded her, and they pressed closer as one, chilling the air. Beyond them, she sensed more spirits, too tired or weak to manifest their human forms.

A man in his thirties floated forward from the rest of the pack. His cheeks were rough with facial hair, but the flesh was gone from the upper left side of his face, exposing an empty eye socket. "Mistress Skybright. We were but humble servants, as you are—"

A chorus of voices echoed.

I served Lady Pan for thirty years.

I took care of the horses and dogs for the Jins.

I was a cook for the Wang family until the kitchen fire took my life.

I'm an orphan but kept my master company!

The last voice was high-pitched and cheery, and Skybright

glimpsed the shadow of a boy no more than eleven years near the front of the crowd.

"What do you want from me?" she whispered.

Their response was an uproar, lifting the loose hair from her head. She staggered back from the force of their sheer need.

Love.

Vengeance.

My wife.

Retribution.

Peace.

Rest.

My Son.

Life.

Tears sprang in her eyes because, inexplicably, she knew their loss, felt their wants and desires as if they were her own.

The man who had spoken to her raised a blurry fist and snarled. The silence that followed was immediate and eerie, and her ears rang with it.

"Please, Mistress Skybright," the man said. It seemed to take great effort for him to speak so clearly to her. Each of his sentences was followed by the restless echo of hundreds of others. "Feed us. We have no relatives left to do so. And those who remain are too poor."

"But the Ghost Festival hasn't started yet," she said. They were a few days from the middle of the seventh moon, when the gates of the underworld were supposed to open for the ghosts to visit the living. The Yuan manor was already beginning to prepare elaborate feasts in remembrance of ancestors, to pay respect and symbolically feed the dead.

We escaped, followed, pushed through. Wanting. Hunger.

"There was a breach between the realms," the man said. "We escaped the underworld early."

Skybright's skin crawled, fearful for the first time in this exchange with the dead.

"But why did you seek me out?"

Us. See you. Are us.

Their crackling chants shivered across her.

"Because you're the only one who can see us," he said, his voice almost gentle. "Hear us."

"The only one ... " she repeated.

He paused. "The other one is too well protected."

"I will. I'll feed you and burn incense in your memory. I promise." Skybright's eyes swept past the hundreds of glimmering ghosts floating before her in the empty road, to the indistinct forms crouched beneath the shadows of the plum trees. "But who's the other one?"

The man grinned, though the flesh dissolved from his mouth and chin, exposing yellow, jagged teeth. He didn't answer her question. Instead, the spirits hissed in delight, as if in acknowledgement of who she was—what she was. *One of us*, they had said. Could they see the monstrous side of her so easily? As easily as she could see them, she realized. They whirled until the pins fell from her hair, freeing her locks.

Then, the air stilled, as sudden as when it erupted.

A cat yowled in terror in the distance.

She was alone.

Something bounced against the cobblestone and rolled into her bare foot. Skybright stooped to pick it up. A copper coin, hundreds of years old, tinged green with age.

A token of gratitude.

Skybright hurried toward Zhen Ni's quarters with the small coin clenched in her hand, and made it back right as the roosters began to crow. She almost bumped into her mistress when she entered the reception hall. The tall girl had a lavender silk robe drawn about her.

"I was just coming to find you." It was clear Zhen Ni was concerned, but she withheld her reprimand.

"I needed fresh air, mistress."

"Look at you, wandering like a wild animal in your bare feet. Really, Sky! Do you not want to get better?"

Skybright smiled, glad that her mistress had reprimanded her after all. It meant things were returning to normal between them. "I didn't want to wake you."

Zhen Ni pulled her into her bedchamber, and Skybright lit the giant pearl lanterns in each corner. Skybright's arms shook, and she did her best to steady them.

"Are you feeling better?" Zhen Ni asked.

In truth, she felt drained and wanted more than anything

to crawl back into bed. Too much was happening to her at once, all inexplicable and strange. Instead she said, "I am. And you?" She had been a poor handmaid these past few days, and it was the only normal aspect of her life now, reassuring in its rituals and cadence.

Her mistress unconsciously pressed a palm to her abdomen. "The worst of it is over now … until the next moon."

"How long do you plan on keeping this from your mother?"

"Forever," Zhen Ni said vehemently.

Skybright's mouth dropped, but she clamped it shut when her mistress shot her a challenging glare.

"My parents already have two grandsons and a granddaughter! And another on the way. Why must I be married off as well? It's not fair!"

Skybright stared at her fists. Her mistress sounded like a petulant child. There was nothing fair or unfair in the way things were. Was there any point in challenging them, when in the end, a girl such as Zhen Ni must accept her fate, no matter what? Just as Skybright must accept her own? Memories of herself in serpent form filled her mind—how *alive* she had felt. She shoved them aside. There was no place for that here.

"You'll help me, Sky? Hide the truth from Mama?"

She led Zhen Ni to the vanity to prepare her for the coming day. "Of course, mistress. I'll help you for as long as you want."

Zhen Ni grinned, her relief plain. "I'll wear the turquoise tunic today, what do you think?"

Skybright retrieved the tunic and matching skirt from her mistress's giant rosewood wardrobe. The color especially complemented Zhen Ni's ivory skin and set off her warm brown eyes. The tunic was embroidered with golden chrysanthemums. "Is it a special occasion? Are we receiving a visitor?"

Zhen Ni's cheeks colored, surprising Skybright.

"Not at all." Zhen Ni brushed her own hair in long strokes. "I just wanted to dress especially nice today, after all that's happened this past week."

Skybright took the brush from her and smiled. "I'll do something fancy for your hair then, to match the outfit."

Zhen Ni folded her hands in her lap and Skybright saw how the flush in her cheeks enhanced her natural beauty. Her face was more rounded, like she'd gained some weight in these past weeks, softening her features. Her eyes shone as she watched Skybright plait her hair, and a faint smile lifted the corners of her generous mouth. Skybright ran a cursory glance of her own reflection, noted how her dark eyes appeared too large in her pale face, before concentrating on her mistress's locks once more, Zhen Ni had turned into a woman as well, seemingly overnight.

The realization struck Skybright with a pang of fear and regret. How long could they cling to their childhoods, ignoring the fact that they had become young women? She twisted tiny braids near the top of Zhen Ni's head, weaving ruby flowers in them, before winding the small braids to join her single, thicker braid.

The color of the dazzling stones reminded her of her serpent scales, and Skybright's hands trembled as she clipped the final hairpin into her mistress's hair. What would Zhen Ni think if she ever discovered the truth? How could she possibly care for her the same? Skybright would be cast out as the cursed monster that she was.

Zhen Ni turned her head this way and that, admiring Skybright's handiwork. She paused when she caught Skybright's reflection in the mirror.

"What's wrong?" she asked.

"Nothing, mistress." She rubbed gardenia musk against her mistress's wrists and behind her ears. "You look beautiful. And you haven't even put the tunic on yet."

Skybright helped Zhen Ni into her thin chemise and silk shorts, then dressed her in the luxurious turquoise tunic and skirt. She drew back when she was done, and her mistress stood in front of the mirror, smoothing the silk, making certain everything was in place and perfect.

"I need to change, too, mistress. I'll meet you in the main hall?"

Zhen Ni turned, and her smile was warm. "Yes. I'll fetch Lan on my way."

Skybright stopped by the kitchen before returning to her own quarters. Cook was busy preparing the morning meal and ignored her as she collected the items she needed in a woven basket. She changed quickly in her own bedchamber before pulling her small rosewood table outside. A narrow unused alley ran behind her bedchamber, along the perimeter of the manor's high stone wall. Skybright pushed the table against it, then placed oranges and apples on a blue porcelain plate. Beside the fruit, she set down three bowls of rice and a bamboo and bean curd dish. Cook's famous nut cakes were her last offering. She lit an incense stick and set a woven cover over the table.

It was a humble offering, food that servants would be used to, except the fruit and nut cakes. Skybright bowed her head and said a prayer, wondering how this could possibly be enough for the hundreds of lost souls she had seen.

The next two days, before Skybright would see Kai Sen again, passed agonizingly slow. She accompanied Zhen Ni and Lan throughout the day, sewing and embroidering, feeding the song birds in their gilded cages in the courtyards as well as the wild ones fluttering among the trees. On occasion, Skybright would hear the distant gong from the monastery, and she'd always turn her head in its direction, wondering what Kai Sen was doing in that moment.

The girls lounged now on the covered balcony of the fish pond room. Skybright leaned over the wooden railing carved with ducks, contemplating the clear water below. The square pond was enclosed by high walls open to the sky, giving the young ladies sunlight yet allowing them their privacy. She couldn't quite reach to trail her fingers through the water as she would have liked—it was a hot day in the seventh moon. Silver and gold fish darted below, and Skybright sang under her breath about lovers separated in the springtime. The lattice woodwork framing the top of the balcony threw sunlit geometric patterns against the walls, adding to the serene, dreamlike quality.

"Sing louder, Skybright," said Zhen Ni. "Your voice is so lovely."

Skybright turned her head toward the two girls, and froze. Zhen Ni was nestled at Lan's feet, her legs tucked beneath her, leaning into Lan's legs like a contented cat. Lan had unraveled Zhen Ni's thick hair, and it fell across her shoulders past her waist, its jasmine perfume scenting the air. The girl ran a brush through her mistress's locks, a dreamy look in her eyes. Skybright tried to choke down the knot that had risen in her throat. No one was allowed to arrange Zhen Ni's hair except herself, not unless Skybright was ill.

Zhen Ni lifted her face and smiled at Skybright. "Doesn't she have the prettiest voice, Lan?"

Lan inclined her head, the movement like a sparrow's, then nodded. "She does. But she's stopped singing."

"Do go on, Sky. But sing something happy. About lovers who are together, not apart and missing each other." Zhen Ni draped an arm over Lan's knees, a gesture that was both familiar and affectionate.

Skybright felt as if she were missing something. As if Zhen Ni and Lan were playing a game that she hadn't been invited to join. Lan was a shy and demure girl, the exact opposite of Zhen Ni. But her mistress seemed to coax Lan out, as only Zhen Ni could, eliciting rich bursts of laughter from her. As high in station as Skybright was and as close as she was to her mistress, she was still only a handmaid and didn't feel comfortable chatting with Lan, befriending her. It wasn't her place.

Skybright lowered her chin and cleared her throat before singing again. This song was about lovers reunited, and the endurance of their love, as certain as the changing seasons. Her voice rose, sweet and strong, as she sang for the two girls. Skybright closed her eyes, and also sang for herself, to try and ease the inexplicable ache in her chest. So much had changed in so few days—Skybright wasn't certain who she was any more. And Zhen Ni, the person who had always known her best, now knew Skybright very little at all.

Zhen Ni and Lan clapped when Skybright finished her song, but she kept her head bowed. Soon after, Rose and Pearl swept in bearing trays laden with tea, fruit and sweets. Zhen Ni and Lan stood as one with identical smiles. Skybright hurried to set the plates for them and pour the chilled jasmine tea. Her mistress winked and patted the enameled stool beside her. "You sang so beautifully, Sky. Are you feeling back to normal?"

Nibbling on a taro rice ball without tasting it, she forced a smile for her mistress.

Would she ever be normal again?

Skybright rearranged the thin sheet on her bed numerous times then opened the lattice window to air out her stuffy bedchamber. She was supposed to meet Kai Sen tomorrow morning and had to think of an excuse to give to Zhen Ni so she could sneak away. Her heart beat faster at the thought of him, and she chided herself over such a pointless crush.

A shadow obscured the moonlight that had filtered into her bedchamber, and a gust of wind stirred the crabapple trees outside. The night whispered to her. She stepped into the courtyard, not bothering to pull a robe on over her sleep clothes. Excited murmurs drifted from the back alley behind her chamber, and she padded toward the sound, barefoot.

Skybright rounded the sharp corner and stopped abruptly. The narrow alley was jammed with spirits crowding close to the makeshift altar she had made for them. They glowed, some wavering like candle flames. She could push through their insubstantial forms if she wanted, but she stood there, stunned that so many ghosts had filled this confined space.

The scent of sandalwood drifted to her. She had lit another incense stick before she had gone to bed. The tall ghost who had spoken to her hovered in front of the small table, directing each spirit as it took its turn. He saw her and nodded with a smile, his broad face morphing into a leering skull. The other spirits seemed to sense her with their leader's acknowledgment.

Thank you, miiiiistress some rice wine next time are there lychees lychees were my favorite. I miss them so.

The voice rose and melded together with others until they were unintelligible to her.

Their leader thrust his fist in the air, and the spirits ceased speaking as one. "Quiet. He comes."

Who comes?

"He can force us back to the underworld if he chooses," the leader told the other spirits. "We must go."

The spirits shimmered, then extinguished into darkness. Just then, a shape rose over the manor wall, crouched at the top. The person dangled, then dropped without sound to the ground below.

The moon was still bright, even as it cast the back alley in shadows. Skybright dared not move, afraid this would catch the intruder's attention. He was dressed in black and blended with the darkness. She caught a quick glimpse of a brow and cheekbone touched by moonlight. The intruder paused in front of the altar, examining it.

Skybright held still, then made the smallest shift to her right, hoping to escape back around the corner. The hidden face whipped in her direction, and within two breaths, he had shoved his hands against her shoulders and pinned her to the wall. She opened her mouth to scream. He clamped a palm over her lips and they stared at each other, eye to eye. Recognition dawned at the same time.

"Goddess. Is it you, Skybright?" Kai Sen asked, dropping his hands from her.

Her knees wobbled, and he caught her by the elbow. "I'm sorry," he said. "I wasn't expecting to see anyone." She shivered from the feel of his palm against the back of her arm. "What're you doing here?" he whispered.

"Me?" She replied too loudly. "I *live* here! What're you

doing here?"

She could sense his surprise despite the darkness. He released her and she leaned backward, propping herself against the wall, her heart racing.

"I was following—" He stopped abruptly. "I thought I heard something."

The spirits. Kai Sen had heard the ghosts.

"But why are you so far from the monastery?" He still stood close enough that she could feel the heat of his skin. "In the dead of night?"

He grinned sheepishly. "You wouldn't believe me."

She glared at him, hoping he got the full effect, even in the shadowed alley.

"All right. I've been hearing strange … noises these past few nights. Voices. They would come and go with the wind." Kai Sen tilted his head and studied her. His features were half hidden, making him seem like a complete stranger. She could not make out the color of his eyes, though she felt his gaze on her face. "I followed the voices tonight. I needed to be sure I wasn't going mad."

Kai Sen was *the other one*, she realized.

"There were hundreds of shimmering shapes, flitting through the trees of the forest," he said. "I thought it was a trick of the light, but the whispers sounded like words at times. I could understand them."

"What did they say?"

"They were … needy. Hungry." He paused. "You can hear them too?"

"Yes … "

Kai Sen leaned toward her, but seemed to catch himself, then straightened. "But how?"

Because she could turn into a serpent demon. Because she was something of the underworld—like them. She shook her head, not able to lie to him out loud. "What about you?"

He bowed his head and his black hair fell across his brow. Skybright wanted to reach over and brush it back. "I wasn't completely truthful with you when I spoke of my parents giving me away. I've had a … strong intuition since I could talk. The abbot calls it clairvoyance. My parents and the village folk thought I had been marked," he touched his birthmark, "because of this." He paused, and even in the near darkness, she could see his throat work. Without thinking, she put her hand on his arm, and she felt the tension seep from him, saw it in the way his stance softened. "I always saw lost spirits and didn't realize no one else could until I talked too often about people who weren't there. Until everyone I knew was afraid of me, including my own parents. And every misfortune that happened, every illness, every misplaced jar or broken bowl was blamed on me. I didn't know. I was only six years."

Her fingers glided down his arm and she slipped her hand into his, gripping it. "Kai Sen. I'm so sorry."

"Skybright … " He tugged her gently to him. "I never feel as if I can speak of my past with the other monks. Because of my birthmark. Because I'm different. But with you, I … " He didn't finish the thought, but instead leaned in and kissed her.

It was like a jolt, quickening her pulse. His mouth was full, firm against her own. He smelled of camphor wood and sweat. Of boy. His tongue flicked across her lips and instinctively she opened her mouth to him. She gasped when their tongues met. Warmth pooled in her stomach and spread, till her entire body was roused.

Lit.

His hands had wound around her waist, sneaked under her sleep tunic so she could feel his rough palms against her midriff. They met at the small of her back and slid upward, till his fingers caressed her shoulder blades, and they were crushed against each other.

They kissed until the blood roared in her ears and she felt drunk with desire. Then something ignited inside of her, that now familiar heat, writhing through and pulsing down her legs. Terrified, she shoved his shoulders hard, and he stumbled back, dazed.

Skybright clutched her head between tight fists, willing the blazing heat away. Willing herself not to change. *No.* Not now. Not in front of Kai Sen. Her body shook with the effort, still trembling from the kiss they had shared. Terror constricted her chest.

His thumb stroked her cheek, and she jerked away from him.

"What was that?" She tried to catch her breath, and the words came unevenly.

"I've always wondered what it was like, to kiss." His voice sounded low and thick.

"So you decided to experiment on the first handmaid you came across?"

The first handmaid he came across *naked* in the forest.

Humiliation and anger wound tight within her, and she welcomed the emotions. Anything to smother the heat that threatened to rise below.

Kai Sen made a choking noise. "No. Of course not. I wanted to kiss you." He lifted his hand to touch her again and she slapped it aside. "I like *you*," he said quietly. "I've seen plenty of servant girls in town, wandering the markets. But you were the only I ever knew brave enough to climb a giant cypress to spy on monks." He smiled. "You're the only one I've felt I could share my past with–"

"You don't even know me," she said. And it felt as if her heart was shattering like brittle porcelain, because Kai Sen could never truly know her. Not ever. "Please go."

He took a step back, and she hated him for obeying her. "Will you still meet me in the morning by the creek?" he asked.

She almost laughed. "Have you found something?"

"Come and I'll tell you." He climbed up the manor wall with ease, although she didn't know how he was able to find any purchase. Crouching low at the top, his dark eyes sought hers, before he said, "Don't be angry, Skybright." Kai Sen dropped noiselessly down onto the other side of the wall. "I like *you*." She heard him say again.

Then there was nothing more except for the soft murmurs of the evening.

CHAPTER FOUR

Skybright purposely overslept the next morning, hoping Zhen Ni would come to her. When her mistress arrived, she made it a point to seem limp while lying in her bed. Zhen Ni rushed to her, hands outstretched.

"What's wrong, Sky? Are you ill again?" She leaned over Skybright, the silver sleeves of her robe fluttering.

"It's only a headache, mistress," she said in a meek voice. "I'm sorry I didn't come to you this morning."

"Nonsense!" Zhen Ni touched her wrist. "That's what I have Rose for. I love your company too much and you never get a break. It's no wonder you've fallen ill. Especially after that—" She pursed her lips, "episode."

Skybright gave Zhen Ni a weak smile.

"Shall I have Oriole send you some rice porridge? Would

you like Nanny Bai to make a tonic?" Zhen Ni fussed with the few cushions on Skybright's bed, and her heart swelled with love for her mistress. It only made her feel worse for lying.

"I think you're right, I just need to rest."

Zhen Ni patted her hand. "I'll ask the household not to disturb you and to be especially quiet if they're outside your bedchamber. Better yet, I'll ban them from coming near this side of the quarters!" She grinned, delighted by her own fantastic idea. "I'll check in on you before the evening meal. You must feel better by then or I shall be worried."

Skybright smiled. It was so like Zhen Ni to command her back to health. "I promise I shall be, mistress."

"All right. You're sure you don't want anything?"

"I really have no appetite."

"Rest well then. Lan and I were going to spend the day composing bad love poetry and attempting calligraphy. She's better studied in the women's language than I am! And her calligraphy is quite impressive for a girl," Zhen Ni said in one long rush.

Skybright had been excluded from the weekly lessons Zhen Ni had with her tutor on the simplified words used in the women's language. Lady Yuan had thought it improper to teach a handmaid how to read or write. Now, it was something that her mistress could share with Lan.

"She can even paint a little! Lan's father taught her how to paint the most delicate plum blossoms. You should see how she purses her lips and squints when she does them." Zhen Ni mimicked Lan's expression then burst into laughter. "Then she dabs the petals in the palest pink—"

Her mistress broke off, catching the sour expression on Skybright's face. "Oh, I've tired you with my chatter." Zhen Ni leaned over and kissed her on the cheek, just as they used to do in parting when they were little girls. She smelled of lemon soap, and the sweet subtle scent that was her own skin. "Do rest, Sky."

"I will, mistress," Skybright lied.

She was becoming quite good at it.

Skybright sneaked into the kitchen again while Cook was away serving the morning meal. She threw away the day-old food that she had laid out for the hungry ghosts, and exchanged it for fresh rice, pickled cucumbers and garlic eggplant, steamed red bean buns, and a cluster of lychees. She grabbed a jug of rice wine and three cups before slinking back to her bedchamber.

Frustrated that she cared so much, Skybright took too long deciding on what to wear to meet Kai Sen, rifling through the wardrobe, discarding one outfit after the other. She had never dwelled before on her own appearance—it only mattered that Zhen Ni was beautifully dressed and put together. She finally chose a tunic the color of pale jade, embroidered with peach blossoms, and pinned silver lotus ornaments into her wound braids—gifts from Zhen Ni.

Peering out of her bedchamber, she saw no one, and hurried to the back with her stash of food. Skybright laid out the new offerings and lit another incense stick. She then ate an apple she had taken, and slipped out of the manor through the servant side entrance.

It was a gorgeous morning, and the giant cypresses soared into the blue skies. Skybright ran toward the forest, feeling unburdened and free, reveling in the majestic beauty that surrounded her. The lotus ornaments in her braids chimed with her every step, but she slowed when the trees' coolness enveloped her.

She'd always felt home hidden within, surrounded by thick trunks and leafy branches, with the dirt beneath and the glimmers of sunshine above. And it wasn't until she heard Nanny Bai's story that it made perfect sense. She was born in this forest, was *of* this forest. Her pulse quickened as she neared the creek. What if Kai Sen didn't come? And if he did, what horrible things would she learn about herself?

Her fingers rose to touch her lips, remembering the feel and taste of him. She frowned and tried to push the memory aside; it only distracted her from her task—finding out what she could about serpent demons. It's not as if she could ever be in a real relationship with Kai Sen—he was a monk, and she was ...

She broke through the trees and entered the clearing, spying Kai Sen immediately. She let out a breath of relief. His back was to her, and instead of his usual wooden staff, he had a giant book tucked against his side. Head bowed, he was observing something in the water, but turned when she neared.

Kai Sen's smile was tentative. "I wasn't sure if you would come."

"I wasn't sure if you would, either," she replied.

Skybright stood beside him, and they watched the clear water ripple over the stones and pebbles of the creek. It was soothing, mesmerizing. She wished that she could stay like this for a long time, in the sunshine, beside Kai Sen, feeling content. Feeling uncomplicated. "The rocks are all different sizes and colors," she said. She saw large gray rocks protruding from the surface, and stones and pebbles in pale pinks and blues or mottled black and white in the creek bed.

"Who knows how long they've been there," he added.

She sat down cross-legged by the water's edge. "So did you find anything?"

Kai Sen sat across from her with the heavy book in his lap. "Not much, unfortunately. The legend of the serpent demon is one of the oldest in Xia, but it's surprising how little information there is on her."

Her.

"It's always a woman?"

"Always."

He flipped to a page in the book marked with a green ribbon. She smelled the must of old paper and imagined she saw dust particles rise as he turned the pages. Kai Sen stopped at his marked page. The spread had a black and white illustration on one side and text on the other. "Here." He shifted so he was sitting beside her, their shoulders touching. "This is a depiction of the serpent demon."

She leaned over the book. The serpent demon had the face of a beautiful woman, but her irises were vertical slits, and they glowed, as was indicated by the lines drawn around her eyes, like rays of sunlight. A long forked tongue dangled from her sensuous mouth. But the only thing remotely human about her was her face, as it melded into a thick snake's head and body.

This wasn't how she appeared. She kept her human shape above the waist while in demonic form, although the long muscular coil ending in a tail was the same.

"What does it say?" Skybright pointed at the text beside the drawing.

Kai Sen began reading aloud:

"The serpent demon is another soulless creature that roams our world. She manifests as a beautiful and alluring woman, preying on unsuspecting men. In human form, she is irresistible, and there are no visual clues as to her true identity to forewarn the victim. By then the victim is usually sound asleep after an amorous encounter and is brutally murdered, either poisoned by her venomous bite or strangled by her coil. It is unclear why she kills. Some legends say she was placed in our world by the gods themselves as punishment for men who are unfaithful to their wives. Others believe she kills for the pleasure of killing. The serpent demon is immortal and can only be slain with a blessed blade or by decapitation. She often travels on deserted roads alone. She is temptress, seductress, murderer, home-wrecker—"

He stopped mid-sentence and cleared his throat.

"What?" Skybright glanced from the text to his face.

Kai Sen's dark brows drew together. "Nothing. It doesn't say much more beyond that."

"But ... can she speak in serpent form? Can she—can she give birth?"

He gave her a peculiar look, then rubbed his eyes. She noticed now the dark circles beneath them. "What a strange question. It's not mentioned in this particular text, but I read about fox spirits in another tome during my research. It said that fox spirits would often fall in love with humans and marry them, sometimes having the mortals' offspring. *Unlike the serpent demon*, the text said. The serpent demon always killed her victims and was incapable of love or bearing offspring."

Skybright's heart sank. None of this made sense.

"As for whether she can speak while in serpent form, there's no mention of that anywhere in the books I've read."

He touched the back of her hand, and she flinched away from him. "Why are you so interested in this anyway?"

Skybright drew her knees to her chest. "I don't know. It's fascinating, don't you think?"

"Fascinating isn't the word I'd choose," he said, and placed the book on the grass beside him, before stretching out his arms and folding them behind his head. "We have thousands of books in the monastery library, and the abbot has a few hundred more in his personal collection. Some of the things I've read about in those books—" He shook his head, then rolled onto his side so he could see her.

"I'm sorry I frightened you last night, Skybright. And … and I'm sorry you didn't enjoy our kiss."

She dipped her face toward him. "I never said I didn't enjoy it."

He stared at her for two beats before falling down on his back again and laughing uproariously. "And here I was worried all night that I'd done it wrong," he said, between gasps.

She smiled into her sleeve, even now recalling his palms caressing her skin, how she could feel his heart hammering wildly against her own.

"Because truly, I could kiss you for days. Of course, we would have to break off to drink water. If I've learned anything from my training, it's the importance of staying hydrated. But I could do without food and fast on your kisses," he said with a big grin, his eyes closed to the sunlight above them.

Skybright groaned, but laughed despite herself. "You're ridiculous."

Kai Sen peered at her with one eye. "Tell me you liked it as much as I did." He sat up, and covered her hand with his, suddenly serious. She didn't pull away this time. "I felt like I was drunk. And floating. It was like nothing I'd experienced before." He laced his fingers through hers, and her hand seemed small clasped within his. "There's something about you. I felt it the moment I saw you standing in that tree." He laughed that full laugh of his. "You're irresistible."

She'd been enjoying the feel of his palm against hers, but her heart dropped with that last word, her stomach clenching. She shuffled back on all fours away from him.

Irresistible.

Temptress.

Seductress and murderer.

Kai Sen scrubbed a hand across his face, but not before she saw the stricken expression on it.

"You're a monk, Kai Sen. Aren't you sworn to celibacy?" He liked her because he had no choice. She liked him because she was a fool.

He snorted. "I'm no real monk, remember?" It was jarring to hear the bitterness in his voice. "So why should I abide by their rules?"

"Well," She dug her hands deep into the dirt, "I'm not who I seem either."

"If you're trying to scare me off, it's not working." He stared at the open book, the drawing of the serpent demon leering back at him. "You can see and hear the ghosts because you're different, too, aren't you?"

Her arms pimpled, as if a cool breeze had swept across her, and she shivered. She wanted to slam the book shut.

"I do know one thing for certain." He lifted her chin with gentle fingers so she would see him. "Whatever power you have, whatever gift, you didn't choose it. Just like I didn't choose to be clairvoyant. When I saw you for the first time, it felt as if something snapped into place. It wasn't a coincidence that I found you asleep in the forest that morning, Skybright. I was drawn to your presence." His gaze was filled with warmth, with concern. "I've experienced many unusual things because of my … ability. But never this."

Skybright shook her head. "We don't even know each other, Kai—"

"You said that before. Ask me anything then," he said with a grin, a note of challenge in his voice.

"Where were you born?"

"Xi Men. In the twelfth moon."

"What's your favorite pastime?"

"Jumping."

She laughed. "What?"

"I like jumping. Leaping off the ground. Or from high up." He shrugged. "I like the freedom in the movement, the rush from the motion."

"Don't you have a less … strange hobby?"

It was his turn to laugh. "Oh, so I'm being judged now?" He sprang to his feet in one swift move. "You tell me something you like to do first."

Skybright rested her chin against her knees, thinking. Her entire life revolved around serving Zhen Ni—what did she do for pleasure? "Singing. I like to sing."

"You do have a pretty singing voice. I hope to hear more of it." Kai Sen began backing away from her, the sunlight a bright halo around his frame. "I'll jump across the creek."

"No. You'll get sopping wet!" The creek was wider than the length of two men.

But Kai Sen was already racing toward the water, and he shot straight up when his foot hit the creek's edge. Skybright covered her mouth as he flew over to the other side, landing gracefully on both feet. He turned around with a boyish grin on his tanned face.

"See? There's no feeling like it." Kai Sen leaped back across the creek with ease, using the few stones that protruded above the water, and sat down beside her. "I enjoy carving too," he said after a pause. "Making things from wood—if that's more acceptable to you."

She smiled. "Your favorite dish?"

"Cold noodles with bean curd and sesame paste. You?"

"Braised pork chops with rice."

"I'm hungry now."

"I almost forgot. I brought something to thank you." Skybright unwrapped a handkerchief, revealing four steamed red bean buns. "Cook just made them this morning." They each took one and ate in silence, both savoring the treat.

It wasn't until they had polished off all four that Kai Sen finally said, "You set up that ancestor altar for the ghosts, didn't you?"

"They asked me to."

"That was kind."

"It seemed the right thing to do," she replied. "They were lost … forgotten. Just because they were poor in life doesn't mean they should spend their afterlife in hunger."

Kai Sen considered her for a moment before saying, "For as long as I've seen the random spirit bound to our realm, it's never occurred to me to help them."

"Our circumstances are different," she said. "I only began seeing spirits recently. You were just a child and given away because of it."

He bowed his head and began pulling stray blades of grass from the earth, his shoulders tensed into a straight line. "Weren't you frightened, Skybright?"

"Not really," she replied. She remembered then what he had said to her the previous evening, right before he had kissed her: *I never feel as if I can speak of my past with the other monks.* She suddenly understood that there was the cheerful Kai Sen, full of teasing banter—the confident young man that the monks knew—and this one before her, hunched as if trying to fold inward to protect himself, still nursing the anger and heartbreak of being discarded by his own parents and taken into a monastery that would not fully accept him. She wanted to touch him, to somehow ease his pain and sorrow.

Finally, she said quietly, "I'm an orphan too, Kai Sen."

His head snapped up.

"It seems so frivolous to say. Because I know it doesn't change anything for you. But my mother abandoned me. And I had never given much thought to her—"

"Never?" Kai Sen said incredulously.

"No. It had seemed pointless to wonder, but now ... "

But now, I wonder.

"I'm sorry, Skybright." He slid his hand across her back and pulled her into him, so that they leaned together. "The monks say that those who can see the dead have one foot in this realm and one in the underworld."

"Is that how you feel, like you've got one foot in our world and the other in hell?" She knew Kai Sen was fully human, nothing like her.

Kai Sen caressed her arm with one hand, in a distracted way. "I don't know, to be truthful. I only know that I've always been marked as different." He lifted his chin in that unconscious way of his, and Skybright traced his birthmark with a light finger. He froze, seeming to hold his breath.

"And do you think your ... clairvoyance is connected to this?" she asked.

He grasped her hand, pulling it gently from his throat. "Yes, I do." His expression was guarded, lacking its usual mirth. And somehow, she knew she was the first person he had ever allowed to touch his birthmark.

"One ghost said that there's a breach in the underworld, that they escaped early," she murmured.

"It's true. The hungry ghosts are already wandering, and the Ghost Festival doesn't start for a few days yet. The monastery has been on alert. Our abbot is concerned by the stories travelers are bringing from across the provinces."

Skybright stiffened. "What stories?"

"Peasants and nobleman alike have seen ... oddities. A man twice the height of any mortal with a bird's head and black wings sprouting from his shoulders. Children without arms and a hand where their mouths should be—"

She shuddered and he leaned in to kiss her softly on the cheek. Skybright smelled again his subtle scent of camphor wood.

"I'm sorry. I shouldn't have gone on."

"No. I'm glad you told me."

Kai Sen rubbed his forehead with one hand, his weariness palpable. "The abbot has sent notices to nearby towns and villages, warning the people that all wards for their homes should be in place. That no one should go out at night, especially past the thieving hour." He reached over to grasp her hand. "Be especially careful, Skybright. I don't know what it means that spirits show themselves so clearly to us both."

She stared at their hands, fingers twined, and wished she could be truthful with him. Or tell him she didn't like him, never wanted to see him again. Make things easier for them both. But she enjoyed his company too much, and his kisses, to give them up.

"Promise you'll keep safe?"

She gripped his hand. "But what does it all mean? Are the demons real?"

"I've not seen them myself, but the sightings have been too numerous. If there truly is a breach between our realms, any demon or monster can come into ours from the underworld." Kai Sen stood and helped her up with a gentle tug. "It means that the monks are going to war."

They took leave of each other reluctantly. Skybright accepted another chaste kiss on her cheek, although she wanted nothing more than to push Kai Sen to the ground and kiss him again like they had the night before, with his arms tightly wound around her.

Her head swam with everything they had discussed—the little information she could gather on the serpent demon, the early appearance of the hungry ghosts and a breach in hell into their own world. Kai Sen had said they might not see each other again for some time, and this had filled Skybright with a sense of longing and dread. More than she should have felt for a boy that she had just met—that she barely knew.

The cheerful sunshine and blue skies seemed a mockery of what was happening around them, what would surely come again at night.

That evening, Skybright lay awake in bed, listening for the return of the hungry ghosts. But there was nothing except for the chirping of crickets. She thought back to what Kai Sen had read to her about serpent demons. If this was what she truly was, there was no way of changing it. But she could try and control when she shifted. Grabbing her hand mirror and stuffing it into a knapsack, she peered into the silent courtyard awash in moonlight, then sneaked quietly out the servant entrance after unlocking the door with her key.

She shouldn't be going into the forest so often. But she had to find out more about who, or what, she was becoming, had to find a way to control her shape shifting. She couldn't risk someone discovering her as a serpent in her bedchamber—she needed to know how to change back. And deep down, if she would admit it, the wilderness called to her.

Running, she was drawn back to the creek where she had met with Kai Sen. The three quarter moon sat high in the sky, giving enough light that she could see what she was doing. Quickly, Skybright undressed, glad for the warmth of the summer air, yet her bare skin still tingled at the thought of being so exposed in the wild. She folded her sleep clothes neatly and placed them in a pile on a stone. The familiar ritual soothed her jangled nerves.

Skybright then sat on the sparse patch of grass near the bank with her legs extended and the knapsack she had brought beside her. She concentrated and recalled that unbearable heat, imagined the feelings that struck her when her tail emerged, the writhing of her flesh, the soft whisper as scales covered her skin.

Nothing happened.

Again, she tried to change into serpent form, imagining the hotness rising below her waist, that sensation of severing then melding together. Something shifted, and she jolted up. Her tail emerged within a few breaths, and she shuddered to see it twisted in front of her, so long it touched the creek's edge. Darting her tongue out, she thought that she could still taste Kai Sen in the air, the lingering scent of camphor wood from his clothes, the distinctive salt and tang of his skin.

She retrieved the hand mirror from her knapsack. The passage Kai Sen had read mentioned venom. She opened her mouth, her forked tongue flicking out. Her heightened vision and the moon let her see her reflection perfectly. Grimacing, her upper lip pulled back to expose curved fangs where her incisors had been. Skybright shrank back from the mirror, but forced herself to look again. The fangs were the length of a finger joint, deadly sharp. With her mouth closed, her face appeared unchanged. Hand trembling, she slipped the mirror back inside her bag.

To distract herself, Skybright focused on what she could sense in her serpent form. No nocturnal creatures scampered around her, like she had felt the other night. Not even the leaves rustled. It seemed impossible that the forest, usually so filled with hidden movement and life, was at a complete and hushed stand still. She ignored the strange quiet and tried to will herself back into a girl. This was what she needed to be able to do, if she wanted to survive. She had always been asleep when she changed back and had no inkling what it felt like.

She imagined her scales vanishing, revealing human flesh, visualized her serpent length shortening and splitting in two. Something faint whirred in her chest, but nothing happened. Skybright squeezed her eyes shut and tried harder, picturing herself with bare legs. The scales of her serpent coil rippled, but the sensation halted when she felt the pounding of many feet from a great distance, like a faint echo. She flipped over and began pushing herself through the trees toward the noise. The vibrations became stronger and stronger, until she glimpsed many torches weaving between the trees.

She sensed danger like a tremor in the back of her throat,

tasted terror and anger the closer she came to the lights. Instinct told her to stay away, that she shouldn't be seen, but she was unable to pull away from the wavering torches before her. Men shouted and grunted, their thundering footsteps carrying to her like stampeding elephants. She stopped a fair distance away from the chaos, hidden among the dark trees. The large clearing ahead was filled with monks battling ... demons. There could be no other word for the creatures that she saw.

Dozens of monks clutched torches, and the bright flames cast a lurid light across the clearing; their flickering bounced off the strained faces of the men and illuminated the murderous rage of the beasts from hell. Even the tall cypresses ringing the battle appeared ominous, silent observers to the bloodshed before them. A muscular monster towered above a group of monks, his body that of a man, but with the head and legs of a goat. The demon's bare chest was a dusky blue, and he swung a giant axe at the attacking monks. The men dispersed like leaping grasshoppers beneath it.

The stillness from before had been replaced with a thousand voices that began as a hum and surged to shrieks, swelling the air and shuddering Skybright's heartbeat before dropping off again. She covered her ears, although that didn't stop her from feeling it just as strongly through her serpent coil. The Xia spoke of ghosts and demons in folklore, in tales of morality, used wards against evil to protect their homes, paid respect to their dead ancestors. But it was all a part of ritual and tradition; never considered as actuality, as fact. But nothing was more real than what Skybright was now witnessing.

She should have been terrified, in disbelief. Instead, she felt only fascination, to see these demons that appeared so much like herself, who had burst into their realm from the underworld. Their existence validated her own. She wasn't going mad. Skybright didn't know why this had happened to her, but at least she still had her sanity.

The demons and monks fought in the clearing, hacking at each other, like in a scene from some nightmare. She caught glimpses of the undead risen from their graves, could smell their musty flesh from where she hid. They shambled in spastic motions, reminding her of broken puppets. The monks set fire to them, and the undead twitched in circles, aflame, before crumpling to the earth.

Skybright tasted his scent before she saw him.

Kai Sen whirled amongst the chaotic mob, a torch in one hand and a saber in the other. He slashed with precision, at throats and shins and the tender insides of arms, while stabbing at torsos and thrusting the torch in an agile dance that was mesmerizing. The entire time he seemed to be chanting, though she was too far away to hear him. But even from this distance, the birthmark on his neck stood out, an angry palm print against his throat.

Captivated, Skybright didn't feel the approach of the undead creature until it was too late. It jumped toward her, arms extended, surprisingly quick despite the stiffness of its limbs. The overwhelming smell of decay turned her stomach. She slid away, but it followed. Instinctively, she thrust her head forward and bared her fangs, hissing deep.

A small part of her cringed that she was acting this way, like the monster she had turned into. But she shoved those human concerns aside, and relied on her intuition for survival. Skybright let the distance between them shorten, until it was close enough for her to whip her long coil out and wrap the length around its torso, binding its arms to its side.

The undead thing grunted, but didn't struggle, seemingly incapable of dealing with this new situation. She constricted the muscles of her serpent body, amazed by how powerful it was, reveling in the feel of her prey caught between her coils. They shifted and curled, writhing along the ground as they snaked their way over the undead creature's neck. Her tail wrapped around its throat. She yanked it in one violent motion, and the creature's head snapped off with a sickening pop.

Her thick serpent length unfurled smoothly, and the undead creature's body twitched on the ground for long moments, even as its head rolled into the darkness. She hissed in triumph, her hands fisted in front of her, the taste of dust and decay like grit against her tongue.

"You are supposed to be on our side."

She whipped toward the deep voice, the tip of her tail slapping against the earth.

A tall man stood behind her, dressed in full armor—silver and gold etched with crimson. The only piece missing was his helmet. His hair was long, pulled back in a top knot, like paintings she'd seen of ancient Xian warriors. He didn't seem to be more than eighteen years, but she felt as if she should bow down to him, as if he were nobility.

Instead she pushed herself back with her coil, so there was more distance between them. This man was powerful and dangerous. Her tongue darted out; he didn't appear as he truly was.

He smiled. "I can take on almost any form I want, it is true. But this is a close representation of the mortal that I was."

She slid further from him. What was he? Could he read her mind?

He closed the distance between them with two long strides. She tried to turn, to escape from this man who wasn't a man, but discovered she was unable to move. Her breaths quickened with panic as he grasped her chin in one hot hand—so hot it could burn her if he allowed it. He turned her face from one side to the other, and Skybright saw how impossibly handsome he was—in the way that gods were—with perfectly chiseled features, a strong full mouth and eyes as black as the night sky.

She swallowed hard, trying to control the tremors that swept through her.

"You look exactly like your mother," he said in a soft voice. "There is no question that you are Opal's daughter." He dropped his hand and she gasped, released from his enchantment, and slithered away from him.

"I did not think it was possible, a serpent demon giving birth. There are so few left in this world now. I have seen many things, but never a halfling such as yourself."

Was this man saying that he knew her mother? That he could confirm what she was?

Skybright threw her hands up, fingers splayed, as if she

could push him away or ward off his words.

"You cannot speak in this form," he said in sudden understanding. "Change back to your human form, and we can talk."

She shook her head and retreated further from him. Was there a glimmer of sadness in his eyes? Of sympathy?

"You have spent most of your life thinking that you are normal—human. You are not. You are one of us." He tilted his head toward the clearing, where the shouts and cries of the fighting monks and the inhuman roars of the demons drifted to them. "Those monks would kill you without hesitation. You are not a part of their world any longer. There is no denying what you are, daughter of Opal."

She twisted from him then and propelled herself deep into the forest, faster than she'd ever done, into the embrace of its darkness. *Opal.* Was that her mother's name? Her mother, the serpent demon? The salt of tears filled her throat, but didn't escape from her eyes. She couldn't cry in this form, just as she couldn't speak.

"My name is Stone," the man's voice said in her ear, and she lurched, lifting high on her serpent body. But no one was near her. "Say it if you need me." And his words whorled into the night.

Stone.

It was what he had tasted like on her tongue. Of earth and gravel and granite. Of dirt and pebbles and the most pristine jade. Of all the life that could spring from it. Or all that it could oppress with immoveable finality.

Skybright clutched herself with both arms, trying to make sense of everything she had seen that night. Trying to ease the trembling that would not stop. She never glanced back as she returned to the creek. She sank into the cold earth near its bank, pressing her bare torso against it, her tail unwinding along the ground. It was frightening how familiar this form felt to her already, how used to being unclothed she'd become. She didn't even think to cover herself when Stone had manifested from nowhere.

Change back to your human form, he had said, and we can talk.

To be naked as a girl was a completely different matter. But Skybright didn't forget her original task. She needed to be able to control her shape shifting, needed to be a girl as quickly as she could change into a serpent. She lay there, with her cheek pressed against the dirt, absorbing the quiet hum of life that reverberated through her senses, the rodents and hares, her fellow brethren slithering along the forest floor, hunting in the warm night.

She drew a deep breath and focused on becoming a girl again, on her tail splitting to give her back her legs. Her fingers thrust in the dirt. A coolness zinged through her lower half, the opposite of the heat she had always felt when her tail emerged. She tingled from the waist down. Rising unsteadily on both feet, she grinned in triumph as she pulled on her sleep clothes.

There was no use fighting fate, fighting the lot you were given in life. But she refused to be ignorant and helpless, halfling demon or no.

CHAPTER FIVE

Skybright sneaked on noiseless feet back to her bedchamber, feeling very awkward in her human form. She did her best to sponge the dirt from her body, then slipped into a peach tunic and trousers for the day. It was still some time before dawn, but feeling too restless to sleep, she slipped on her embroidered cloth slippers and stepped outside, with the intention of going to the kitchen to replenish the hungry ghosts' offerings.

She wound her way through the enormous manor, but slowed out of habit outside her mistress's quarters. A faint sound made her pause by the door panels carved with lotus. There it was again—a low moan. Was Zhen Ni having a nightmare?

Skybright slid the door panel aside. The reception hall was in complete darkness, but she walked through it with the familiarity of someone who could navigate it blindfolded. She pressed her ear against the bedchamber door. There was the rustling of silk sheets, a soft murmur and gasp. Surely, her mistress was having a bad dream.

She pushed the bedchamber door aside and the golden glow of lantern light spilled into the reception hall. Surprised that Zhen Ni had kept the lantern burning, Skybright stepped inside. The chamber was warm, tinged with the scent of peach cream and jasmine perfume, sweat and—

The bed sheet writhed in front of her, obscuring a giant lump, some kind of beast or monster. Uttering a cry, Skybright rushed to the bed, tearing the sheet back, ready to do whatever she had to to defend her mistress. But what she saw stopped her dead. Confused, she stumbled back.

Zhen Ni and Lan clutched one another, their eyes standing out in their white faces. Their hair was disheveled, floating in wild wisps around their heads. Both girls mouths and cheeks were smudged with faint rouge. Hadn't she removed the cosmetic from her mistress's lips before Zhen Ni retired to bed the previous evening?

Skybright staggered back another step, really taking in the scene. The flush in both girls' cheeks. The faint musk of pleasure that hung in the air. The fact that Zhen Ni and Lan were completely unclothed. Skybright bit her knuckle hard to keep from wailing out before running into the reception hall.

"Sky!" Zhen Ni cried. "Wait!"

She stopped, so used to obeying her mistress's commands. Skybright paced the dark hall, her fist still shoved in her mouth, feeling as if she couldn't get one full breath into her lungs, her hands numbed by shock and betrayal.

Zhen Ni rushed out a few moments later, tying a lavender robe around herself. "Sky, I wanted to tell you." Her mistress tried to grasp Skybright's hand, but she twisted out of her reach.

"Tell me what?" The words came in a rasp. She had to hear it from Zhen Ni's own mouth.

"It only happened tonight. We didn't plan... "

How could she have been such a fool when it had all been clearly laid out in front of her? She'd been so distracted by her own problems these past few weeks, she'd neglected to notice that her mistress had—she had—

"Do you love her?" Skybright's voice was so soft that Zhen Ni had to lean forward to hear her.

Her mistress shook her head, her loose braids unwinding further so that her thick hair tumbled across her shoulders. "Oh, Sky. What does it matter?"

"So it means nothing to you?"

Tears sprang into Zhen Ni's eyes, those expressive soulful eyes that shone now even in the dim reception hall. "It means everything to me." She brushed her fingers across her eyelids, her hand then straying to her mouth, lingering there. "Lan means everything to me."

"But she's a *girl*."

Zhen Ni's laugh was short and strangled.

"What would your mother say?" asked Skybright.

Zhen Ni winced as if Skybright had slapped her. "I'd tell her I was practicing for the sake of my future husband."

Skybright turned from her mistress. How could she

explain? She'd known her entire life that her mistress would be betrothed to a good boy from a well-respected family. That she would follow as her handmaid. She had prepared for this eventuality, that her mistress would give herself to her husband, that she would fall in love. Still, this future husband would be excluded from their lives within the inner quarters—from the world of women.

But this. She had never imagined this. That Zhen Ni's affections would be for another girl. Another girl just like Skybright, only higher in station. That *a girl* should steal her mistress's heart and be both friend and lover to her. What did Zhen Ni need her for now then? Not for companionship. Not even to serve her. Rose could easily replace her as handmaid. "You've no need for me any longer." Her voice quavered, even as Skybright fought against it.

She felt Zhen Ni's hand on her shoulder, and she gently turned Skybright so they were facing each other again. "Of course I do."

Skybright bit her lower lip and stepped away from Zhen Ni so that her mistress was left with her hand still raised, clasping nothing. "No matter what you say, I will always only be your handmaid, and you, my mistress." Her entire life had revolved around serving Zhen Ni, and it meant nothing. Skybright's only other alternative to this life—the only life she had ever known—was abnormal and monstrous. "You use me to conspire. To keep your secrets."

Zhen Ni's fingers clenched into a fist. "We're sisters, you and I."

"Everything I've ever done is because you commanded it of me," Skybright whispered.

Her mistress's hand dropped, heavily and without grace. "You love me because I command you to?"

No.

She loved Zhen Ni because she was full of irrepressible life and adventure, of wild notions and mischief. Because she was brave yet irreverent, utterly selfish but totally giving. She loved her mistress because it was she who tended to her scraped elbows and knees (even if they were mishaps due to Zhen Ni's ambitious exploits). She was the one to rush to Nanny Bai when Skybright, at seven years, had swallowed her front tooth by accident, dribbling blood all over her chin and screaming at the top of her lungs, the one to insist that she be dressed in the prettiest tunics and shoes possible, so they appeared more like sisters rather than mistress and servant. She loved her mistress for all of this and more.

But she didn't tell her any of these things. She wanted to hurt Zhen Ni as much as she had hurt her. Instead, Skybright said, "Come. The rooster has crowed. I should dress you for the day."

Head bowed, Zhen Ni shuffled back into the bedchamber.

Feeling wrung out, Skybright followed, and opened the lattice windows, as she did every morning. The faint light of dawn washed the bedchamber in muted dream-like colors. The large platform bed stood empty, strewn with brocaded cushions and a crumpled silk sheet.

Lan had sneaked away without either of them noticing.

The mood was subdued that day. Zhen Ni and Lan spoke very little and laughed not at all. They sat far from each other, making sure no parts of their bodies ever touched, their faces pinched in misery. Lan actually seemed physically ill, unable to look at anyone, her complexion sallow. She folded into herself, as if her stomach ached, and she appeared even younger than her sixteen years.

Zhen Ni spent the entire day casting anxious glances in Skybright's direction, worrying her lower lip until the skin broke and bled. Normally, Skybright would have stopped her before she drew blood, would have given her reassurances, massaged her shoulders, but today, she kept her distance and remained silent.

Her mistress should know her well enough to realize she would never give her and Lan's secret away. Her loyalties, no matter what happened, were to Zhen Ni. But then, she thought she had known everything about her mistress as well, until this morning. And it wasn't as if she didn't now conceal secrets of her own.

Was this what growing up, becoming a woman, meant? To show only certain, acceptable sides of yourself to others, even to those you love?

Skybright dozed throughout the day, emotionally and

physically exhausted. Zhen Ni didn't request any tasks of her, so she followed her and Lan from the fish pond room into the garden pavilion, from there to the main hall, and then to the stone benches beneath the crabapple trees by the waterfall. They drifted from one location to the next like silent ghosts, with Pearl and Rose chattering behind them.

She dreamed strange, intense dreams during her short naps. Being chased by giant looming shadows as she slithered, the terror heavy against her chest. Lying by the creek kissing Kai Sen until it felt as if her soul was pulled taut with desire. Stone's perfect and handsome face hovering above hers, like she had just woken and he was peering down at her.

You are one of us, daughter of Opal. The monks would kill you without hesitation.

Skybright jolted awake, the cushion she had leaned against falling from the bench. Zhen Ni was watching her intently, her embroidery sitting neglected in her lap. Her shoulders slumped, but she straightened when Skybright woke. Her mistress attempted a timid smile, but Skybright dropped her chin and didn't return it. How could Zhen Ni have fallen in love with another girl? Did her mistress have the same feelings for Lan as she did for Kai Sen? Did her skin tingle from Lan's touch? Did blood roar in Zhen Ni's ears, too, when they kissed? The notion seemed so strange to Skybright. But she knew her mistress well, and she knew from observing Zhen Ni that her feelings for Lan were true.

She was still angry with Zhen Ni. But Skybright missed her mistress like she missed a part of herself—a limb or organ—

missed the ease and familiarity of their relationship. Although what was the point of a true reconciliation now, of growing close again? Skybright wasn't the girl Zhen Ni had grown up with, the one she said she loved as a sister, the one she thought she knew.

What would happen if she told Zhen Ni the truth, if Skybright revealed her serpent form?

It wouldn't just be the monks, she was certain, who would turn on her.

They went through the usual rituals of preparing for bed. It wasn't a bath day, and Zhen Ni didn't ask for it specially. So Skybright undressed her, then washed her mistress's hands and feet in rose water before wiping her torso and back with a damp cloth. What had been routine for years was awkward this evening, in their strained silence, as Skybright sponged her mistress's skin, knowing Lan had seen and touched Zhen Ni in a very different way. She then fetched another bowl of scented water so her mistress could wash her face.

After, they sat in front of the vanity and she unwound Zhen Ni's hair, brushing it over and over until it gleamed in the lantern light. "I won't tell anyone," Skybright murmured.

Their eyes met in the bronzed mirror. "I know," Zhen Ni said. She took the brush from Skybright's hand and set it on the vanity. "You have a right to be angry. We tell each other everything. It's just … you haven't been yourself lately."

Skybright's heart constricted with longing to tell her mistress the truth, knowing that she never could. Her secret was as effective as any high wall, separating them, driving them apart. Finally, she said, "You can't wed a girl, mistress."

Zhen Ni pulled a face, then pressed her lips together. "You're right. I can't. But I need not wed at all."

Skybright shook her head, feeling worn. Weary.

Zhen Ni turned and caught her wrist. "We can go into town tomorrow to buy ornaments for our hair? Or take a picnic to the creek?"

"We're in the midst of the Ghost Festival. The abbot has warned us of evil omens and dangers this year. I think it's safer to stay within the manor—enjoy your time with Lan." Skybright drew the silk sheet back and arranged the cushions on the bed just as Zhen Ni liked them. "I won't interrupt you again, mistress."

Zhen Ni glanced down, but not before Skybright caught the deep flush that spread across both her cheeks. She bade her a peaceful evening and left Zhen Ni standing by the platform bed alone, reminding Skybright of a bride without a groom.

"Skybright." The whisper was so hushed she thought she imagined it.

She had snuffed the lantern a while ago, but, although she was exhausted, found that she had too much on her mind to fall asleep. Someone whispered her name again, and it was nothing like the murmuring chaos of the ghosts. It sounded like Kai Sen. She quickly pulled her cloth shoes on and slipped into the darkened courtyard. The sweet fragrance of honeysuckle filled the air, and she breathed deep, admiring the scent.

"Skybright?" His hushed inquiry came from the back alley.

She walked down the narrow corridor and peeked around the corner. Kai Sen stood, like a dark phantom, in front of her makeshift ancestor altar. She had replenished it before retiring for the evening, and the sandalwood incense still lingered in the air.

"What're you doing here?" she whispered.

He was beside her in a few quick strides, sweeping her into his arms in a tight embrace. Her cheek pressed against his chest and she drew in the familiar, comforting scent of him. They stood like that for a few moments before she disentangled herself.

"I didn't know where you slept. I came hoping that perhaps you'd hear me calling you." He cupped her cheek in one hand and she felt her entire body warm to his touch. "I thought it unlikely but I had to try … "

"My bedchamber is just on the other side of this wall." She tilted her head so she could see his face, but his features were obscured in shadows. "What's wrong?"

"The hungry ghosts were right. There's a breach in the underworld; the undead and demons have arisen too. I've seen them." He had been cradling her elbows and his grip tightened as he spoke. "I've killed them."

Skybright remembered seeing Kai Sen battling in the distance while she hid within the trees. "Goddess. Are you all right?"

His head dipped lower, so she could feel his breath when he spoke. "It's gruesome. I had never killed anything. I'd thought the abbot's notion of actual demons existing was … absurd. Those texts are hundreds of years old, some over a thousand years. What relevance could they possibly have?" Kai Sen gave a rueful chuckle. "He always did say I was too flippant in my attitude. I learned a hard lesson last night."

"What happens now?"

"I don't know. The abbot has received word from the other monasteries—the demon sightings extend across the entire kingdom. Monks are fighting in every province to keep our people safe. Traditionally, the gates of the underworld close again two weeks after the Ghost Festival begins. But who knows what will happen with this breach between our realms."

She pressed a palm against his chest. "Do take care."

She caught the flash of his teeth when he smiled. "That's why I came. To warn you. It's most dangerous at night, but you shouldn't be wandering outside the manor any longer, even in the day. Especially within the forest."

Skybright was glad for the dark, so he couldn't see her expression as a host of different emotions flitted through her. Kai Sen was killing demons—slaying monsters exactly like herself. Ignoring the knot in her stomach, she twisted the front of his black tunic in her fists and pulled him down for a kiss. He obliged, grazing her mouth softly at first, so her lips tingled. His hand slipped behind to caress her nape as the other brushed across her lower back, and he drew her even closer to him. Their kiss was slow and deep. And when she felt her insides quiver, followed by that dangerous heat, she imagined coolness drenching her legs, keeping them separate.

Human.

He could never know. No one she cared for could ever know. But she would have this one kiss, because she desired it.

It was Kai Sen who broke away first, releasing her and flinging his arms to the sides as if checking his balance. "Goddess," he said in a low voice. And for the next few moments, there were no other sounds except for their ragged breathing. "I admit I was going to ask for a kiss before I left—" He threw a hand up. "All right. Beg for one if I had to."

She laughed, then winced as it had been too loud. "Kai Sen, I like you. But—"

He pressed his fingers to her lips. "Don't. I'm going demon hunting tonight. We've started a war against the underworld. The proper things to say here are: Be careful, Kai Sen, or I'll miss you, Kai Sen." He stepped back and grinned at her. "I'll wait for you, Kai Sen," he said and climbed the wall in two breaths, crouching low at the top. "I hope we see each other again soon, Skybright. Keep safe."

She stood alone in the dark, listening for his retreating footsteps, and heard none. He moved as silently as the ghosts.

"Be careful, Kai Sen," she whispered. "I'll miss you."

But only after she felt certain that he had gone.

The Ghost Festival kept the entire manor occupied in the following days. Not only was a magnificent feast laid out for all the Yuan ancestors, hell money was burned for the dead to use in the underworld. Incense was kept lit day and night, and the fragrance of sandalwood drifted on the wind. Because of the strict warnings from the monastery and the strange sightings that had been reported, Lady Yuan hired monks to chant prayers for the dead throughout the day. Performers were also hired for shows of dancing and opera to entertain the wandering ghosts. The manor was large enough that a small stage was built in the main courtyard, and neighbors were invited to attend.

The girls kept within the manor all day and planned no secret adventures. Even servants, when they had tasks that took them outside the manor, went in pairs or more. No one from the Yuan manor besides Skybright had seen anything unusual since the Ghost Festival began, but they all took the abbot's warning seriously. For that, Skybright was relieved. She didn't encounter any more hungry ghosts, although at night, she'd sometimes catch the murmur of hundreds of voices upon the wind or glimpse shimmering light in her peripheral vision. But if the hungry ghosts feasted, they did so without bothering her.

Her relationship with Zhen Ni slowly returned to normal,

even if Skybright remained more reserved than before. If her mistress noticed, she didn't comment on it. She watched as Zhen Ni and Lan fell back into their close friendship, laughing together, their cheeks blooming again with color. Zhen Ni tried to include Skybright in all her conversations and pastimes with Lan, but Skybright felt awkward around the quiet girl, less refined. She was keenly aware that she was unable to read the simple women's language that had been taught to both girls, couldn't grasp the literary and poetic allusions they referred to in conversation. But least penetrable of all was the closeness that bound the two girls, affection, desire, and ... something more that Skybright could neither pinpoint nor describe. It was as if Zhen Ni and Lan existed in their own world, communicated in their own language. She saw it in their sidelong glances, the way their fingers would linger on each other when they passed the embroidery, how they each unconsciously leaned toward the other, like two orchid stalks on the verge of twining.

Skybright's thoughts would then turn to Kai Sen and wonder how he was. She'd say a prayer for him every time she imagined him fighting against those towering demons. Choosing to heed his warning, she remained within the manor. Skybright wanted to be a better handmaid to Zhen Ni. She still had time alone with her mistress in the mornings and before bedtime, as she prepared Zhen Ni, when they could gossip and laugh as they did before Lan had come. But after eight days had passed and still no word from Kai Sen, she began to worry. She'd started the habit of lighting the final incense stick for the hungry ghosts in the narrow alley, then pacing the length of it until she became too weary, hoping that he would come to see her.

He never did.

Zhen Ni was lying across her large platform bed with a deep purple cushion beneath her elbows. Her eyebrows knitted together as she studied the black and white stones on the board in front of her. She was playing her usual afternoon game of Go, but Lan had taken the place of Skybright as her partner. Skybright tried not to dwell on the fact that her mistress had not asked her to play since Lan had arrived. It made things easier for her, Skybright reasoned. Let Lan face the repercussions if she were foolish enough to win a game over Zhen Ni!

Skybright wiped the jade jars and boxes on Zhen Ni's vanity, arranging then rearranging them perfectly on the rose wood table. She didn't sing while she worked, her mood too heavy after over a week of not seeing Kai Sen and worrying for him. And from never knowing exactly how she should act in front of Lan, always feeling as if she were intruding. Always feeling awkward and irrelevant. She knew deep down that she was truly an outsider now, different than everyone. Skybright could never marry, but neither would she ever get her monthly letting, a passage into womanhood that was so fraught with meaning for other girls.

Zhen Ni and Lan whispered behind her on the bed, their fingers entwined.

Skybright had opened every lattice window in the large bedchamber, and a soft summer breeze stirred, bringing the subtle fragrance of orange blossoms. Afternoon sunlight cast diagonal patterns against the pale green walls. Skybright had just begun wiping the large bronzed mirror hanging above the vanity when Zhen Ni touched her shoulder, startling her.

"Could I speak with you in the reception hall, Sky?" her mistress said.

Placing the cloth she had been cleaning with on the vanity, Skybright followed her mistress into the spacious reception hall. The doors leading out to the courtyard were pulled closed to allow the girls their privacy.

"Yes, mistress?" Skybright said, unable to deny how truly happy Zhen Ni appeared, her cheeks rounded and glowing with natural color. Her expressive eyes seemed to hold an inner light.

"I'd like you to speak with Lan," Zhen Ni said in a hushed voice.

Panic surged through Skybright. "About what?"

Her mistress laughed softly and touched Skybright's sleeve, in the way she always did when she wanted to cajole Skybright into doing something. "Don't be silly. About anything," she whispered. "I want you to get to know her better. You're so quiet and withdrawn when she's around. I want you to be friends, Sky."

Skybright almost let out a sigh. "I'm your handmaid,

mistress. It isn't my place to chatter on with Mistress Fei—"

"Do this for me, Sky. Please?" Zhen Ni had her by the wrist and was pulling her back toward the bedchamber. "I'll leave you two alone for awhile," she said, and pushed the door aside and scampered out into the courtyard before Skybright could reply.

This time, Skybright did let out a long breath of exasperation.

Zhen Ni always got what she wanted.

Skybright straightened her shoulders before stepping back inside the bedchamber. Lan had moved to sit on the edge of Zhen Ni's bed, and it seemed to swallow her petite frame. Aside from her robust laugh, Lan was soft spoken and much more reserved than Zhen Ni. But then, she was a guest in the Yuan manor. The two girls studied each other silently before Skybright said, "Do you need anything, mistress? Tea? Or perhaps fruit or something sweet?"

Lan's bow-shaped mouth curved into a smile, and Skybright had to admit Lan had a beautiful smile, bright and open. Still, she imagined her mistress kissing Lan's full lips, saw again the rouge that had smeared across their cheeks when she had found them that early morning, and Skybright remembered once more her own shock and confusion. She was jealous. Not because her mistress had chosen to share her bed with another girl, but because Lan had obviously filled Zhen Ni's heart so completely. Was there any room left for her?

"Please call me Lan."

Skybright bristled. This girl was asking her to break one of the most fundamental rules of decorum. "I'm not allowed to call you only by your given name, mistress." Skybright bowed her head in acquiescence to emphasize her point.

An uncomfortable silence.

Finally, Skybright lifted her chin to see Lan red-faced, Zhen Ni's embroidered sheet twisted in both fists. "I apologize, Skybright," she said in a husky voice. "I come from a humble home, and we have no personal servants. We're fortunate to have a cook and a housekeeper who come and help Mother, but neither of them live with us."

"Please don't apologize, Mistress Fei." Skybright had known from the start that Lan's family was not as wealthy as the Yuans, but didn't realize how much so until now. They stared at each other awkwardly.

"Perhaps we are more alike than not?" Lan said after a long moment, smiling shyly.

No, Skybright thought, and bit her tongue. No matter how poor Lan's family, how low her stature, it was still above that of handmaid. Even if Skybright wore a fancier tunic and more elaborately embroidered slippers, it was only because Zhen Ni wished for her to have them. Her mistress treated her well, and they loved each other, but this conversation only stressed more to Skybright how different she was from Lan, each of them trapped within their own stations.

Seeing that Skybright had no intention of replying, Lan swallowed and tried again. "Zhen Ni speaks so highly of you." Lan's face softened just from saying her mistress's name. "You're like a sister to her."

"We grew up together since we were babes," Skybright replied. "We've never spent a day apart." Her voice wavered at the end, and the threat of tears gathered in her eyes. Saying these simple truths drove deeper just how much had changed for Skybright and Zhen Ni in the past month. How much Skybright could lose. It felt as if it were all slipping from her, because Zhen Ni had fallen in love and refused to marry. Because Skybright had discovered that she wasn't truly mortal. And she saw no way to close this widening chasm between them.

"I'm envious," Lan said. "I have just one sister, and she's six years older than me. We were never very close, and now I'm fortunate if I see her once a year."

What did Zhen Ni want from her? For Skybright to jump on the bed and ask Lan to join her in a game of Go? As shy as Lan was, Skybright could see she was truly making an effort to be friendly, but Skybright found it impossible to respond other than formally—as a servant. A servant was all she had been her entire life, and it seemed unfair that Zhen Ni expected her to do the impossible and break decorum simply because she desired it.

Mercifully, Zhen Ni returned just then, bearing a tray laden with sweet buns, salted walnuts, and sliced pears and oranges. She beamed at each of them in turn, as if she had played matchmaker and made a successful pairing. "Have I interrupted something?" she said brightly. "I've asked Oriole to bring in a pot of tea as well."

Relieved to have something to do, Skybright took the tray

from her mistress and began setting the dishes on the enameled tea table.

"What shall we do for the rest of the afternoon?" Zhen Ni asked, throwing an arm over Lan's shoulder.

"A game," Lan replied, "Something so Skybright can join us too."

Zhen Ni tapped her chin with one finger. "We can't do a poetry composition or recitation contest. Obviously Go and chess are out." Her mistress pursed her lips and Lan did the same, making fish faces at Zhen Ni. They burst into laughter and Skybright turned from them, feeling weighted down, extraneous, wishing Oriole would hurry with the tea so she could pour it and have something to occupy her time.

"A card game," Zhen Ni announced triumphantly. "After we're done with our tea." Her mistress looked around the bedchamber and frowned. "We only have two stools in here. I never noticed before. Could you bring in another, Sky?"

Skybright murmured yes and went into Zhen Ni's reception hall, but there were only heavy sitting chairs and no other stools. Frustrated, she left to search for one in the manor, while Zhen Ni and Lan took their tea together.

It was the last day of the seventh moon, the last day to celebrate the Ghost Festival before the spirits were supposed to return to the underworld. The quarter moon was still low against the sky when Skybright decided she needed to find Kai Sen, to be sure he was all right. She hadn't changed to serpent form in over a week, having learned how to quench the heat that wanted to rise by concentrating on coolness instead, and envisioning her legs staying separate. It took all her will to fight the urge, to deny that part of herself.

But tonight, she would shape shift.

Skybright ran into the looming forest, comforting as a lover's embrace. How much she'd missed it this past week! Stopping by one of the big gnarled trunks, she stripped off her sleep clothes and shifted, taking on the serpent form as if she were pulling on her favorite pair of embroidered slippers. The night opened itself to her, humming with life and overflowing with the ancient aroma of the forest. She lifted her head and tasted the air, felt the foxes and rats scatter as she slithered between the cypresses, using her heightened senses to search for any humans near. Or demons.

She returned to the clearing where she had first seen the monks fighting, but the space was empty and silent. Nothing larger than a rodent was within a half league of her. Cautiously, she slid into the forest opening, feeling the ruts and grooves beneath her tail from the fight that had taken place. The scent of those killed, mortal and demonic, was so faint it tasted like a distant memory. And the site had been cleansed by the monks after the bodies had been cleared. Even the zombie she had slain had disappeared.

Had the monks defeated the demons and closed the breach

in hell? Where was Kai Sen now?

Just the thought of him sent a vibration of pleasure through her, starting in her chest, the warmth winding leisurely to the tip of her tail.

"I was hoping you would return in your human form," a deep voice said from behind her.

Skybright reared, hissing, her hands drawn into claws at her sides. Stone stood like a statue at the clearing's edge, his form glowing subtly. He appeared in the same resplendent armor that he had worn when they first met. He shimmered, vanished, then manifested again right in front of her, quicker than she was able to blink. She fought the urge to prostrate herself before him. Instead, she slithered back, fangs bared.

His expression was inscrutable, like the carvings of the gods. She found herself comparing him to Kai Sen. Stone, perfect and remote—the most handsome man she'd ever seen. Kai Sen, brimming over with warmth and life—who stirred so many conflicting emotions within her.

Stone didn't try to close their distance again. She was grateful, for she knew she could never outrun him.

"It is so curious that you cannot speak in this form. Your mother was known for her eloquence in her serpent form. The things she would say before she killed her victims." Stone gave a low chuckle. "She would draw on classic literature and poetry, from *The Book of the Divine* and *The Book of the Dead*. She spoke with so much passion and wrath, she would bring the men to tears, sniveling and groveling at her tail before she slew them."

The passage Kai Sen had read to her said most victims died in their sleep. It obviously got it wrong when it came to her … mother. Skybright mentally stuttered over the word.

"Among all the temptresses the gods created, yours was always my personal favorite." Stone walked a slow circle around her, his hands held behind his back. His every movement hinted at the immense power he held in check. Skybright kept still, refusing to show any fear, to let him know that she was intimidated. "Devastatingly beautiful in human form, the most stunning women I've ever seen, yet still sublime in a different way in her serpent form. So lithe and powerful. So lethal."

He stopped in front of her. They were not a hand width apart. His scent overwhelmed her, an aphrodisiac, deep as earth and high as any heavenly peak. She bowed her head, trying to slow her racing heart.

"I would give you your voice back if I could, Skybright."

She flinched, and it took all her will not to rise on her serpent coil. He knew her name.

He smiled, and seemed to hold the moon in his black eyes. "I am not a mind reader. Although after so many centuries, I am good at gauging people. And I have an infinite number of spies." He raised a hand and a silver robe glimmered into existence, smelling of stars and moonlight. "Won't you shape shift back so we can talk?"

She shook her head.

"I understand. You feel exposed in your human form. It is as it should be. But know that even though you appear mortal on top, unlike other serpent demons—" Stone gestured to her naked torso and arms, "make no mistake that you are fully demonic." He stroked her face and her lower half leaped, resonating to his touch. "I will be here when you are ready to talk," he said, and disappeared.

The only indication that he was ever there was his unmistakable, lingering scent, and the flourish of warmth upon her cheek.

Skybright remained for a long time in the empty clearing after Stone had gone. Who was he? It was clear to her that he was immortal and powerful. But why did he take such an interest in her? And could she believe what he said about her mother? Instinct told her that Stone wasn't lying about knowing Opal, and that he did believe she was Opal's daughter. And that was as far as she was willing to take his word.

The rest of the night she explored the vast forest, searching for monks or monsters, but she sensed and found nothing. Disappointed, she hoped that Kai Sen was all right. In the hour before dawn, she lay by the creek and concentrated on shape shifting from her serpent form back into a girl, then into serpent again. She did this until she could change with ease and little thought, almost by reflex. Finally satisfied, she pulled on her sleep clothes and returned to the Yuan manor, as the birds began to greet the day with morning song.

Skybright had drifted to sleep without meaning to. She had only wanted to lie down for a moment, to rest her eyes, but the night's activities had exhausted her, and she woke with a start, not knowing what time it was. She changed quickly and hurried to Zhen Ni's quarters. The angle of the morning light told her she was a quarter of an hour late.

The panels to Zhen Ni's reception hall were thrown wide open, and she could hear shouting from within. Alarmed, Skybright ran inside.

Lady Yuan stood in the middle of the bedchamber, gripping a pair of silk shorts in one hand and a bamboo switch in the other. Zhen Ni crouched in front of her mother, long hair obscuring her face, completely unclothed.

"Did you think I would never find out? I'm your mother! How long were you going to lie to me? To your father?" Lady Yuan said, her voice rising with each word. Skybright cringed, shocked. She had never heard Lady Yuan raise her voice. "To hide this!" Lady Yuan waved the silk shorts, and Skybright saw that it was stained with dried blood. Goddess, where had she found that? Why hadn't Zhen Ni given them to her to wash? "That you've come into womanhood and deliberately refused to fulfill your duties as a daughter." Lady Yuan shook with rage. "How long have you kept this from me?"

"It only started this month, Mama. I swear." Zhen Ni was hugging herself, speaking to the stone floor. It broke Skybright's heart to see her this way.

"Your oaths mean nothing to me. You're a liar and … and to think I come and find you in bed with her!"

It was only then that Skybright noticed Lan cowering in the large bed, the sheet drawn over her mouth so only her round eyes peered out.

Goddess have mercy. What had they done?

"Not only do you refuse to fulfill your duties as our daughter, but you give yourself to a girl." The bamboo switch made a swishing sound as it slashed in Lan's direction. "I welcome you into my home as a guest, and you show your gratitude by seducing my daughter? Some households might approve of two girls sharing a bed, but not mine."

"No! It's not Lan's fault!" Zhen Ni screamed, rising to her knees.

Lady Yuan struck the switch across Zhen Ni's bare back. Her mistress crumpled forward, refusing to cry out. "I've spoiled you too much. Been too indulgent. And this is what it gets me." Lady Yuan raised her arm again and Skybright sprang forward, throwing herself between mother and daughter.

She wrapped her arms around Zhen Ni's shaking body, shielding her.

"You! Worthless handmaid. Of all the ungrateful creatures. I raised you as my own, as part of our family, and you betray me like this." The switch came down hard across Skybright's back and arms, again and again, and Zhen Ni cried out with each thrash. "My daughter could never have done this without your help."

"No, Mama, no! I'm sorry!" Zhen Ni and Skybright clung to each other. Her mistress's arms were wound around her waist, and she sobbed into Skybright's shoulder. "I'm so sorry!"

"You need to learn a lesson, youngest daughter. You don't go through life shirking your obligations, only doing things which please you." Slash. "You grow up, and you accept that you do things because you must." Slash.

Skybright kept her face buried in the crook of Zhen Ni's neck, biting her lip hard as the throbbing pain increased with each bamboo stroke—she lost count after ten. Lady Yuan hit her as if she were possessed. Skybright smothered a moan when the switch sang through the air, striking her again across the back. Her demonic side writhed, a whisper in her chest. She could shift, kill Lady Yuan in a matter of seconds. The thought filled her with terror, and a sob finally escaped, wracking her body, as she ignored the physical pain on the surface and wrangled with her monstrosity within.

A flurry of footsteps clattered into the bedchamber. "Lady Yuan, Lady Yuan! Stop, I beg you! They're just thoughtless girls."

Nanny Bai.

"Please, give me the bamboo switch. See, poor Skybright is bleeding." It was Golden Sparrow, the head servant who managed the household. "The young mistress can't stop shivering. She'll catch her death kneeling on the ground without clothes."

Between her own labored breaths, Skybright could hear people sniffling behind her.

"She needed to learn," Lady Yuan said, then broke into a deep, long sob.

Skybright turned her head. Zhen Ni's mother stood alone, her face pressed into her hands, the bamboo switch on the ground beside her. Nanny Bai and Golden Sparrow had thrown themselves onto their knees, crouching by Lady Yuan, their arms raised in supplication.

"She needed to learn," Lady Yuan said again in a trembling voice, brushing the tears from her cheeks. "We don't do what we want. We do what we must ... "

Nanny Bai and Golden Sparrow led Lady Yuan out of the bedchamber, followed by wide-eyed handmaids who had come to see what the commotion was about. Zhen Ni and Skybright did not let each other go for some time, as they tried to control their shaking limbs.

It was Lan who finally broke the silence. "Zhen Ni?" she said in a tremulous voice.

Skybright had forgotten she was still in the room.

"Lan," Zhen Ni replied softly, and the tender way she spoke her name told Skybright everything.

Skybright gritted her teeth, trying to manage the pain

that shook from her arms and back through her entire aching body. A sheet rustled and she heard Lan's light footsteps as she handed her mistress her robe, then gently swept Zhen Ni's black hair from her brow and caressed her cheek. "I'm so sorry," Lan said, her voice breaking. Her mistress nodded once and drew on her robe.

Zhen Ni stood and took Skybright by the hand, led her to the vanity, and sat her on the padded stool in front of it. "Oh, Skybright," she said with a sharp gasp. "Lan, could you bring warm water and some washcloths?"

The girl hurried out.

"We need to get this off of you before the blood dries." Zhen Ni unhooked the buttons on Skybright's tunic. Her hands trembled, jumping like nervous finches. "You'll have to raise your arms," she said, after she had undone all the buttons.

Skybright did so, wincing as the muscles on her shoulders and upper back tightened. Zhen Ni slowly peeled the tunic from her. The silk was wet and sticky, like shedding a second skin. She cried out as the material lifted from her.

"Oh, Skybright," her mistress said again, and dropped the tunic at her feet.

Skybright saw that the back was shredded, smeared in her own blood. Zhen Ni's fingers fluttered over her shoulders, her arms, as if she didn't know where she could touch her without causing pain. Skybright caught her mistress's wrist. "I'm all right. I'll heal."

Tears streamed down Zhen Ni's face, and she shook her head. "I'm so sorry. It should have been me taking those thrashings. It's my fault."

Skybright managed a small smile. "What kind of handmaid would I be, if I didn't take my mistress's place?"

Zhen Ni bowed her head, silent sobs shaking her body, and there was nothing Skybright could do but clasp her mistress's shoulder in comfort. Finally, when her mistress's crying slowed, she asked, "How did your mother find the silk shorts?"

"I was a fool," Zhen Ni said in a tired, bitter voice. "I panicked that morning and shoved it in the back of my wardrobe and forgot about it completely. Mama must have found it when she was taking an inventory of my clothing." She grasped Skybright's fingers and peered up at her. "I love Lan, Skybright. Do you understand? I *love* her."

Skybright sighed but said nothing as her mistress laid her head in her lap, and she stroked her hair. She remembered asking Zhen Ni if she loved Lan that morning she had discovered them together. What does it matter, Zhen Ni had replied.

We do what we must.

Lan returned with a large porcelain bowl filled with warm water, and Zhen Ni tenderly wiped the blood off of Skybright's back and arms as best she could. Skybright hunched on the stool, gripping a sheet to her chest, and gritted her teeth against the pain. Nanny Bai came a little while after to apply a salve onto her wounds.

Lan was sent away the next morning.

CHAPTER SIX

It was only the daily rituals and routines that kept Zhen Ni going in the days following Lan's banishment from the Yuan manor. She rarely spoke. She didn't eat. She never laughed. The mischievous shine in her eyes dulled to a blank stare that saw nothing around her. It was as if Skybright was watching her mistress wither away. She tried to cheer Zhen Ni, by suggesting her mistress play the lute while she sang for her—something that she had always enjoyed. But she refused. Skybright requested all the dishes that Zhen Ni loved to eat: crab meat soup, braised pork ribs with carrots, deep-fried shrimp in a spicy sweet sauce. But her mistress ate as if she tasted nothing, if she remembered to bring the food to her mouth at all.

The one thing Zhen Ni never forgot was to help clean

Skybright's wounds and apply Nanny Bai's salve each day. It pleased her mistress that she was healing well. Skybright, in turn, was physically exhausted, and spent each morning sleeping in, allowing Rose to take over the task of dressing Zhen Ni for the day. Her mistress had insisted that she take all the rest she needed to recover. But she made a poor companion to her mistress due to her injuries, when this was the time Zhen Ni needed her the most.

Twice in the night, Skybright had woken in serpent form, only to shift back with ease by recalling the coolness winding through her lower body. She had long since taken to sleeping unclothed, and would drift back to slumber as a girl once more. Her last waking thought was always of Kai Sen, of the warmth of his laughter, and the heat of his embrace.

Nine days passed like this, each a mirror image of the other, dragging so slowly it was intolerable. It was now the middle of the eighth moon, and the nights had become oppressively hot. Skybright's back was full of scabs, and they itched horribly. She tossed from side to side on her narrow bed, unable to sleep. Giving up, she dressed and wandered out into the warm summer night and into the narrow alley behind her bedchamber. The ancestor altar she had set up was gone, but she still came, hoping that Kai Sen would visit, that she would see his dark form crouched low on the top of the wall, that she would hear him whisper her name.

She wondered how he was, and hoped that he was well.

A shadow shimmered in the blackness, and the ghost she recognized as the leader of the spirits she had seen flashed into view. He appeared alone. "Mistress Skybright," he said, and bowed his head.

"I'm afraid I've taken the altar down since the Ghost Festival ended."

The spirit nodded. "Most spirits have returned and stay in the underworld now that the festival is over. Our gratitude for your offerings. But the breach is still open, so I escape once in a while to roam this realm and gather news."

"The demons are still escaping then," she said.

The ghost floated toward her. He had been a large man in life. "Yes. The monks are battling day and night. I've seen the young man with the mark on his throat, the one who can see us too. The one you call Kai Sen."

A surge of emotions flooded her so strong she pressed a hand over her heart. Kai was all right.

"I can lead you to him."

"Could you?" She could see Kai Sen again, make certain that he was well. "I've tried to find him myself, but have had no luck."

The spirit led her into the forest, a glowing orb. Skybright paused beneath a giant tree to strip off her clothes, heedless of modesty. She wasn't able to travel safely or fast enough through the trees in human form, and was useless without her serpent senses. The spirit hovered over her when she stopped, then zipped off again when she was unclothed. She chased after it, morphing into her serpent form while she ran, shape shifting seamlessly. The world opened to her as she slithered after the bright ghost, and her body vibrated with pleasure to be so free again, so filled with life.

Oh, how she'd missed this!

The spirit flew through the trees at a breakneck speed, but Skybright was able to keep pace. They delved deep into the forest, moving down Tian Kuan mountain, further than she'd ever gone. Finally, the spirit halted where the forest abruptly ended, opening into a wide clearing. A low plateau jutted from the mountain's slope across from them. Some monks had converged on the plateau, while others were spread below. They held a torch in one hand and a sword in the other, reminiscent of the last time she had seen them. Only this time, the number of demons and undead that were attacking appeared endless.

Fetid undead swarmed like locusts, hoping to spread their disease to the living with a bite or lingering touch. Giant demons with goat, ox and horse heads overran the battlefield, all swinging enormous axes. Skybright caught sight of a demon with a vulture's head and black wings sprouting from its massive shoulders. The creature's muscular thighs were covered in brown feathers, and tapered to two talons, which the demon would use by thrusting its knife-like claws into a monk, disemboweling him with one sharp twist.

She searched the chaotic scene for Kai Sen. He was on the far side of the slope, a blur of motion with his torch and saber. Had he been fighting every night since the last time they had seen each other? He was as fit and lithe as ever, but she could see the strain in his features even from this great distance. His arms and tunic were covered in black smears.

The bright spirit orb had winked out when they reached the

battle, and Skybright said a few words of gratitude to the ghost in her mind, even if he couldn't hear her. She slithered along the tree line, hidden, winding her way closer to where Kai Sen was fighting a hoard of undead, decapitating then setting them on fire. The night was lit by the stumbling creatures wreathed in flames. Skybright kept a safe distance in the trees, so no one would see her. She'd give a small triumphant hiss each time Kai Sen slew a demon or undead creature. Then something strange began to happen.

An undead thing seeming to sense her hopped into the thicket, arms extended. She slithered deeper into the forest, but it followed. Skybright strangled it as she had done once before, snapping its head from its body with her coils, and slid closer to the fighting again. Each time she drew near, another undead creature would veer toward her, sometimes followed by others. Skybright lured them deeper into the forest again and again, and killed them each the same way, until the earth was littered with corpses, the air thick with their musty stench.

Finally, there was a pause in their pursuit, and she hovered, hidden amongst the trees. Kai Sen was battling the vulture-headed demon alone. The monster towered over him, almost twice his height. Skybright had seen the thing kill another monk tonight, and her heart thudded hard against her ribs. How could she help Kai Sen? She slithered closer to the forest edge as an undead creature jumped toward Kai Sen, whose back was turned to it. Skybright hissed softly and it pivoted toward her, and she killed it with ease by snapping its head off with her thick coil before hefting the body into the trees.

The demon and Kai Sen circled each other, eyes locked, the demon's glowing a fiery orange and Kai Sen's so intensely dark they seemed to gleam. He began chanting a mantra in archaic Xian in a deep, strong voice that she barely recognized. The demon swung its giant axe and Kai Sen sprang out of the way, slashing his saber across the demon's torso as he did so. It shrieked, an inhuman cry that reverberated into the night. The demon bled a thick black ooze. It kicked out a lethal talon in fury, and Kai Sen dodged it easily, thrusting the saber deep into the demon's thigh. It screeched again, swinging its axe wildly, and Kai Sen flipped out of the way, as if carried by invisible wings. He never ceased in his chanting. The demon turned to track its prey when its wounded leg gave out, and it crashed onto one knee. Kai Sen darted in at that moment to plunge the saber into the beast's throat, and it was as if time stood still before the monster fell forward and Kai Sen leaped away, pulling his saber just in time.

He kneeled to swipe his blade across the demon's thigh, wiping the blood against the feathers. He was breathing hard, she could tell, by the rapid rise and fall of his chest. Another undead creature hopped toward Kai Sen's bent figure, arms outstretched. Oblivious, he remained by the fallen demon, head bowed.

Without thinking, Skybright slithered past the tree line, hissing. It twisted around, as if called to, and jumped toward her. She slid backwards into the safety of the forest, but before it reached cover, a torch lit its ragged clothes, and its long hair caught fire. The thing stumbled in a tight circle twice before crumpling to the ground.

Kai Sen stood behind it, illuminated by the blaze.

Skybright gasped—a gasp that erupted as a long hiss. He leaped over the flames and was upon her in an instant, chanting again in that strong voice. She tried to slide back, face averted. The words of his mantra lilted and swelled. It was a spell, she realized, and it immobilized her, rooted her serpentine body to the earth. She threw an arm up to protect herself, only to see Kai Sen raise his saber in one smooth motion.

Terrified, unable to speak, her arm jerked aside and she looked him full in the face. Kai Sen's dark brown eyes widened even as his saber fell. It was only in the last moment, and with amazing deftness, that he checked his stroke, and the blade sliced across her cheek instead of decapitating her. He had stopped chanting as he stumbled back and released her from his spell. She didn't feel the cut, but tasted the warm blood on her lips. Skybright swiped her muscular coil, knocking him from his feet, and slithered into the forest.

He sprang up in one breath and chased after her. She felt his pounding footsteps vibrating through the earth. He was fast, faster than any man she had ever seen, but she was faster. Her serpent senses let her know exactly where all the obstacles were in the vast forest, and she could have navigated it with her eyes closed. Her heart was in her throat as she slid amongst the ancient cypress trunks, feeling the distance increase between herself and Kai Sen. Blood pounded in her ears.

Then something sharp pricked the side of her neck. The world grew hazy, and darkness seized her like a giant fist.

"She hasn't woken?" The rich voice resonated, echoing across the chamber.

Skybright opened her eyes to mere slits, trying to gauge where she was. It was still night, and torches blazed along the cavern walls. A squat man stood some distance from her, dressed in crimson robes. He spoke to a tall, young monk beside him. She was in a cage with thick wooden slats. A small twitch of her tail let her know that she was somehow still in serpent form.

"We'll interrogate her when she wakes. Imagine what we could learn from her. She might even change into her human form. If so, do not let her beauty deceive you."

"Yes, Abbot Wu."

"She's the first shape shifter we've seen since the demons began crawling out of the underworld. The opportunity is too great. Call me the moment she wakes, brother."

The young man inclined his head. "Yes, Abbot Wu. But what will we do with her after?"

Skybright closed her eyes before the abbot turned to consider her. "Kill her, of course. Then we can cleanse the site."

She heard the crunch of gravel as the two walked away, and her stomach twisted. She tried to rise, push herself up with her hands, but was too weak. Her vision blurred, and the world tilted. Skybright laid her head down and lost consciousness once more.

When she awoke next, she felt someone scrutinizing her so intensely it was like sunlight on her skin. Cautious, she opened her eyes to slits again, not wanting the person to know that she was awake.

Kai Sen crouched in front of her, his hands gripping the wooden slats.

She almost jerked back to see him, and it took all her will power to keep still, to keep her face smooth, as if she were asleep.

"Skybright?" he whispered.

Her chest ached to hear his voice, to feel his presence so near. She could smell him, his wonderful scent made stronger by her serpent senses, and it stirred something primal within her.

"Is it … truly you?" His voice broke. "It can't be. This is the hell lord's work."

Skybright didn't breathe, too afraid that she would give herself away with a hiss. She was grateful she couldn't cry in serpent form, because then Kai Sen would have seen the tears slide down her face.

He rose and ran out of the cavern, his footsteps light.

She watched until he vanished into the darkness, although she could feel his easy tread for some time after. Skybright curled her coil tighter after she lost track of his vibrations, and her chest felt hollow, as if he had carried her heart away with him.

Skybright awoke to faint morning light, her mouth dry and bitter, like it had been stuffed with dirt from the graveyards. No one was inside the cavern, and the torches burned low. She pushed herself up with shaking hands. Her body ached, and it felt as if her face was pulled too tight, like a poorly fitted mask. The cage wasn't tall enough for a person to stand in, but she could rise on her serpent body. Skybright gripped the thick slats of the cage with numb hands. They would be impossible to break.

But the center slats weren't resting flush against the rest. Skybright touched one, and it swung outwards a little, a square door that wasn't latched.

Kai Sen.

Her heart raced as she pushed through the cage. The only nearby human was outside the cavern, pacing. She slithered to the opening and glimpsed the tall monk who had been speaking with the abbot. His back was half-turned to her, and she slid as fast as she could toward the tree line in the distance.

He caught the motion and shouted in surprise, giving chase. But he ran slower than Kai Sen.

Skybright's head pounded and her cheek stung, but she slithered faster than she ever had across the forest floor, as squirrels and rabbits leaped out of her path. She lowered herself so her long serpentine body fully connected with the ground and gathered its power, propelling herself at an inhuman speed through the trees. She drew her arms close to her sides, and tucked her chin, so she was more streamlined. The monk was no match for her. It wasn't until she glimpsed the tall monastery walls that she got her bearings and veered toward home. Her clothes were still where she had left them when she followed the ghost the previous night—what seemed like a lifetime ago. She shifted into human form and pulled her clothes on before running back to the Yuan Manor.

Everything was comfortingly familiar. Servants bustled as they tidied bedchambers while others carried lacquered trays, ready to serve the midday meal. Skybright kept her head down as she hurried to her bedchamber on trembling legs, and no one took notice of her. She ducked into the safety of her quarters and almost cried out when she saw Zhen Ni sitting on her bed like a statue. Her hands were folded in her lap, and the sunlight from the lattice window emphasized her cheekbones and chin.

She had lost weight since Lan had gone.

"Mistress," Skybright said, bunching her tunic in sweaty hands.

"I didn't tell anyone," Zhen Ni stated simply. She rose and drew closer, then grimaced when she saw her face. "What happened, Skybright? You'll need stitches. That cut is deep."

The cut.

Skybright picked up the hand mirror and stared. She barely recognized herself. Her face was dirt-smudged and bloodied, her braided hair in wild disarray. A cut ran down the left side of her face, from the top of her cheekbone until it was level with the corner of her mouth. The wound was split, an angry red, pulling her face tight. It throbbed, and the pain seemed to increase the longer she stared at it.

"Where did you go?" Her mistress asked.

She laid the mirror down with a quivering hand. "I went into the forest. And a branch cut me."

"I never thought the day would come that you would lie to me," Zhen Ni said.

Tears blurred Skybright's vision and she crossed her arms, trying to steady herself.

"You've changed. I was too distracted to notice while Lan was here. But I've been watching you this past week … "

"Mistress—"

"Is it a boy?"

Skybright choked, lowering her chin.

"A girl then?"

She lifted her head and her mistress arched her delicate

eyebrows. "You're right. It's a boy," Skybright finally whispered.

"Sky, how could you keep this from me! Are you in trouble? Are you with child? Did *he* do this to you?" Zhen Ni gestured to her face, worry conflicting with anger.

Oh goddess.

"No! No, we haven't … done that. And this, this was an accident."

Zhen Ni put a light hand on her shoulder and examined her face more closely. The scent of her jasmine perfume filled Skybright's senses. "I'll fetch Nanny Bai."

"Don't!"

"It must be stitched. We can't risk an infection. Leave the talking to me. You don't say a word, understand?"

Skybright nodded dumbly as Zhen Ni left her bedchamber.

Zhen Ni returned with Nanny Bai soon after. The older woman tutted loudly as she turned Skybright's face this way and that. "You'll have a scar for life." She shook her head and let out a long sigh. "Such a waste of a pretty face."

Skybright nearly snorted aloud, weary and sick from exhaustion. A scar seemed the least of her worries.

Nanny Bai forced Skybright to drink a deep cup of hard liquor, then she cleaned her wound. She screamed in pain, and

Zhen Ni clutched her hand, trying to show a brave face. When Nanny Bai began stitching the cut with needle and thread, Skybright thought she would pass out from the agony. The older woman had given her a bit of leather to bite on, so only her haggard groans could be heard.

Skybright didn't know when Nanny finished. She only recalled Zhen Ni gently laying her head on the pillow, and pulling a sheet over her before she sank, once again, into oblivion.

Zhen Ni came the next day in the late morning, bearing a tray with rice porridge, pickled cucumbers and bean curd with minced pork. Oriole followed and set down a pot of hot tea. They left her after Zhen Ni examined Skybright's wound, saying she'd send Nanny Bai soon to check on the stitches.

She was just finishing her meal when someone knocked.

"Yes?" Her voice sounded weak and rough.

Golden Sparrow popped her head in. "You have a visitor at the main gate. A young man called Kai Sen?"

Skybright almost spat out her last mouthful of food. "Tell him I'm not here."

Golden Sparrow gauged her with interest. "I'm afraid I already gave you away. I said I'd ask if you were taking visitors." She pursed her lips, her curiosity plain. "I didn't realize you were avoiding him."

"Tell him no then. I can't see him."

Golden Sparrow nodded. "Are you all right, Skybright?"

"I'm fine. Thank you." She did not look at the head servant.

She had lain down again to rest, her cheek throbbing, when she heard someone whisper her name too loudly.

No. It couldn't be.

Skybright slid her door aside to find Kai Sen in the courtyard, neck craned and face alert. He stuck out like a bamboo stalk amidst lotus blossoms.

"Kai Sen!" She waved an arm and he ran to her, his shoulders loosening with relief. Skybright dragged him in by the tunic when he was near enough.

"What do you think you're doing?" she asked, closing the panel. "Why are you soaking wet?"

The entire front of his tunic stuck to his chest, and it looked like he had just dunked his head into the creek for a bath. "The woman I spoke to threw a bucket of dishwater to get rid of me. I tried coming through the front gate, but she turned me away. So I climbed the wall again instead." Kai Sen took a step closer and the blood rushed to her head. "I had to see you."

He winced when he saw her wound, lifting his fingers so they hovered near her cheek, tingling her skin. "It's true then." His tanned face had gone pale. "I didn't want to believe it. I *couldn't* believe it."

Her chin sank toward her chest, her head felt so heavy. It was too much to hold it upright. Why were they all here, tormenting her, when she only wanted to be alone?

"I almost killed you last night, Skybright." The words came in a choked whisper.

She raised her face. "You won't tell anyone?" He looked physically ill, like someone had punched him in the chest. "Please, Kai Sen. No one knows but you."

"How can this be?" he asked.

"I don't know. Nanny Bai said she found me in the forest. I believe my mother was one."

"And you're here, like the rest of the—the demons from the underworld, to attack us?"

"No! This only happened around the time I first met you. I never knew I was … I always thought … " It was too much. She swallowed her tears, struggled to keep them at bay. They would only sting her wound. "I always thought I was … normal."

"You distracted the undead creature that was about to attack me."

"I killed many undead last night," she said, forcing a tight grin. "But I would never hurt another person. You have to believe me."

Kai Sen shook his head, swiping a hand over his eyes. "What were you doing there then, if not to fight with them?"

"I … I wanted to see you." It sounded so foolish. What had she been thinking? Showing up at their battle in serpent form, appearing exactly like all the other monsters from hell?

"Ah." Kai Sen swallowed. "Skybright, your cheek. I'm so sorry."

"It'll heal."

"But the scar—"

"I'm not vain."

Kai Sen laughed. A pained laugh that was cut short, awkward and unfamiliar. "You are all right?"

Skybright nodded, staring at the floor. She could not look at him. "What is happening then, with the breach?"

"We've been fighting every night. They keep coming, an endless army." He paused, and the silence was thick. "The abbots from all the monasteries have met, and they're devising a plan. The attacks are spreading, moving down Tian Kuan mountain. We have no choice but to follow, and hope to kill them all before they reach the base and the towns and cities below."

They were standing so far apart they might as well have been on opposite sides of the creek. She wanted more than anything to reach out and grab his hand, to press close for one of his strong embraces that took the breath from her. "Are you well then?"

He smiled, and it was strained, like her own. "I've been better."

"You're a strong fighter."

They stared at each other, and she began to feel light headed.

"I'm sorry, Skybright," he said again.

"It's not your fault. And thank you. Thank you for setting me free."

They had begun leaning toward each other, drawn like puppets on strings, but he straightened then, and blinked. What was it that flashed in his eyes? Regret? Shame? He felt shame for releasing her.

"I have to go. We'll be fighting tonight."

She nodded.

"Don't come again, Skybright. To the battles. It's too dangerous. Especially as you did last night. I—" His jaw clenched, and the anguish on his face was as plain and raw as the wound on her cheek. "It was truly you? How—"

"I don't know either, Kai Sen. I—I'm sorry too."

He bowed his head for a brief moment. "Your secret is safe with me. Just don't come again," he repeated.

"But—when will this all end?"

When will I see you again?

"I wish I knew." Kai Sen slid the door ajar. "Promise me you'll keep away."

Skybright turned from him and sat down on her narrow bed, she was too woozy to stay standing. By the time she glanced up, Kai Sen was already gone. He hadn't touched her once during their entire exchange. This was the end between them. She wanted to bury her face in the pillow, to sob her heart out, but her cheek stung too much. Instead she remained on the bed's edge, staring at her trembling hands.

Trying to force his face from her mind.

His scent and his touch.

It felt as if she fell into an exhausted trance when her door pushed open again, and her heart leaped with hope that Kai Sen had returned. Instead, Zhen Ni came in, her face even more pale than usual. Was Rose not putting cosmetics on her in the mornings?

"He's very handsome," Zhen Ni said.

Goddess have mercy. Not her mistress now.

Skybright sighed. Why did she ever wake this morning? "Yes, he is," she replied. "But no matter, it's over between us." Whatever it was that they had. Laughter and fun. Shared kisses.

Trust.

"Do you want it to be over?" Zhen Ni remained near the door.

"I'd rather not talk about it, mistress."

"I saw the way he looked at you, Skybright. He cares for you."

"You were spying on us?" She would have been aghast, if she could gather the strength.

"And you care for him. I've never seen you gaze upon anyone like that before." Zhen Ni took one step closer, and seemed to vibrate with restrained energy.

Skybright tilted her head back to stare at the wood-beamed ceiling, wincing when her stitches tightened with the motion.

"Where did you go last night?" Zhen Ni waved a hand at her face. "Why did your lover do this to you?"

"He's not my lover," Skybright snapped.

"But he did cut your cheek? How can you be with someone

like that, Sky?"Skybright dropped her head between her fists. "Please just leave."

"No," Zhen Ni said.

Skybright clenched her jaws. She hated lying to Zhen Ni, but there was no other choice. Her demonic side had driven her to this. "You've seen the warnings issued by the monastery. There are ... unpleasant things wandering through the roads and forests. We're lucky they haven't attacked the villages or towns yet, but only because the monks have been battling them," Skybright said. "I ... I went to find Kai Sen and got caught in the fighting."

"He spoke of demons as if they were real," Zhen Ni said.

"They are. I've seen them with my own eyes."

I am one.

"He's a monk?"

"Kai Sen trains and studies at the monastery, but hasn't taken his vow."

Zhen Ni twisted her hands nervously. "What of Lan? She left almost two weeks past and I've had no word from her. How am I supposed to know if she arrived home safely? That she wasn't attacked by these demons you spoke of?"

"I'm sure she's all right, mistress. Wait and a letter will come."

Zhen Ni pulled the wooden stool near the bed, so they sat across from each other. She gently grasped Skybright's chin and tilted her face to study her wound. "Tell me why it's over then. If you both care for each other?"

Skybright twisted her face, and her mistress's hand

dropped. Zhen Ni hadn't heard the entire conversation, thank the goddess.

"When have we ever kept secrets from each other, Sky?"

"Zhen Ni." She forced herself to meet her mistress's gaze, and Zhen Ni's eyes widened to hear Skybright speak her name. She hadn't done so in over ten years, not since they were little girls. "If you truly care for me, you won't ask again. You've kept your secrets before; I'm allowed mine."

Zhen Ni pounded her fists against her thighs. "It's because I care for you that I'm asking. I'm worried for you, Sky!"

"I'm all right. It's nothing I can explain." Skybright touched her knee. "Please."

Zhen Ni rose, her shoulders slumped, a shadow of the vibrant young woman she had been only a few weeks back. "Nanny Bai said she would come soon. She's making a tonic and salve for you."

Skybright exhaled, trying to release the tension she'd held in for so long.

"You know you can tell me anything, Sky, and I would still love you."

Skybright nodded, head bent, staring at Zhen Ni's beautiful slippers embroidered with dragonflies until the shining thread and bead work began to blur. After a long silence, Zhen Ni's feet finally shifted, and she left the room.

CHAPTER SEVEN

Skybright's growling stomach woke her. She stepped gingerly out of bed and opened the lattice window. It was already a few hours past dawn. She had slept the previous day away. Skybright dressed slowly, brushing her hair then winding it into braids close to her head. The scabs on her back had healed almost completely, revealing pale new skin, striping her flesh like she was some exotic animal.

She rubbed coarse salt against her teeth and carefully swiped a damp cloth over her face, avoiding her stitches. The wound didn't throb as much as it had the previous day, but her skin still felt stretched too tight.

Skybright was headed for the kitchen to find some food when Rose ran up to her. She gasped and covered her mouth when she saw Skybright's face. "Lady Yuan is asking for you."

It was rare that Lady Yuan called for her, and they hadn't spoken much since ... that morning.

"She's in her bedchamber."

And she'd never called Skybright to her private quarters before. Alarmed, she caught Rose's sleeve. "What is it?"

"It's the mistress. She's disappeared—"

Skybright ran toward Lady Yuan's quarters before Rose finished her sentence, leaving the handmaid alone in the corridor, gaping after her.

She forced herself to pause in front of Lady Yuan's reception hall. The door panels, carved with peonies, were closed. She tried to catch her breath, wiping the sweat from her forehead and upper lip with a handkerchief. Her cheek was throbbing again. She finally knocked on the door panel, and Lady Yuan's head handmaid, Nightingale, slid the door open.

Skybright had always admired Nightingale. She was four years older than Skybright, always calm and capable, performing her tasks with a dignified elegance. But the fresh powder on the handmaid's face didn't disguise the redness around her eyes. "Skybright. We've been expecting you."

Nightingale's obvious distress increased Skybright's own anxiety. Zhen Ni had never left the manor on her own, and certainly not without Skybright accompanying her. Now her mistress was wandering on the roads alone, an easy target for bandits and demons alike. If only she had warned Zhen Ni more of the monsters and bloodshed she had seen in these past weeks, perhaps she would have listened, and stayed. Perhaps if she had been more truthful to Zhen Ni, and a better friend ...

Skybright swiped her damp palms against her trousers and stepped inside. The subtle perfume of roses filled the air. Ceramic bowls full of the flowers, in pinks and yellows, adorned the tables around the reception hall. Lady Yuan's quarters were papered in the lightest blush of pink, and two huge landscape paintings hung on the far wall. Four deep curved back chairs faced each other across a dark walnut table inlaid with pearl. Brocaded cushions in each chair added to the plush feel of the space. It was more intimate than the main hall but every bit as opulent.

"Lady Yuan is waiting for you in her bedchamber."

Skybright entered the bedchamber alone. Lady Yuan's platform bed was even grander than Zhen Ni's, with silk drapes in a light sage tied back at the sides. The bedchamber was large enough to include another seating area, and Skybright found her there, alone on a cushioned chair.

Lady Yuan nodded to the seat across from her. She dabbed at her eyes with a handkerchief. Fighting the sick feeling in her stomach, Skybright sat and Lady Yuan recoiled when she saw her face. "Zhen Ni had told me you hurt yourself yesterday. But I had not realized to what extent. Is Nanny Bai taking care of you?"

"She is. Thank you, Lady Yuan."

The older woman slanted her head, a gesture that reminded her of Zhen Ni. They had the same eyes, beautiful and expressive. Why had she never seen the similarity before?

"It was the last time I spoke with her, when she came to tell me about your accident. Rose went to Zhen Ni this morning to find her quarters empty, her bed not slept in." Lady Yuan straightened. She was impeccably dressed as always, the stiff collar of her emerald tunic beaded with pearls. But no amount of cosmetics could disguise the blotchiness of her skin. "It was my fault," Lady Yuan continued with a trembling voice. "I was too harsh with her when I discovered her deception." She pressed the handkerchief against her face.

Skybright shifted her feet, not knowing what to do. As close as she was to Zhen Ni, she had never been close with Lady Yuan.

"I knew she was hurting after I sent Lan away. I read her suffering so clearly in her eyes. But I didn't go to her, didn't comfort her. She cared for Lan beyond just friendship, and there's no future in that. I believed she needed to be taught a lesson. She's a woman now, not to be coddled. I was only trying to make up for my lax ways." The tears came freely, and Lady Yuan didn't even bother to dry her cheeks. "Do you know what it feels like to be a mother? It feels like I carved a piece of my heart for every precious child that I conceived. I hurt when they hurt. And like any mother, I only want the best for them. Now she's gone."

"Why didn't you call me earlier?" Skybright asked. The question was both bold and rude, but she was trying to control her panic over Zhen Ni's disappearance.

Lady Yuan's response was unexpected. She half laughed, and picked up a piece of rice paper rolled up on the tea table. "Zhen Ni left a note. She asked, or rather instructed me, not to."

"Was that all it said?" Skybright wanted to snatch the letter from Lady Yuan's hand, but what use would it be when she couldn't read?

Lady Yuan unfurled the short piece of paper and read it aloud: *Do not worry for me. I will return home. Do not wake Skybright. She knows nothing and is ill.* Lady Yuan sighed and put the letter back on the tea table. "My daughter didn't even sign her name. I waited two hours after dawn, then sent Rose to fetch you. Thank the goddess Master Yuan will be away for another week at least tending to business. It'll be a disaster if he returns and Zhen Ni is still gone."

It was so like Zhen Ni to leave demands even in this terrible instance. And yet, she was still looking out for Skybright's well being. Skybright was desperate to find out everything. "You have searched—"

"Since after dawn. In the forest, in the city, in the town. I've hired ten men I trust to help the manor staff. An artist has been drawing a likeness of Zhen Ni all morning to accompany the announcement of her disappearance. These have been distributed and pasted everywhere." Lady Yuan drew her back even straighter, as if she could armor herself by stiffening her spine. "I care little for decorum now. My daughter is wandering out there alone and I just want her home safe again. The reward for finding her alive is one thousand gold coins."

Skybright flinched at the word alive. "She's probably on her way to Lan's home."

Lady Yuan nodded. "I've sent Golden Sparrow with an escort of eight men to the Fei manor. We're hoping we'll intercept her along the way." She touched Skybright's hand and she jumped in her seat. "Is your face all right? It looks painful."

"Yes, Lady Yuan."

"Skybright, I was harsh with you as well. I know how much Zhen Ni cares for you. You've been nothing but an exemplary handmaid and companion to her."

Skybright recalled how despondent Zhen Ni appeared when she had left her bedchamber the previous day. It was her fault that her mistress had run away. She'd been a terrible handmaid to her in these last few weeks, and an even worse friend.

"I shouldn't have beat you, Skybright," Lady Yuan said, interrupting her thoughts.

Skybright inclined her head, so the woman could not glimpse her expression. "It was your right as the lady of the manor."

"Even so—" Lady Yuan struggled for composure, to rein in the distress written so clearly on her face. "I know you're as worried as I am. Please pray that Zhen Ni will return home to us safely."

Skybright left Lady Yuan's beautiful quarters in search of Nanny Bai. She was housed on the other side of the manor with a large front room filled with drawers of medicinal herbs. She didn't visit often, as the sharp and bitter scent of the chamber would often linger in Skybright's clothes for days.

She found the older woman at her square blackwood table, grinding something with mortar and pestle. The chamber was infused with the pungent scent of sage. Nanny Bai glanced up when Skybright pulled another wooden stool to the table.

"You've heard," Nanny Bai said in her grating voice.

"I just came from Lady Yuan's."

"They did not get you sooner?"

Skybright swallowed with guilt, and she had to wait a moment before replying, "Rose had been tending to Zhen Ni."

"Zhen Ni was very concerned about your face. She came yesterday to give me specific instructions on taking care of you." Nanny Bai snorted. "As if *I* needed guidance. Now I know why. She was planning to leave even then."

"When did she come see you?"

"Midday. She had just come from your bedchamber."

It was as Skybright thought. Her refusal to speak truthfully to her mistress was the last aggrievement Zhen Ni could endure. "I have to find her."

Nanny Bai sighed. "Lady Yuan has taken care of that. The reward is so generous I think the entire province is in search of our mistress."

"I'll have better luck. Zhen Ni had always said it, and she was right. We *are* like sisters. And I've failed her in these last weeks."

"Lady Yuan would worry." Nanny Bai had not ceased in

her rhythmic motions of pounding pestle against mortar.

"She would understand. I'm useless here without Zhen Ni. A handmaid goes where her mistress goes. Will you tell her tomorrow, after I'm gone?"

Nanny Bai set the pestle down and rested her gnarled hands on the table. "It's dangerous out there in the world, Skybright. Especially now."

"I can take care of myself, Nanny. But Zhen Ni can't. She's smart and brave, but she's never left the manor on her own before." The more she spoke, the more terrified Skybright became for her mistress's fate. Demons had escaped from hell, and there's no knowing what Zhen Ni might encounter. "She needs me."

"I can't argue with you. Lady Yuan will be upset with me. But I'll tell her tomorrow that you've gone, and the reason why." She stood and fetched a jar from one of the low shelves. "I made this ointment for you just this morning. It should be enough to see that the cut heals."

The jar felt cool and heavy, and she had to hold it with both hands. "Thank you, Nanny Bai."

The older woman patted Skybright's hair, scrutinizing her wound. "It still breaks my heart to see that cut on your lovely face."

"No matter. The pain has eased."

Nanny Bai gave a low chuckle. "You've always been practical to a fault."

Skybright kissed Nanny on the cheek before she left, wondering how practicality could ever be a fault.

Skybright packed a knapsack with a few changes of clothing, a light blanket, and food that would keep for the journey. She retrieved a satin pouch filled with coins from her dresser, a savings of her allowance from Zhen Ni. But she had rare occasion to spend the coin, as the Yuans provided everything that she needed.

It was evening when she sneaked out the side entrance of the manor, making her way down the main road. Zhen Ni had left in the dead of night, and Skybright wagered that she took this more direct path the previous evening to travel as quickly as she could, before moving into the trees when daylight broke, to avoid searchers once her disappearance had been discovered.

Skybright had taken a map from Nanny Bai with detailed drawings of their province, Shi Lin, named for the dense forest that covered most of the region. Lan's home was in a town three days away by carriage. But it would take much longer on foot. The roads took a more direct path from their town of Chang He in the Tian Kuan mountain down to Lan's town of Hong Yu near its base. Skybright knew that there were no clear trails within the actual forest, and it was especially dangerous now with the breach in the underworld. She wished again that she had emphasized the danger to Zhen Ni, even though it probably wouldn't have deterred her. Once her mistress set her mind to something, she'd follow through no matter what.

The forest beckoned, and Skybright couldn't resist. Although it was a less direct path through the trees than on the main road, she'd travel much faster as a serpent. She ran into the thickets and undressed, carefully folding her clothes and placing them in her knapsack. Reaching for that searing heat within, she felt it meet her mind with a powerful surge. She shifted in an instant, and the world expanded through her serpentine senses. Skybright picked up the knapsack and slung it over her shoulder; it felt bulky and odd, like something that didn't belong to her. But she kept it, knowing she needed it to survive while in human form.

Slithering beneath the massive trees, she caught the low buzzing of bees high above, their drone prickling her scales like a caress. It brought to mind a particular day, early this summer, when she and Zhen Ni had snuck away for a picnic in the forest. It was during that outing when her mistress had first suggested they could spy beyond the tall walls of the monastery to see what went on behind its grand facade, to find out what the monks did hidden inside each day.

To prepare, Skybright would only need to practice climbing trees.

At first, she had refused, but Zhen Ni wheedled her into it, as she always did. Skybright had been quite high off the ground on her third attempt when she heard the low hum of the beehive and let out a cry. She had scrambled down as fast as she could, even while Zhen Ni asked her to try and get some fresh honey.

Skybright had glared at her mistress when she set foot back on the ground. And Zhen Ni had sniffed, indicating her disappointment. Suppressing a smile at the memory, Skybright blinked, tasting the tears that did not reach her eyes.

She paused after dawn to gauge her progress. She had a very clear sense of direction as a serpent, and hadn't taken a drink of water since she was in human form. These mortal concerns obviously didn't touch her as a demon.

A creek wound its way in front of her, maybe the same one that was near the Yuan manor. She glided past a grove of sandstone pillars, stretching high enough into the sky to block the sunlight, standing like silent sentinels. They were marked on the map with a few oblong shapes drawn in a circle, but not named. She ran a hand down the rough, tan rock, wondering how they got there and at their significance. Stone suddenly sprang into her mind, the mysterious immortal with the powerful presence. The man who claimed to have known her mother, Opal.

Skybright left the grove, trying to sense Zhen Ni or others. But no humans were near. She veered toward the next town before midday, hoping to gather some news there. Thirst and hunger struck her like physical blows when she shifted back into a girl. Her muscles ached as if she had been running non-stop for leagues. Skybright smiled wryly and ate two cabbage buns and an apple. Her stomach growled in reprimand as she gulped down mouthfuls of water from her flask. She patted her hair, still wound in tight buns at her nape, and smoothed the tunic and trousers she had pulled on. Her face throbbed again.

She cautiously applied the ointment Nanny Bai had made for her, wincing as she dabbed it over the stitches. It was another hour before she walked through the open gates of a small town called Chun Hua. The main street was quiet. Merchants fanned themselves by their bamboo stands or perched outside their stores on stools, eyelids drooping.

The midday sun was hot and blinding. Skybright paused near an announcement pasted outside a restaurant's wall. She couldn't read it, but recognized the portrait of Zhen Ni drawn by the brush artist. It was a good likeness, capturing her spirit with a few strokes. Her chest tightened to see the slight upturn at the corners of Zhen Ni's wide mouth, as if she were about to burst into laughter.

She pushed through the swinging wooden doors and stepped inside the restaurant. It was almost empty. A few patrons sat in the far corners, enjoying small dishes with rice wine or tea. Skybright approached the server girl, who didn't look more than thirteen years, leaning lazily against the back wall, keeping cool with a paper fan. "Have you any news about that missing girl?" Skybright asked.

"Some men came through yesterday looking for her." The girl stared at Skybright's wound, not bothering to hide her grimace. At least she didn't ask how she had gotten it.

"And what did you tell them?"

"Nothing. Except an hour after they left, a girl did come in." She stopped and puckered her lips. "Might've been her."

Skybright fished a gold coin from her pouch and held it in front of the girl, pinched between two fingers. "What did she look like?"

"Tall. Thin. Wore her hair exactly like yours. Her clothes and face were dirty. Her hands too. But she spoke educated, like you."

Skybright lifted her eyebrows at that.

"She asked about the poster too. I told her about the men who had come in earlier and pasted it on our wall."

"What time of the day was it?"

"Early evening yesterday. She bought some food, and gave me two gold coins, she did." The girl snapped the gold coin from between Skybright's fingertips and slipped it into a pocket. "I offered her our washroom so she could clean up a little, since she had been so kind with her coin, but she said no and left."

It had to have been Zhen Ni. Here less than a day before!

"Did she say anything about where she was going?"

The girl shot her lips out again and shook her head. "She was nervous. Fidgety. She left the moment she got her food."

"Can you tell me what she was wearing?"

"Sky blue tunic and trousers. I could see it was good quality." The girl paused, considering Skybright. "Another gold coin and I'll give you what she left behind."

Skybright lifted her chin, trying not to betray her racing pulse. What could Zhen Ni have left? Certainly not a note? She held out another gold piece for the server, but did not let go of it at once. "It better be worth the coin," Skybright said.

Although they were the same height, the girl shrank back a little, and drew something from her pocket. "I would have kept it, but it's not very well done." She held out a pale gold handkerchief.

Skybright recognized it immediately, and took it from the server, smiling. "I made this." She ran her thumb over the emerald dragonfly stitched in the corner.

"Your embroidering is awful," the girl said.

"I know." Skybright ignored the sting behind her eyes. "It was a birthday gift."

"Your friend dropped it. By the time I picked it up, she was long gone."

"Thank you," Skybright said.

Skybright left the restaurant and spent the rest of the afternoon wandering the town, hoping to gather more information, but had no luck. Finally, in the late afternoon, Skybright left the small town and walked back into the mountainous forest of Shi Lin. She fought the urge to change into serpent form the moment she was deep enough within, surrounded by towering cypresses. Retrieving a small wash cloth, she sat beside the creek she had passed earlier that morning and wiped her face and neck. She remembered Kai Sen leaping over the water, his figure limned in sunlight, as if he were flying. Remembered how he twisted and jumped before he plunged his saber into the giant demon with the vulture's head. She shivered as the forest darkened around her. Zhen Ni wouldn't be traveling tonight—she was almost certain, felt it in her core. Skybright needed to gather her thoughts.

She lit the small travel lantern she had brought and perched it on a smooth rock, setting the light by her feet. Her mind flew over everything that had happened to her in these last weeks. Who was she? What was she turning into? Only one person could answer these questions for her.

She spoke his name aloud before she could stop to reconsider. "Stone."

Skybright kept still, and waited. She heard nothing but the soft stir of the forest. And then, everything went silent, as if she had suddenly been robbed of hearing. The dirt near the creek began to whorl, caught in a tight twister, spinning and rising in a funnel. The twister gathered more earth, pebbles, and rocks, even larger stones around it, until it solidified into the shape of a tall man.

Stone.

He materialized a lifeless dark gray at first, a statue. Then in a moment, he was flesh, armored in magnificent silver and gold. She could recall the taste of his scent on her tongue, even now, the memory sharp and potent.

"I did not think you would ever speak my name." He strode forward so the faint halo of lantern light touched his boots. But she needed no light to see him. He glowed. "I have been waiting," he said.

She had never encountered him while in her mortal form, but his presence provoked the same emotions, awe and an indefinable sense of longing. He drew one step closer, and all the hairs on her arms stood on end.

"Your cheek," he said in that deep voice and dropped to one knee, the movement so swift she was unable to follow it. One moment he was towering over her, and the next, he was crouched before her. "He did this to you. That boy, the false monk."

Her mouth went dry, and her throat worked before she could speak. "It was an accident."

Stone's fingers touched her right cheek—the uninjured one—and his black eyes swept over her face. She held still, resisting the urge to jerk back from him, knowing she couldn't escape even if she wanted to. His fingertips traced her jaw line, and she could feel the heat in his touch, tamped down because he willed it. His fingers brushed to the other cheek, and he cupped his hand over her wound.

She gasped, as a tremor convulsed through her, and her cut tingled, feeling of fire and ice.

Stone dropped his hand after a moment and tilted his head. Her breath caught, he was so handsome. Frightening in his perfection. "I have healed you, but the scar remains."

Her hand flew to her cheek, and she felt the raised scar, a smooth painless ridge across her face. "Who—what are you?"

Despite his impassive features, she didn't miss the wry humor that touched his eyes. "A thank you would have sufficed."

"Thank you," she mumbled, her fingers still pressed to her cheek.

He caught her wrist and drew it aside. His touch was always gentle, but firm. She suspected he rarely needed brute strength. "You're more beautiful now because of the scar. It emphasizes the symmetry of your face."

Skybright pulled her arm back and rolled her eyes to the

night sky. All this talk of beauty. Did beauty help her make beds neatly or apply Zhen Ni's cosmetics with more expertise? Beauty did nothing to make her a better handmaid—and only caused trouble in other areas.

Stone chuckled, and the humanness of the sound surprised her. "You think it is frivolous?" He draped an elbow across his knee, still managing to appear majestic while hunched in front of her. "The beauty of your kind is precise and deliberate. Specially crafted to suit your purpose."

Seductress. Temptress. Murderer.

"What is my purpose?" she asked.

He slanted his head and scrutinized her for so long she was certain he could see into her mind, read her thoughts. "I do not know. You are unique. I have met none other like you." He pressed a hand into the dirt and the air filled with the pungent scent of earth and deep roots. "You do not behave as I would expect from a serpent demon ... like your mother did. She preyed and killed men with such finesse. She perfected it to an art form. You, I have only seen you kill the undead." He chuckled again, amused for some reason.

"Is that ... wrong?"

"Wrong?" He lifted his broad shoulders. "There is an endless supply of undead as long as there are human corpses. But you take pleasure in killing them. I find that interesting."

Stone was right. She did take pleasure in killing them. He had spies everywhere, he had said. Did he see everything that she did? He seemed to read her so easily. She didn't like that. It put her at an even greater disadvantage during their exchanges. Then she almost laughed aloud at herself, because she was trying to outwit an immortal.

"Do you know where my mother is?" She wanted answers that only he could give.

"Opal." The way he spoke her name was weighted, but with no emotion she could identify. "It is difficult for me to gauge time in human years. But our paths have not crossed since she became pregnant with you." He continued to twist the earth with one bare hand, and it vibrated with life—she felt it through the large rock she sat on. "You are sixteen or seventeen years?"

"I just turned sixteen."

Stone nodded, thoughtful. "She was well when I last saw her. Eager for her next kill. How she became with child will always be a mystery. It is supposed to be an impossibility." He paused. "To be truthful, I do not believe she survived the birth."

She recoiled, not knowing how to feel. "Why?"

"I have not sensed her presence in this realm for some time, Skybright. It is as if she winked out of existence."

She dropped her head into her hands. She was so tired. Tired of not knowing why she had turned into a serpent demon, tired of hurting those she cared for because of what she was. Tired of lying. Tired of hiding. Her feet hurt and her legs ached. She felt empty inside.

Stone lifted her chin with one hand. "May I?"

Skybright's chest seized. He wanted to kiss her and had only asked as a courtesy. But she realized she wanted to, was curious to see what it would feel like to kiss an immortal. He continued to cup her chin in his warm hand and tilted his face, pressing his perfect, sensuous mouth against hers. His lips were hot, as if he had a fever, and she caught too long a glimpse into his infinite eyes. She closed her own, head spinning.

Then it felt as if she literally leaped into a well of rushing starlight, both hot and cool, and she was plunging endlessly into its brightness, exultant, cradled within its vast glow.

Suddenly she slammed back into herself, bulky and weighted. Stone had pulled away, studying her. She gulped for air as her eyelids fluttered uncontrollably. She gripped the rock's edge, trying to steady herself.

"That was not what I expected," he said.

Skybright barked a short, strangled laugh. "Nor I. Do you kiss all the serpent demons you meet?" Then she blanched at the thought that he might have kissed her mother. And more.

Stone cocked one black eyebrow and stood, pulling her up with him. He didn't release her hand until she was firm on her feet. "Walk with me," he said. Again, it was more a command than a request. She wanted to say no just for the pleasure of refusing him, but did not.

It was full dark now, but the forest seemed to light a path for Stone as he weaved amongst the giant cypresses. As elaborate and heavy as his armor appeared, he made no noise as he walked, treading lightly. He kept his stride short, so she could walk beside him. The top of her head didn't even reach his shoulder.

"Why do you befriend me?" Skybright asked after a long silence.

"Because you intrigue me." He paused. "Because you are Opal's daughter."

"You have a history with my mother? Did you ... love her?" Her stomach knotted to be asking such intimate questions. But she had to know.

Stone did not answer immediately, and she swallowed, wondering if she'd gone too far. "I am incapable of love, Skybright. And my history is as endless as the evening sky." He stopped and she turned, drawn to him like the pointer on a compass. "But I did admire her. I cared for her in my own way. Mortals are too bound by their emotions, caged by them. They lead their entire lives ruled by emotions, by ephemeral feelings called love or hate, jealousy or desire. They make choices and do things on a whim, swayed by those emotions."

"And you feel none of these things?" she asked.

He gave a slight shake of his head. "I am too far removed. You do not live as long as I have, and survive, by feeling deeply. I sometimes wonder, from my observations, if mortals do not often die from broken hearts."

"That sounds rather poetic, coming from you."

He threw his head back and laughed, again catching her off guard by how human he sounded.

"So you wouldn't understand why I search for my mistress?" she asked. Did Stone know where Zhen Ni was? Would he offer to help her?

"I do. Because I have searched for your mother."

Skybright opened her mouth, then closed it again, stunned into silence. Stone was a complete enigma to her, even if he seemed to speak truthfully.

"With regret, I must leave you now. There is much I need to attend to," he said, leaning in. And for one terrible and thrilling moment, she thought he would kiss her again. "A peaceful evening," he said, and vanished.

The forest dimmed in his absence, along with the pungent scent of deep earth.

Skybright had never felt so alone.

CHAPTER EIGHT

S kybright wandered back to the travel lantern, grateful for the small beam of light it gave to guide her. As forthright as Stone seemed to be with his answers, she still knew so little about him. Was he of the underworld? An immortal demon? Had he and her mother been lovers? She perched back on the rock and withdrew Zhen Ni's handkerchief from her knapsack, running her palm across the smooth silk.

She studied the crooked dragonfly on the handkerchief and smiled. It truly was terrible embroidering. But Zhen Ni had lit up when Skybright gave her the gift, pressing it against her chest before giving Skybright a hug. "I'll keep it with me always," Zhen Ni had said.

Skybright scowled, an attempt to force the tears away.

Instinctively, she pressed the silk to her nose. It smelled of faint jasmine, and something deep within her chest stirred. She jumped to her feet and stripped, tucking her clothes neatly into her knapsack before shifting within two breaths into serpent form. She lifted the handkerchief to her nose again and her forked tongue darted out. An impression of her mistress still lingered in the silk and she sensed her like a mild taste at the back of her throat. She gathered her belongings and slithered through the dark trees, guided by that subtle connection, clutching the handkerchief in one hand. There was still hope of catching up with her, if she was certain of the path Zhen Ni had taken.

She traveled all night, using the connection that tugged her toward her mistress. Skybright thought over what Stone had told her about her mother—that she might be dead. She wouldn't feel regret or loss, not now, not when she still felt so conflicted over everything that had happened to her in these past weeks, since she changed. Why did she even exist, when Stone said it wasn't meant to be possible? She was a fluke, an aberrant mix of mortal and underworld. And she had no one to guide her except for Stone, whose intentions she couldn't gauge, and whom she could never fully trust. But she had little choice, for he was the only one who knew what she truly was.

Except for Kai Sen. And that was why she would probably never see him again.

Skybright followed her mistress's trail through Shi Lin, never ceasing, until past midday, when the faint taste in her throat bloomed into something much stronger. She skidded to a stop, her coils gathering behind her in a sinuous line. Zhen Ni was near. Skybright changed back to a girl, and was instantly bowled over by hunger, thirst and exhaustion. She gulped water from her flask and dressed, then stumbled on her feet, calling for her mistress. Skybright took large bites of dried beef as she walked on wobbling legs, unable to run. Being in human form was so inconvenient.

She'd lost the strong connection she had to Zhen Ni after she shifted. Tripping over a tree root, Skybright propped herself against the trunk, breathing heavily, blinking the bright spots away. She had felt her mistress near, and she refused to lose her when they were so close.

"Mistress!" She straightened, determined, and pushed herself off the tree. "It's me! Skybright."

There was a noise in the brush to her left, and Skybright went toward it, but lurched and fell to her knees. Frustrated, she wanted to scream. Zhen Ni's eyes peered over the foliage, and relief flooded her. "Mistress!"

Zhen Ni emerged through the riot of branches and prickly leaves, looking even grimier than Skybright felt. She had never seen her mistress so unkempt. "Skybright, is it truly you?" she asked, her voice trembling.

Skybright pulled herself to her feet and the two girls fell into each other's arms, hugging tight, both crying onto the other's shoulder. Finally, her mistress drew back, swiping the tears from her cheeks. "How did you find me?"

"I ran all night." Skybright paused and swallowed. "I

prayed to the gods for a miracle, mistress. We are all so worried for you. Your mother's devastated."

Zhen Ni tensed, but then her face softened. "I only wanted to see Lan again. Make sure she was all right."

"I know, mistress." Skybright's vision began to take a strange shine along the edges.

"You're shaking, Sky! You've exhausted yourself searching for me." Zhen Ni guided her to a giant cypress and made her sit against the gnarled trunk. "Have you not slept?"

"No. I needed to make up for lost time."

"And I'd wager you haven't eaten either." Zhen Ni made disapproving tutting noises and Skybright leaned her head back against the tree, almost smiling. "Eat this," Zhen Ni said, and passed a large bun to her. "It's a day old but still delicious. Taro, your favorite."

Skybright bit into it and sighed, chewing slowly, savoring the treat. When she finished, Zhen Ni passed her a flask filled with tea. She drank half the flask, comforted by the familiar scent of jasmine leaves.

"Mistress," she finally said, after Zhen Ni was done fussing over her. "I'm supposed to take care of you."

Her mistress folded a blanket into a rectangle and placed it on the ground, patting it so Skybright could use it for a pillow. "You've looked after me my entire life, Sky." And Skybright suddenly realized that Zhen Ni had cared for her in turn, in her own way. "Sleep now, for a few hours. You need the rest."

She laid her head down and didn't argue, and was asleep before she heard Zhen Ni say anything else.

ᏩᎧᏩ

It was near dusk when Zhen Ni woke her with a gentle shake of her shoulder. The birds sang in a clash of melodies above them. Skybright stretched, feeling the ache and pull of her body, but when she sat up, she felt much more refreshed. Her mistress passed the tea flask to her again and she took two long sips. "Thank you, mistress."

The two girls both lit their travel lanterns and huddled beneath the hulking tree. Skybright felt protected beneath its branches. "Have you been sleeping in the forest at night?"

Zhen Ni had her long legs drawn up, her knees tucked beneath her chin. She seemed even thinner than when she had left only a few days before. "I didn't sleep the first night and rested a bit in one of the towns yesterday. But the men Mama sent in search for me almost found me, so I slept in the forest last night."

"Weren't you scared?"

"I was terrified. There are so many noises in the forest after dark." Zhen Ni chewed her lower lip, and Skybright refrained from tapping her chin to stop her. "I'd think about seeing Lan again to give me courage."

Skybright nodded. "I was in Chun Hua and spoke to that girl in the restaurant."

"I've been lucky so far, with the one trip I've made into

town for food. Everyone's looking for me, with such a huge reward for my return." Zhen Ni smiled ruefully. "Thankfully, no one is staring too hard at this dirty servant girl."

Skybright laughed despite herself. "I think I've fared better than you have, mistress."

"That's so. But I'm in disguise." Zhen Ni grinned, and Skybright glimpsed her mistress's fierce spirit again, her determination. "I have to see Lan. I'll go home after, but I must see her one more time. Just to make sure she's all right." Zhen Ni glanced toward a lantern, and Skybright saw that her eyes were bright with unshed tears. "So I can say a proper goodbye." Her mistress rubbed her face against her sleeve, then lifted it. "You'll come with me?"

"Of course." Skybright reached across the arcs of soft light between them for Zhen Ni's hand. "We'll send word to your family when we arrive at Lan's house?"

"Yes, we can send word when we arrive."

The girls shared a meal of salted biscuits, sugared walnuts, red dates, and a bruised apple and pear for dinner. Zhen Ni cut a taro bun she had with a dagger she kept at her waist, and gave half to Skybright. Skybright stared at the silver-handled knife, the length of her forearm, amazed her mistress owned anything so lethal. Zhen Ni, wiping the sharp blade against a cloth, grinned. "I stole it from Nanny Bai." She tucked the dagger back into its sheath. "I couldn't wander about alone without some sort of weapon."

"I'm so glad I found you safe, mistress." Skybright kicked at the dirt. "I'm sorry I wasn't a better handmaid—a better friend to you in these last weeks."

The small lanterns did nothing to disperse the dark shadows that enveloped them, and Zhen Ni's eyes appeared even wider in their dim halos, too big for her thin face. "Nonsense, Sky. Here we are together again, on our most perilous adventure yet!" Her mistress squeezed her arm, and smiled. Skybright would feed Zhen Ni well when they returned to the Yuan manor, until those cheeks were rounded and flushed again.

They settled down, Zhen Ni's back tucked into Skybright's front, feeling safer for each other's nearness, and chattered on about inconsequential things, until Zhen Ni fell asleep, drawing long, even breaths. Skybright listened to her mistress for some time— listened to the noises of the forest—before she finally closed her own eyes.

It was the first full night of sleep Skybright had had in a long time, and she woke thick-headed. Zhen Ni had rolled away from her in the middle of the night and slept on her back, an arm flung out to the side. Her face was peaceful in the gray morning light, and she appeared young again, vulnerable. For when Zhen Ni was awake, she was alert and shrewd, her countenance tinged by a weariness and heartache in these past weeks that she was unable to hide.

Skybright began packing their few belongings and was

ready to go when her mistress finally woke. "I can take us to the creek to wash up," Skybright said. She then helped Zhen Ni to brush and plait her hair, pinning it close to her head the way Skybright wore it, in the style of a servant, before making the trek through the forest to the creek. The forest floor was a sea of ferns that reached as tall as their calves, and the girls picked their way carefully through it.

Skybright and Zhen Ni washed their faces, hands and feet at the creek, and rubbed coarse salt against their teeth. Then they studied Zhen Ni's map, which was better rendered than Skybright's, to see where they should head next.

"We need to buy more food. I've nothing left but a few biscuits and dates," Skybright said. "I could go into the next town to restock." She pointed at the map.

"We'll be lucky if we make it there by evening," Zhen Ni replied.

Skybright agreed. She'd be much faster in serpent form, but that was no longer a possibility. "Maybe we can risk boarding at an inn tonight."

"Oh, I'd give anything for a hot bath." Zhen Ni swept her hands across her dust stained tunic. "But I'm not sure if I can chance it."

"They aren't expecting another girl to be traveling with you."

Her mistress smiled, hope coloring her cheeks. "That's true."

Using Skybright's compass as a guide, they took as brisk a pace as they could through the forest, stopping in the late afternoon to nibble on a smoked sausage that Zhen Ni had wrapped in paper smeared with grease. She cut it in slices with her knife, and said, "This is all I've got left besides some dried dates I found at the bottom of my knapsack."

The forest was dense and wild where they had stopped. It didn't seem as if a person had ever passed through. "According to the map, if we descend westward, we should cross the main road leading to Shan An," Zhen Ni said.

The girls pressed on without rest after their short meal, both hoping to reach the town while the inns were still open. By the set of Zhen Ni's shoulders, Skybright knew that her mistress was tired. Skybright tried not to drag her own feet as she walked.

The bird song of dusk gave way to the sounds of night insects and the rustling of nocturnal creatures. An owl hooted in the distance. They continued on, carrying their lanterns, fighting through thick brush and low branches at times. But the foliage only seemed to grow denser as they headed westward. Finally, Skybright stopped them, pausing to drink from a shallow stream. She had heard its trickle, and was relieved when she actually found it in the darkness, guided by its burbling.

"I think we're lost, mistress. We should rest for the night."

Zhen Ni sat down without a word, removing her shoes with a sigh. Skybright wet a cloth for her and wiped her face and neck. Her mistress smiled, dipping her hands into the shallow water. "You're too good to me, Sky."

Skybright didn't answer, but squeezed Zhen Ni's shoulder.

"Your wound healed," Zhen Ni said after a long silence.

"Very quickly."

Startled, Skybright touched the scar running across her left cheek. She had forgotten about it. "Nanny Bai made me a special ointment," she muttered.

"You appear different somehow. Same, but different." Zhen Ni gave a low laugh. "That made little sense." She lifted her lantern as she leaned closer to examine the scar. "It's so long, and raised." Her fingertips hovered over it. "Does it hurt still?"

"No, not since the stitches came out."

"It healed well. I'm even more impressed by Nanny Bai's abilities now." Zhen Ni pulled a wooden brush from her knapsack. "Come, let me brush your hair for a change. You're looking disheveled."

Skybright turned her back and let her mistress remove the pins from her hair and brush it in long, even strokes. She remembered Stone's warm palm cupping her cheek, healing her, saw again the flash of Kai Sen's saber as he raised it to kill her. Her scalp prickled at the memories, spread until her face felt hot. She was glad that her mistress could not see, as Skybright drew a long breath and tried to forget it all.

Skybright had found a spot sheltered below overhanging boughs, so they could be protected on one side by a giant trunk, at least. She fell asleep instantly, worn from the long day of walking.

She woke in the middle of the night in demon form and jolted, whipping her serpent length away from Zhen Ni. She was about to change back when she felt the vibrations in her coil, the stomping of hundreds of feet in a heated battle a league away. Kai Sen had said the last time she saw him that the battles were moving down Tian Kuan mountain, just as Zhen Ni and she were traveling in the same direction toward Lan's home town. Skybright knew with certainty in her heart that Kai Sen was fighting in this battle.

Peering down at Zhen Ni, she saw that her mistress was deep in sleep. She always had been a heavy sleeper. The demons and undead never strayed too far from the actual battle, and her serpentine senses told her they were tightly converged in their fighting tonight. Zhen Ni would be all right as long as Skybright kept her senses on alert. She moved faster than any demon or undead she'd encountered, and if one began wandering in her mistress's direction, she could intercept it.

She slithered silently into the glooming thicket, guided by the pulsations in the earth, her thoughts on Kai Sen. The dense trees opened onto a shallow valley anchored between two forests, strewn with sandstone pillars similar to those she had seen earlier. But over half of them had toppled, making for an uneven fighting ground. Many monks stood on the fallen sandstones so they were better matched in height with the giant demons. Skybright guessed there were at least fifteen of the towering half-human monsters, more than she had ever seen before.

Undead jostled, listless and hungry for mortal flesh. But for the first time, she glimpsed other terrible creatures: spiders the size of large sows with children's faces and giant insect eyes, shadowy figures drifting in bloodstained robes, without feet or faces, their long hair unbound behind them. Both emitted an unbearable keening that Skybright could feel in the roots of her teeth. While the monks set fire to the undead, they decapitated the spider children and faceless demons. The creatures spewed thick black blood from the stumps of their necks and continued to scurry and float for a long time after, headless.

It was a grotesque sight, yet Skybright felt no horror or fear for herself, only concern for Kai Sen. She scanned the mobs for him, unable to place his scent in the chaos of smells that rose from the carnage. Hundreds of monks fought against hell's creatures, and the valley nestled between the thick trees was littered with corpses of mortals and monstrosities alike. She glimpsed the bloodied bodies of dead monks, still grasping their swords, mingled with the severed heads of the bestial and mutant, mouths gaping in hatred. She dared not look too long at the slain men, terrified that she might recognize Kai Sen's face among them.

The vibrations from the battle shuddered through her—and Skybright knew that no creatures wandered beyond that tight circle of intense fighting. Zhen Ni was safe asleep a league away. The pungent reek of black blood shed by the slain creatures mixed with the metallic taste of human blood assaulted her senses. She finally saw Kai Sen standing on one of the fallen pillars on the far left of the fray, fighting another giant demon. This time it was one with the head of a goat, its horns curving forward into dangerous points. It swung a sword that was twice as long as Kai Sen's saber, and she watched, her heart in her throat, as he leaped on the pillar beyond its wide swings, then dashed back to slash at the demon, drawing blood each time.

The goat demon roared, loud enough that even Skybright could hear it from this great distance. Without thinking, she slithered behind the tree line toward Kai Sen, hidden enough so no one could see her. She heard his chanting when she was parallel to him, heard the strong surge of his voice. But it lacked the warmth she was familiar with. He seemed leaner in the face, although his arms were wiry as ever, ropes of muscles working as he attacked his foe.

The goat demon stomped its cloven hooves, but it was clear that it could not move from where it stood, rooted by Kai Sen's spell. It continued to defend itself, determined to stab Kai Sen with its longer sword, even as he danced out of reach every time. But Skybright could see that he was tiring. How many hours had he fought like this, over how many nights? She watched, the tip of her tail writhing anxiously in the dirt. Then the goat demon lunged again, and Kai Sen lost his footing.

Skybright was sliding toward him in an instant, even as Kai Sen twisted out of the way, and the demon's sword sliced neatly across his torso. Kai Sen continued to chant, his voice never wavering, while he backed away on the stone pillar, trying to reorient himself. She saw how fast his chest rose and fell beneath his bloodied tunic, how tightly he gripped his saber.

Then she was upon the goat demon, and she reared high on her coil, sinking her fangs into the back of its naked thigh. Her venom shot into its muscular flesh, filled her mouth with bitterness. It roared again, and turned, sword raised to plunge straight into her. But she had already slithered beyond its reach. It swayed on its feet, fiery eyes piercing Skybright's, before crashing like timber. The goat demon twitched for a long time, its hooves marking deep grooves in the dirt. Finally, it stilled. Skybright knew it was dead with a flick of her tongue. She hissed in triumph, only to lift her face and see Kai Sen, standing near the pillar ledge once more, staring at her with those dark eyes ablaze.

She whipped around, sliding back toward the forest, as fast as she could. Multiple feet seemed to stomp behind, and she threw a backward glance; four undead were jumping toward her, arms thrust stiff in front of them. Wretched things.

"Kai Sen!" Someone shouted from the distance.

His friend Han tossed a torch to Kai Sen. Skybright felt Kai Sen's footsteps, then heard the grunts of the undead and familiar crackling sounds as he set them on fire. She didn't turn until she was within the forest, and saw Kai Sen decapitate all four with clean strong strokes of his saber. He didn't pause after killing them, but ran to the forest edge and stopped at the tree line, peering into its impenetrable gloom. She slid further back, silent, and he scanned the shadows, seeming to look directly at her for a moment. Warmth rose in her chest, crept up her neck.

His mouth was drawn into a tight line, his shoulders

bunched and tense. Kai Sen stood like that for a long time, the muscles of his jaw flexing, before he finally lowered his head and turned away from the trees. Away from her.

He retreated, back straight, a blazing torch in one hand and a blood-stained saber in the other. Han and another monk ran up to Kai Sen, and he passed his weapons before removing his tunic. He raised his arms so Han could wrap a bandage around his torso before pulling the dirty tunic back on and taking his weapon, without so much a pause for rest.

Skybright watched as he ran back to the fray to slaughter more undead and monstrosities.

And she didn't think it possible that she could, in that moment, miss him more.

It was a few hours before dawn when Skybright returned to their small makeshift camp. She sensed Zhen Ni during her entire journey, stirring in her sleep. Safe. Skybright changed back to human form and pulled her clothes on before settling beside her mistress again. She tried to fall asleep but couldn't, too filled with the rush of killing the goat demon and the ache of seeing Kai Sen again.

If the breach was not closed, the attacks would go on endlessly. The monks were fighting a losing battle. How long before Kai Sen was more seriously injured? Or killed?

She tightened her fists, trying to force the thoughts from her mind. Birds began chirping above them, welcoming the new morning. Skybright lay curled on her side, away from Zhen Ni, stiff and unmoving until she felt a hand on her shoulder. "A peaceful morning, Sky." Skybright swallowed the lingering bitterness of venom in her mouth and sat up, feeling stiff in her joints. "A peaceful morning, mistress."

"I think I woke in the middle of the night," Zhen Ni said, "and didn't find you beside me."

Skybright pretended to be too intent on combing her hair to glance at her mistress. "I stepped away for a moment to relieve myself," she lied.

Zhen Ni nodded. "I was so exhausted, I wasn't sure if I was dreaming."

Skybright patted the blanket and her mistress sat cross-legged in front of her so Skybright could arrange her hair in servant style. They then rose and began gathering their belongings before Skybright offered Zhen Ni the last of her salted biscuits and dates. They drank from their flasks and stretched their aching limbs. "Let's find our way back to Shan An. It's worth it to go into town to restock and perhaps find an inn where we can wash up properly and rest," Skybright said.

"That would be wonderful," Zhen Ni agreed.

"The men your mother has sent are at least a day ahead of us. But we still need to be cautious."

It was a mist-filled morning, which made their trek more challenging. They paused to consult the compass and map several times while slowly picking their way through the wilderness. The girls didn't speak for some time, intent on reaching the town.

Finally, when they paused mid-morning to sip from their flasks, Zhen Ni asked, "Is my mother very angry with me?"

"She's worried. But no, I think she blames herself that you ran away."

Her mistress gaped at her, before closing her flask and wiping her mouth with the gold handkerchief. Skybright had returned it to her.

"She felt she was too harsh in her punishment," Skybright said. "She apologized to me … for the beating."

Zhen Ni winced, then sighed, and they continued on their journey. "I knew I was being selfish, Sky. And a poor daughter. But I didn't care. I only wanted to enjoy my time with Lan." Simply speaking Lan's name aloud shadowed her mistress's face. "We'll both be married off when the time comes, and I doubt our paths will ever cross again. If she were of lower stature, I might bring her into my husband's household as a handmaid. But she wasn't born of that class. Her family is not as wealthy as ours, but neither can she ever be a handmaid."

Skybright's heart dropped. She had been right all along, Zhen Ni preferred Lan to her.

Zhen Ni glanced at her face and stopped midstride. "Oh, Sky." She grasped Skybright's elbow. "That wasn't what I meant. You're irreplaceable to me!"

"I've been so jealous … " It was difficult for Skybright to admit it; she felt as if she would choke on the words. "It would have been better if she had been your handmaid. Then you could be together."

Zhen Ni laughed and embraced her, holding Skybright tight. But Skybright stood still, arms hanging heavy at her sides. "Stop your foolish talk. You've been there for me since before I can remember—a sister, companion, my friend who's always looked out for me. Lan could never replace you in my heart; I love you both for different reasons. I'm only glad that Lan and I met as we did this summer, that we got to have the time that we did." Hearing the wistfulness in Zhen Ni's words, Skybright relented and wrapped her arms around her mistress, feeling the delicate shoulder blades in Zhen Ni's back, the sharpness of her collarbone against her cheek. "You need to eat, mistress. You've lost too much weight."

They pulled apart and Zhen Ni said, "I know. I haven't had much appetite these past few weeks. But running away, being alone, has helped. I've had a lot of time to think. And I'm glad I can see Lan one last time."

Skybright squeezed Zhen Ni's arms. Her mistress couldn't be with the one she loved either. "One last time. Aren't you angry? Aren't you—"

"I'm furious, Sky. Devastated. My heart aches constantly, a true pain. And I often feel as if I live outside of myself, like my soul isn't tethered to my body any longer." Zhen Ni bent to retrieve a large rock from the ground. "If I could pick up the world and smash it to pieces, I'd consider it, to ease my misery. Out of selfishness." She let the stone slide from her hand, and it thudded dully against the earth. "But what good would it do me? I've thought long and hard in these few days on my own, and I understand now what Mama was trying to tell me—what she was trying to teach me. Running away and seeing Lan one more time are my last selfish acts. Mama is right. I'm a grown woman now, with responsibilities to my family." Zhen Ni pressed Skybright's hand. "Come. We'll eat well together when we reach town."

They picked carefully through the brush and gnarled cypress trunks with thick roots. Skybright's heart felt full, filled with gratitude that she and Zhen Ni were together again, yet weighted with sorrow that her mistress had been faced with such a wrenching revelation and decision on her own.

We do what we must.

Dusty and travel-worn, they reached Shan An in the mid-afternoon. From the outside, it looked more like a village than a town, with low mud-colored walls surrounding it. There wasn't even a guard at the bamboo gate. The girls walked through and stopped dead at the entrance. The small main street was empty—not a person in sight—and an eerie silence descended upon them, sending pin pricks of unease down Skybright's spine.

Zhen Ni took a step forward. "Where is everyone?"

Two dogs barked ferociously in the distance, but the noise fell into frightened whimpers after a few moments. A goat dashed onto the main street from a side road, bleating in terror, kicking up clouds of dust as it ran blindly away from them.

Her mistress took another tentative step forward, and Skybright touched her arm. "Something terrible has happened. Can you smell that in the air?" Skybright lifted her chin and drew a small breath. The air smelled musty—rank. It smelled of the undead.

"What?" Zhen Ni asked. "What do you smell?"

"Unsheathe your dagger, mistress. I think this village has been attacked."

Zhen Ni drew her dagger and clutched for Skybright's fingers. They walked together slowly, hands clasped, down the abandoned main street. The stores lining it were two-storied, faded and weather worn. Weak from hunger, Skybright led Zhen Ni toward the first tea house they saw. She pushed aside the dark blue cloth overhanging the entrance and stepped inside, blinking against the dimness for a few moments until her eyes adjusted.

The tea house was empty, with overturned chairs and tables littering the floor, as if a big brawl had taken place. Skybright released Zhen Ni's hand and approached a table still filled with uneaten dishes and a pot of tea. She touched the teapot; it was cold. "All this must have happened near midday." Skybright gestured to the many tables cluttered with dishes. "See how many people were eating."

"But where did they all go?" Zhen Ni asked, and rubbed her hands over her arms, as if chilled.

"I think the undead attacked the—"

"Undead?" Her mistress stared at her, as if she were speaking in archaic Xian.

If Zhen Ni even knew half the truth ...

"Undead are reanimated corpses risen from their graves. A bite or lingering touch from them can taint a person—turn them into the same. I think the people that were in this town have been turned."

Her mistress's eyes widened. "But there must have been hundreds of people living here. Are you certain?"

Skybright nodded grimly. She should have felt fear, but after all that she'd seen and been through, she was numb inside. Nothing mattered but their survival.

"How do you know all this?"

Skybright stooped to pick up a man's leather boot, kicked off during his struggles. She avoided Zhen Ni's glance. "Kai Sen. I've talked about this with him. He's been fighting the undead and demons since the Ghost Festival began." Skybright straightened. "Come. No matter what, we still need to find something to eat."

They pushed past the swinging bamboo door into the cramped kitchen. A small fire still burned beneath a giant metal pot with a round lid. Skybright threw a cloth rag over the handle and lifted it, jumping back from the rising steam. The delicious scent of steamed buns filled the kitchen. At least a dozen were nestled within the pot, the sweet ones dotted with red on top.

"They're still fresh," Zhen Ni exclaimed.

Skybright found a beige linen and began picking up the

buns with long eating sticks, placing them on the cloth. "We can eat some and save the rest." She put one onto a chipped plate in front of Zhen Ni, and her mistress drew a stool to the square chopping table in the middle of the kitchen. Zhen Ni poked at the steaming bun with one finger. "I think I've lost my appetite."

So had Skybright. But, always practical, she took a bite from a cabbage bun and chewed slowly, forcing herself to swallow. It would have been delicious under any other circumstance. She nodded at Zhen Ni. "Eat. We need our strength." Her mistress obeyed, chewing like it was a chore, just as Skybright had.

Skybright found a pot of cold tea and poured a cup for each of them. She then wrapped up the remaining buns in the rough linen and tied a twine around it.

"The abbot warned us about the strange sightings, but I found it so hard to believe. Even when you had told me you'd seen it yourself, Sky. I thought you were still in shock from your face wound and delirious. What's become of everyone?" asked Zhen Ni. "Do you think we're in danger?" She plucked at the edge of her sleeve, the gesture betraying her nerves.

"I think they've moved on. Taking all the people they've turned with them. We can check the rest of the town, but we must still be careful." Skybright walked over to the wall, where knives hung from hooks over the sink. She took a knife the length of her forearm with a long triangular blade for slicing meat. Its tip ended in a dangerous point, and she stabbed the blade mid-air, testing its heft.

"The goddess have mercy," Zhen Ni murmured from behind her.

"I'll need a weapon too. The undead can only be killed by fire or decapitation." She returned the knife and lifted a giant cleaver. She made chopping motions with her arm, liking the feel of this one. "I can't tell you how dangerous the world is right now. We have to protect ourselves as best we can." She turned back toward Zhen Ni, who was staring at her, her expression solemn. Zhen Ni's face was dirt-smudged, and her hair escaped from the tight braids Skybright had wound against her head.

"Let's find an inn, mistress. I think we could use the cleaning up and rest." Skybright picked up the bundle of steamed buns and put it into her knapsack. She slipped the bag over her shoulder, still clutching the cleaver in one hand, and Zhen Ni followed her back onto the main street.

The girls saw no other person as they wandered down the main street, knives poised in their hands. They stepped over bundles of carrots and cabbage, eggplants and mushrooms, a tied stack of cut bamboo—all discarded in the middle of the road. An orange tabby followed them for part of the way, yowling inconsolably. Zhen Ni fed it small bites of a pork bun, quieting the frightened cat. But when Skybright tried to reach down to pet it, the cat thrashed its tail, hissing. She jumped back, and Zhen Ni laughed, giving it another piece of pork bun. "I don't think it likes you."

Skybright wondered what the cat had witnessed a few hours before. And if it somehow sensed her demonic side. The cat's anxiety seemed to be infectious, and Skybright felt her hands tingle as she wondered where the undead had gone. Down the main road to attack the next town and grow in strength and size? Skybright grasped the cleaver tighter, stilling the shudder that threatened to overtake her. Her main concern was keeping Zhen Ni safe, and guiding her to Lan without harm befalling them. She would have suggested they turn back toward Yuan manor, but knew that Zhen Ni would refuse.

The sound was imperceptible at first, a soft stirring of wind over dusted cobblestones. But then it became a scrape, a rhythmic thumping. Skybright whipped around in time to catch an undead creature emerging from a side street, its feet thudding spasmodically. The orange tabby shot away, disappearing beneath an overturned barrow. "Where are you going, cat?" Zhen Ni asked, making kissing noises.

"Mistress—"

Zhen Ni turned and almost dropped her knife. She took a step back, shaking her head, lips moving soundlessly in horror.

"They're stupid and slow." Skybright passed her knapsack to Zhen Ni, trying to keep her tone level. "Just stay a safe distance away, and I'll take care of it."

The undead thing continued to lurch toward them, arms held out stiff and straight. It was a woman, its face and torso bloated beyond recognition. Its skin had turned a greenish black while buried beneath ground, and some of it seemed to slough off as it staggered along. A jade comb still clung to its disheveled tresses, and the peonies embroidered on its blue funeral dress were like new, the fabric pulled taut against its swollen stomach. Its distended eyes were rolled to the back of its head, and it rasped a low noise as it closed the distance between them. The thing was horrifying in the brightness of day; she felt frightened of the undead for the first time as it veered straight for Zhen Ni.

Skybright didn't wait for it to get any closer to her mistress. She ran up and buried the cleaver in its forehead, right between the eyes. It felt just like she was splitting a hard melon. The thing stopped midstride, head lolling so her wrists rolled with the motion, as she tried to yank the cleaver from its skull. Its protruding tongue seemed to mock her. Skybright finally wrenched it free. Disgusted and terrified, she stood back and kicked it square in the stomach as it teetered, staring sightlessly at her.

Her aim was poor, and the kick was weak. The undead creature stumbled back a step. This would be so much easier if she were in serpent form. Frustrated, and afraid she'd lose momentum from fear, Skybright ran behind it and shoved her shoulder against its back with all her might. It toppled, arms snapping beneath its own body. Zhen Ni let out a short cry, then covered her mouth. Skybright kneeled down beside the thing and sank the cleaver into the base of its neck. It took five forceful whacks before the head rolled from the twitching body, and Skybright was assaulted with the sickening stench of death and rot.

Skybright turned from it and retched. Then Zhen Ni was beside her, pulling her away from the corpse. "Goddess, Sky! Are you all right?" Her mistress still clutched her knife in one hand, and there was a sheen of sweat on her mottled face. "Is it ... dead?"

"Yes." Skybright wiped her mouth with a trembling hand. "The monks usually set the corpses on fire, but I think cutting its head off is enough."

"You said there are hundreds of those things." Her mistress gripped Skybright's shoulder so hard it hurt. "We have to get out of here!"

Skybright rose unsteadily to her feet with her mistress's help. Zhen Ni gave her a flask so she could rinse out her mouth and wash her hands. "No. We're safer in the town. Out in the open, we'd be easy targets with nowhere to hide."

Zhen Ni stared at the crumpled corpse, and Skybright reached over to grasp her fingers. "I'll keep us safe, mistress."

They walked further down the main road, but didn't go far before the orange tabby dashed out from beneath the barrow to sidle along Zhen Ni. Skybright felt her mistress's shoulders loosen just a touch as the cat wound its body around her legs. "Smart cat," Zhen Ni murmured, scratching between its ears. The tabby still pointedly ignored Skybright.

"Let's try this inn," Skybright said, leading them down a side street to a three-story inn tucked between a tailor and book shop. Bolts of beautiful jade and ivory brocades had been knocked over, the gleaming fabrics unfurled on the dirt in front of the tailor's. Skybright pushed the door of the inn aside and peered into the empty main hall. As with the tea house, stools and tables lay overturned, like someone had come and picked up all the furniture and hurled it against the floor in a rage.

"Come," Skybright said over her shoulder in a soft voice, and Zhen Ni followed so closely she kicked Skybright's heel twice as they walked through a door in the back of the main hall. They stepped into a clean kitchen with a few plates of cold cuts set out on the counter. Zhen Ni picked a slice of beef tongue from the plate and gave it to the tabby. It meowed in appreciation, eating it with delicate bites. Skybright scanned the room. "There. The bath house is connected to the kitchen, as I thought. I'll heat some water so you can wash."

Zhen Ni shivered in anticipation, and helped Skybright fetch water from a giant cistern.

The large pots took a while to boil, and the girls spent some time wiping their faces down with wet cloths and brushing each other's hair, their cleaver and dagger within easy reach. The tabby had curled up beneath the kitchen table, and it watched them through half-lidded eyes. After Skybright helped Zhen Ni bathe, she stepped into the wooden tub herself, scrubbing the grime and the cloying stench of the undead from her skin. She felt revived after, and even Zhen Ni appeared less pale.

"What do you think we should do now, Sky?"

Skybright tilted her head. The small town was still utterly silent, much quieter than the forest, which was always alive with noise and movement. The musty scent of the undead lingered, but had faded. "I think we should rest for a few hours, mistress. I don't believe the undead will be returning here, and it's better if we stayed awhile and put some distance between them and us. What I killed was a stray."

"Where are they going? What do they want?" Zhen Ni's voice began to rise with panic. "What if they attack Lan's town?"

"I don't know what they want, mistress, other than to wreak havoc. If they're stopping in each town and village on the way down Tian Kuan mountain, we'll pass them and reach Lan first. Don't worry." In truth, Skybright had no inkling what the undead or demons' intents were, and how they would be moving. She only hoped that Kai Sen was all right, battling enemies that seemed incapable of being beaten.

They climbed the narrow wooden stairs to the topmost floor and selected the largest room in the inn. It contained two narrow beds, a wide window overlooking the faded roof tiles of the small town, and a lopsided vanity and chair. The tabby leaped onto the worn cushion of the seat. It kneaded it before curling up, yawning ostentatiously so its fangs showed. Zhen Ni sat down on one of the beds, gripping her hands in her lap. "I'm frightened, Sky."

Skybright kneeled before her mistress and touched her arm. "It'll be all right. We've got weapons and a demon-sensing cat on our side," Skybright jested.

Zhen Ni gave a short laugh. "It's an adorable cat, but I doubt her abilities."

Skybright stood and tugged her narrow bed toward the door. Then went to the head and pushed it the rest of the way, until it blocked the entrance completely. "There. Nothing can come in now. Not past me. We're on the third floor, and safe."

"What would I do without you, Sky?" Her mistress flashed her a smile, a wishful, melancholic smile that caused Skybright's throat to tighten. "You should have seen how you attacked that dead thing, like some warrior. Madame Lo said you were strong, and she was right."

"You're strong, too, mistress."

Zhen Ni lay on her side on the bed, tucking her knees against her chest. "I would suffer heartache. And—what was it that she said—cause trouble and grief for my family?" She laughed bitterly. "Mama wasn't fooling when she said Madame Lo was the best seer of our time."

Skybright lay down on her bed too, facing her mistress. "Do you regret it? Loving Lan?"

Zhen Ni was quiet for some time, watching the tabby licking its paw with intense concentration. "No. No matter what happens, I'll never regret it. How can one ever regret falling in love?" She smiled again, a small smile, but a genuine one.

"I think you've softened since falling in love," Skybright said.

Her mistress clutched the thin blanket in her hand. "You're probably right. I've not been denied anything I wanted in life until now. And I would trade every frivolous thing I ever thought was important to be with Lan instead. I wish I had something of hers, a keepsake." Zhen Ni eased her grip on the fabric, as if she had to force her fingers to relax. "What about this boy called Kai Sen? Do you love him?"

Did she love Kai Sen? Skybright knew he was never far from her mind, that he lingered in the dark and warm recesses of all her dreams each night. "It doesn't matter. It's over," she murmured. "We only met a few times, and ... and we never truly knew each other."

"What is there to know, Sky? You're loyal and kind and trustworthy. You're forthright and sing beautifully. I'd wager Kai Sen knows all these things—and it's no wonder he's so taken with you."

Skybright said nothing.

"You believe he's been untruthful to you?"

"No. Never."

"He's probably feeling guilty for that scar he gave you, then. I know you said it was an accident, but it's still a terrible thing to have inflicted on someone you care for."

Skybright ran her fingertips over the ridge of the scar, from beneath her left eye until it was flush with the corner of her mouth. She hadn't thought of it since Stone had healed the wound, and each random glimpse at her reflection was a small shock. "He didn't mean to hurt me," Skybright said. "He ... he saved me." If it hadn't been for Kai Sen opening the cage for her, she'd surely be dead by now, after an awful interrogation with Abbot Wu.

"Then maybe it'll work out," Zhen Ni said. "You won't tell me what happened that night—when Kai Sen cut you by accident?"

Skybright shook her head. "I'd rather not speak of it."

"Madame Lo was unable to see your fortune clearly. What

could you possibly have to hide? Perhaps the seedlings of love have been planted for this boy called Kai Sen and you're too shy to admit it to me? To admit it to yourself? I would not begrudge you a lover, Sky." Zhen Ni closed her eyes, her features relaxing. "We have a lifetime together, and you can tell me one day."

Skybright watched her mistress until her breathing became slow and steady, before she closed her own eyes, wishing her secret could be as easily told as Zhen Ni believed.

The tabby's terrified shrieking startled Skybright awake. Its orange fur stood on end and its tail was thrashing wildly. The carved panels of the bedchamber window had been flung wide open, and a giant demon with a black bull's head towered in the middle of their room, red eyes blazing beneath its pointed horns. The demon had thrown one coarse-haired hand over Zhen Ni's mouth so she could not scream. Zhen Ni struggled on the bed, wide-eyed with horror, but she was no match for the huge beast. With one swift motion, the demon slung Zhen Ni over his shoulder and leaped out the window.

It all happened so quickly that Skybright had no time to think. She shifted and launched herself after the demon. She eased her landing by gripping the ledge of the third-story window with her muscular coil, then she gathered all its power to give chase. The bull demon was pounding its way down the narrow alley, its hoof beats echoing against the empty buildings.

Zhen Ni dangled head down over its massive shoulder. She beat its back with her fists, but didn't scream. Skybright could hear Zhen Ni's ragged breaths and fury ignited within her. Skidding, the demon rounded the corner onto the main street, and Skybright followed, flying across the cobblestones. It was fast, but she would catch up soon enough.

The demon suddenly roared. Zhen Ni had unsheathed the dagger at her waist and plunged the blade into the monster's back. But it hadn't gone deep, even as her mistress used all her strength to try and thrust it in further. The demon paused midstride to grab the knife and flung it forward; it skittered against the ground. Skybright closed the distance between them and Zhen Ni finally made her first noise since being taken—a low terrified moan as black blood began to ooze from the demon's wound.

Hearing her mistress's desperation, Skybright surged forward, almost at the demon's heels. And in that moment, she could feel Zhen Ni begin to lift her gaze, and Skybright instinctively changed back to a girl. Losing the momentum she had had with her serpentine length, Skybright stumbled forward, falling hard on her knees.

"Sky," her mistress cried out. The blood had rushed into Zhen Ni's cheeks, but her face still blanched.

Skybright scrabbled on her hands and knees, trying to launch herself toward the bull demon, but lacked the speed she had as a serpent. She was completely bare, and could feel slick blood on her knees, but was too frightened to register pain. Deep down, she knew she had to shift back to her serpent form if she were to have a chance on saving Zhen Ni, but in those precious few seconds, she was incapable of doing it—of revealing her grotesque demonic side.

Zhen Ni's eyes were dark shadows now as dusk deepened into night around them. She threw a hand toward Skybright, fingers splayed. "Skybright! No!"

Skybright leaped to her feet and ran, agonizingly slow, her own arms outstretched.

"No!" Zhen Ni cried again. "Stay back!"

The salt of tears filled Skybright's throat as she realized Zhen Ni hadn't thrown her hand out to plead for rescue, but to stop Skybright from chasing her. So she could keep Skybright safe. Her mistress flailed against the demon's shoulder like some rabid animal, sobbing as she slammed her fists against his wound, her palms sticky with black blood. "Let me go!" Zhen Ni screamed.

The demon growled, slowing, and Skybright dove for the discarded dagger on the ground, clutching it with a death grip. She vaulted toward the demon, an inhuman scream ripping from her throat. Then the air tore like paper in front of them, revealing a gaping hole that glowed an intense red. Skybright skidded to a stop, stunned. And in that moment of hesitation, the demon hurtled through with Zhen Ni, and the rip closed, as if it had never existed.

Skybright was left alone on the empty main street with only the sound of Zhen Ni's screams ringing in her ears.

CHAPTER NINE

Dread knotted in Skybright's stomach as she paced again and again across the point where Zhen Ni had vanished into the air with the bull demon, but there was nothing except cobblestones. Heart heavy, she shifted to her serpentine form in hopes of gathering more clues with her heightened senses. Perhaps if she hadn't changed to a girl, she could have saved Zhen Ni. Instead, she had let her own dread of revealing her true identity taint her judgment. She dug her nails into her hands, welcoming the pain, and gave a low hiss. If Zhen Ni was hurt—tortured or ravaged—it would be her fault.

Skybright stilled, but could feel no other human or demon within leagues. Terrified for her mistress and furious with herself, she returned to the inn and propelled herself back through the third story window of their chamber, where she was greeted by the yowling tabby. Its pupils were dilated in its clear green eyes, its hackles rising. The cat hissed at Skybright before darting beneath a bed.

Somehow, this made all that had happened seem even worse, and she was tempted to shift back to a girl, curl up on the bed, and cry until she fell asleep again. But there was no time for such nonsense. She needed to save Zhen Ni. Wrapping the dagger in a cloth, Skybright tucked it into her mistress's knapsack before retrieving Zhen Ni's handkerchief, then drew it to her nose, taking a deep breath. And although Zhen Ni's image was as clear in her mind as if her mistress stood in front of her, nothing stirred within her chest as before—the inner compass that had guided Skybright to Zhen Ni the first time.

Were they too far apart for Skybright to track her?

Or had Zhen Ni been taken to a place that was impossible to reach?

Skybright thrust the handkerchief back into Zhen Ni's knapsack and slung the two bags across her shoulders, thankful for the human half of her upper body while in demonic form, if just for practicality's sake. She pushed the bed out of the way with her arms, so the cat wouldn't be trapped, and slithered down the stairs back onto the main street.

The scent of the undead still lingered, and that of the demon and her mistress was even stronger. The rent in the air had left a burnt, smoky taste, and Skybright circled the spot again, knowing it was pointless but still unable to believe the demon had disappeared with her mistress. Finally, she slithered out of the deserted town and back toward the forest. She paused at its edge, quieting her mind. She felt a twinge of Zhen Ni's presence, the taste so faint in her throat she wondered if she imagined it. But Skybright clung to that whisper in her chest, desperate for anything. Anything at all.

Skybright traveled the entire night in her serpent form, stopping only to gauge that the quiet glimmer of Zhen Ni was still within her. She hoped that with constant motion she'd somehow draw closer to her mistress and her connection to her would grow stronger. But after covering many leagues, her sense of Zhen Ni remained a faint twinge at her core.

The giant cypresses near the monastery had given way to massive ginkgo trees, some with trunks as wide as she was tall. Interspersed between them were younger saplings with slender trunks and sparse branches. She had never traveled this far within the forest, and only recognized the trees from their pale green fan-shaped leaves. Nanny Bai had used both the ginkgo nut and seed in her concoctions. For a brief moment, she thought about the manor and Lady Yuan, and the life they had led there. Her heart ached knowing how much she had failed them all in losing Zhen Ni. What did the demon want with her mistress?

All the possibilities Skybright envisioned were violent and horrific. She'd seen these demons fighting Kai Sen and the monks, knew how merciless they were. She would never forgive herself if something happened to her. She had promised she'd keep Zhen Ni safe—only to let her be carried off. Skybright paused by a rushing river, its water glinting in the afternoon sunlight. Several giant gingko trees were rooted right at the river's edge, tilting toward the water, their leaves rustling softly overhead. The sound soothed her tired mind, and Skybright tried to capture this moment of quiet.

I'll come for you, mistress.

There was no response, but the flicker of her mistress remained, and Skybright vowed she'd keep searching for Zhen Ni for as long as it took to find her.

The faint shuddering beneath her coil broke her from her reverie. She twisted from the riverbank and sought the noise, sliding so quickly between the trees it felt as if she were flying. She recognized the hard stomping of the undead almost immediately, but this time there were more than a thousand of them. The number was so staggering Skybright didn't trust her senses—which had never been wrong. She felt the monks' steps among the undead, less than fifty altogether. How could they possibly survive with these odds?

Was Kai Sen fighting among them?

For once, Skybright was grateful her sense of Zhen Ni didn't grow stronger as she neared the battle. Breaking through the trees, she burst onto a main road choked full with undead. With one glance, she saw that the newly turned were amongst them, hundreds that had been tainted in the town of Shan An. These undead wore bright clothes and had pale faces and sightless eyes, but had not yet begun to decompose like those who had risen from their graves. They jostled against each other, arms stretched stiffly in front, tongues lolling from their mouths as they tried to find a human victim to bite or clamp onto. The monks were banded in small groups of four with their backs to one another, forming tight circles, each wielding a torch and blade. As easy as it was to dispose of the undead, Skybright knew the chances of the monks' survival were slim because of sheer numbers. The humans would tire soon, and it wouldn't take more than a moment of carelessness for each to be turned as well.

Angered, and fueled by the helplessness she felt over Zhen Ni's abduction, Skybright struck with her massive serpent body, knocking several undead over before snaking her thick coils around one neck and snapping it like an eating stick. She did this without thought or pause until the dirt around her was littered with decapitated bodies, some still twitching, trying to snatch a living person in their clawed hands. She slid between the corpses, thumping against some and thrusting others aside with a strong flick of her coil. Slithering on the outer edges of the pressing throngs, she stayed out of the way of the monks and continued to destroy the undead, one after the next.

The air was thick with the fumes of burnt flesh and hair, filled with the hoarse chanting of the monks, and Skybright was glad that the undead uttered no sounds, were as voiceless as she was in demon form. They shuffled and hopped, stupid but doggedly persistent. She reared high on her coil to better gauge her surroundings, hoping for a glimpse of Kai Sen. Was he here? Was he all right? The undead pressed around her, gathering, and she decapitated another two, then hissed. There were no other demons among them on this stretch of stench-tainted road and her hiss carried above everyone's heads—humans and undead alike. The moment seemed to freeze, like a scene captured in the brief lightning flash before a storm, and Skybright ducked low again, hoping she hadn't drawn attention to herself. She killed more undead as she slithered along, as swiftly as when she'd yawn or sneeze as a girl. The undead never reached out to grasp her, never opened their maws to try and bite her—as if they sensed she wasn't mortal.

But then Skybright noticed something strange. The undead in front of her, those who had had their backs to her, were all beginning to turn to face her. She glanced behind and saw a huge throng of more undead lurching in jerking motions, as if following her. Not as they would pursue a target, but as a dog would trail after its master. She hissed again at the wall of undead blocking her path, killing another half dozen and flinging their bodies away to emphasize her point. But the others didn't know fear, and hopped aside to let her pass.

What was happening?

With her heart in her throat, Skybright slid through the narrow channel the undead had cleared for her, then reared high on her tail again to see her surroundings. The undead had all pulled away from the clusters of fighting monks and were jumping in her direction. Not wanting to believe it, Skybright hissed again, low and long, and the sound shivered across her bare human skin, from her arms and breasts down through her crimson-scaled tail. The undead who hadn't been facing her now all turned and began their erratic hopping in her direction. The monks' chanting faltered, ceased, and a slow murmuring began to rise among them.

Skybright sank low and shot between the lumbering corpses, sliding far from the monks, upward on the wide mountain road until it bent and met the dense ginkgo forest. She had slithered past the thick of the battle, and finally turned to face the awful truth. The hundreds of undead that still remained had all followed her, were even now pressing around in a tight circle, so she was surrounded. But they gave her space, and each stopped its hopping and stilled when it drew as close as it could.

And they waited.

Skybright wanted to retch.

Instead, she rose on her coil and saw that the monks had gathered together as well, a safe distance from the undead crowded around her. Their expressions were drawn and grim beneath their torch flames. She swept her gaze across the undead, their faces tilted toward her, some with clouded eyes and others with no eyes at all in their exposed skulls. All turned to her, waiting for her instruction as if she led them. As if this army of fetid, mindless creatures was *hers*.

She wanted to scream. Wanted to beat their rotten faces until they caved. The monks watched from a distance, and she sensed Kai Sen amongst them, even though she could not pick him out—was too stricken to do so, too ashamed. The silence that had descended was absolute. Nothing stirred, living or dead.

Skybright lifted higher still on her serpent body, until she towered more than a head over everyone and hissed again, loud enough that it resounded in her throat.

Go! she screamed in her mind. *Away and back to your graves! Or dig a hole and bury yourself inside! GO!* She shouted it so loudly in her head she could feel her eyes bulge, her lips pull back so her long fangs jutted out.

The silence seemed to stretch on forever. In truth, it was probably only a few moments. Then all the undead turned from her and stumbled back into the forest. At first there was no sound except for their awkward movement, then a monk said, "The serpent demon is their mistress! She's sent them elsewhere."

Still trying to grasp the meaning of what had happened as she watched the undead retreat, her attention snapped back toward the group of monks. They had fanned out, their weapons still poised to slay, uncertain if they should pursue. Skybright could tell in one glance that they were all exhausted from fighting.

"We kill the serpent demon first," a tall monk standing near the front of the group said. Skybright's heart sank when she recognized who it was.

Han, Kai Sen's friend.

He ran forward, saber raised, and three others followed right behind. The forest was too blocked with hundreds of meandering undead for her to escape. She slithered backward up the mountain road, eyes never leaving Han and the others bounding toward her, trying to put enough distance between herself and the masses to be able to dart back into the trees.

"Stop!" Kai Sen leaped out from behind the group, then twisted to face them, planting his feet. "No one touches her." He extended his own saber until it was a mere hand-width away from Han's chest, who had skidded to a halt. "*Ever.*" Han stared at him, astounded, as a soft rumbling rose from among the other monks.

"Are you mad, Kai? She's a demon! How many monks has she killed?" Han tried to push Kai Sen's saber aside with his own, but Kai Sen held firm. "How many innocent people has she murdered?"

"None. She isn't one of them," Kai Sen said. His tone was soft, but there was steel beneath. "She's not killed anything except the undead."

Han pulled his arm back, his saber raised. "Get out of my way, Kai Sen."

"Make me."

"You *are* mad! You've been bewitched somehow by that thing," Han said. "Take him away, brothers."

Three monks stepped forward, their hesitancy obvious. Kai Sen thrust his torch out at them and they jumped back. "I don't want to hurt anyone, Han. But I'm serious. No one touches her."

Han gave an imperceptible tilt of his head and the other monks fell back before Han raised his saber, swinging it. It met Kai Sen's with a loud clang. "Her? I think you mean *it*."

Skybright flinched. She had stopped when Kai Sen had broken from the crowd, as astounded as everyone else. What was he doing? He'd get himself killed over her. She retreated further up the road now, her serpent senses resonating with each clash of metal against metal. Kai Sen and Han were circling each other, eyes locked. But she couldn't leave; she had to be certain that Kai Sen would be all right.

"You can be sure that Abbot Wu will hear of this." Han lunged forward and struck. Kai Sen parried and thrust his own blade. The two young men engaged in a complicated series of attacks and parries, neither landing a blow. Both drew apart, breathing hard. They had tossed their torches to the side.

"What's the worst he can do? Expel me from the monastery?" Kai Sen feinted, then hit the flat of his blade against Han's temple, stunning him and drawing gasps from the other monks.

"Stop this!" someone shouted from the crowd.

Kai Sen brought the hilt of his saber down hard against the inside of Han's forearm and Han grunted, taken off guard by the blow to his head, and dropped his weapon. "When he would never accept me as a true monk in the first place," Kai Sen said.

Several monks ran up to the two young men to pull them apart. "Enough!"

"It's obvious why the abbot never accepted you as a true monk now, isn't it?" Han spat out, shaking his arm that had been struck, as if trying to bring feeling back into it, before retrieving his saber from the ground.

Skybright slithered behind an outcropping of rock, beyond sight, feeling sick to her stomach.

"I should have you strung up for treason." Han's voice shook with anger.

"Do what you will, brother, but she saved us." Kai Sen sounded resigned, tired. "She sent those undead away."

Han snorted as Skybright sped into the shade of the ginkgo trees. "I don't know what enchantment holds you, *brother*. But demons do us no favors. They kill us. They *turn* us."

And then she slid beyond hearing distance, unable to listen to any more, unwilling to acknowledge what Kai Sen had given up to protect her.

Skybright slithered blindly through the forest, not knowing where she went and not caring. Zhen Ni's presence never dimmed within her, but neither did it grow stronger. Her chest felt too tight and her head throbbed. Her vision was hazed. Finally, she stopped beneath a massive pine tree with branches so thick and twisted that they bowed to the ground to form a small shelter against the trunk. She shifted, desperate to be human again, desperate to crawl out of her own skin. Hunger, thirst, and exhaustion knocked Skybright to her sore knees. Hands trembling, she took a long drink from her water flask then pulled her travel blanket tight around her shoulders, not caring enough to even dress. She ignored her hunger and the aching of her limbs, and dragged herself into the tight enclosure created by the tree's overhanging boughs. Pine needles prickled her back, and she curled up tight, breathing in their wonderful scent.

Hot tears slid down her cheeks and she dashed them away with an impatient gesture. It seemed that she was only capable of failing those she cared for. What would happen to Kai Sen now, after he had defended her so publically? And where was Zhen Ni? Skybright sensed she still lived from the faint taste at the back of her throat, by the delicate connection she still had with her mistress through her supernatural senses. But how much time did she have?

She should rise, shape shift, continue searching for Zhen Ni. But the thought of changing into a serpent again caused bitterness to rise in her throat. She had heard the contempt and loathing in Han's voice, could taste it in the air, like something sour wafting to her from the group of monks. Stone had been right all along—she wasn't human. She could never belong. She was something to be interrogated then slain, a demon without a name. These monks cared nothing that she was loyal to her mistress, that she felt affection for Kai Sen, that she enjoyed singing and loved freshly steamed taro buns. It meant nothing to them.

The tears continued to fall unbidden, and she was too tired to wipe them away. Skybright tried to push herself up, to change again so she could save her mistress. But her limbs were stone heavy, unresponsive. Instead, she forced her eyes shut, humming to herself a lullaby that Nanny Bai used to sing to her on rare occasions when she was a small girl.

Skybright began singing, her voice soft and wavering at first, then steadying, gaining strength. She sang of the stars shining at night while the crickets made their evening song, lulling the animals to sleep.

It was nearly dusk when Skybright woke. She was starving, and ate a cabbage bun then a custard one without pause, washing the food down with water. Had it only been the previous day when she and Zhen Ni had found them, still steaming? She wiggled from her shelter, reluctant to leave its safe confines, but she couldn't hide forever.

Skybright stood on her toes and stretched her arms wide, shaking the pine needles from her blanket, when a rustle from beyond the trees startled her. She took a step back and pulled the blanket tight, cursing herself for not sleeping with Zhen Ni's dagger out. The weapon was still wrapped neatly in her mistress's knapsack.

And for the briefest moment, she thought—hoped against reason—that perhaps it was Zhen Ni hidden in the wild forest.

A figure emerged from between the trees.

Kai Sen.

Skybright blinked, certain that her mind was playing tricks on her.

But the grin that spread across Kai Sen's dirt-smudged face was very real. "I've found you," he said, before sweeping her into such a tight hug that her nose was pushed against his chest. Her arms were trapped within the blanket, and she struggled against him, like a fish wrapped in banana leaves. But his arms were too strong, and she finally gave in, leaning against him.

The steady thudding of his heart beneath her ear calmed her.

"How did you find me?" she murmured into his tunic.

Kai Sen finally drew back a step so he could see her. "I couldn't discern your tracks the entire way."

She tensed, her mind suddenly filled with the awful image of dozens of monks carrying torches, storming through the forest to hunt and kill her.

Kai Sen's dark eyebrows pulled together, and he squeezed her arms. "No one followed me. I came alone, Skybright. I used my … clairvoyance to find you. Just as I had sensed you that first time, in the forest."

She shook free and stumbled back from him. "Why are you here? Han's right. You *are* mad. Mad to chase me. Mad to talk to me. You shouldn't be—"

"Don't." He lifted a hand to stay her words, but it was the firm tone of his voice that stopped her. "You saw our fight then."

Skybright pulled the blanket closer, cocooning herself; she missed the feel of his arms around her. "I saw everything. You shouldn't have risked so much for me, Kai. It isn't worth it. Don't you understand who—what—I am?" Her throat tightened, but she pushed on. "You read that book with me. I'm a serpent demon. I *kill* people. I'm a seductress. A murderer."

Kai Sen rubbed his palms over his face, and she saw how weary he was. How long had he walked, ran, to find her? When he dropped his arms, there was a slight smile on his lips. "Come here."

She shook her head.

"As the goddess breathes, you are stubborn, Skybright."
Then he was behind her with both hands on her shoulders,
guiding her to her previous shelter. The blanket hindered her
movement and she waddled, eliciting a chuckle from him. He
helped her ease down against the gnarled trunk before sitting
beside her.

"So you've started killing people since I last saw you?" he
asked in a casual tone.

"No. No!" Without the use of her hands, she slammed her
shoulder into him and he grunted in surprise. "It's not funny,
Kai Sen. I don't even know who I am anymore." Her voice
had become gruff, and she wrenched her body away from him.

"I'm sorry. I didn't mean to anger you. It is a serious thing.
But I was serious too. Have you become a murderer?"

"Why would you even believe me if I said no?" she asked.

Kai Sen leaned back against the tree and tilted his face
toward her. "I have a knack for gauging people, Sky. *I* know
who you are."

She flushed, to hear him use her shortened name in such a
familiar way. Only Zhen Ni had ever called her Sky.

"You sent those undead away to protect us, didn't you?"
Kai Sen asked.

Skybright nodded.

"How?"

"I ordered them to leave. In my mind. I … I can't speak
in demon form. And I don't know why they followed me as
if I were their leader. I only realized right before I sent them
away. I had killed so many of them." She had thought they

were approaching to attack her, when they were drawing near because they believed she commanded them.

"Do you know why?"

She sighed and rested her head against her raised knees, face slanted so she could see Kai Sen. The sun had vanished, and she barely made out his features in the dim light. She was grateful that she was wrapped so tightly in the blanket still, as she wanted more than anything to reach out and touch him. "I have no answers. Other than what … someone told me."

"Who?" he asked.

Stone. She wouldn't speak his name aloud. "An acquaintance who said he knew my mother, a serpent demon." She felt him examining her.

"I see," Kai Sen finally said, not pushing her to reveal more. "So you did save us. You aren't what a book tells you. You're defined by your actions, by the choices you make. And I've only ever seen you fight for our side."

Our side. The human side.

"That won't stop the other monks from hunting me. From the abbot putting me in a cage if he ever has the opportunity again," she said and thought she saw Kai Sen flinch, but wasn't certain in the fading light. "I came across you while searching for my mistress. She was taken by a demon. Have you heard or seen anything at all in the last day? I'm terrified for her."

"I've not seen any girl in these past few days, only hordes of demons and undead. I'm sorry, Skybright."

Her chin dropped, even as Kai Sen pressed her arm in an attempt to comfort her. She knew it was unlikely he knew anything, but she had hoped …

"Do you carry a lantern in your knapsack?" Kai Sen asked. "May I?"

She nodded and Kai Sen retrieved her small travel lantern, lighting it and setting it beside them. They turned toward each other, she with her knees drawn up and he with his legs crossed in front of him. She was grateful for the soft glow of light, so she could see his face again. Grateful that they could talk like this, if only for a short time, between the chaos and killing that punctuated their lives. They sat there for a long while, silent, studying each other. Kai Sen's dark brown eyes were liquid in the lantern light, open and guileless. She finally spoke, because she could no longer hold his gaze.

"No matter what you say, there's no denying what I truly am. Do you really want to be … be friends with something like this?" She shifted, not caring if she would be naked before him, she had become so used to her bare body. Surprisingly, the blanket she clutched around her didn't disappear as her clothes always did, but her long serpent length snaked from beneath it, glittering red in the faint light. Kai Sen jerked instinctively from her, unable to control his very human reaction. She swept her muscular coil in front of him, draped the tip of her tail over his ankles, before changing back to a girl. "Do you see now?"

"You can control the changing." His voice sounded hoarse. "You could choose not to be a … serpent demon? You could choose to stay human."

Skybright stared at the pine-covered floor, where her serpent body had been. Kai Sen was right. She had full control of her shifting now, and could probably suppress the urge to become a serpent demon if she had to. But she remembered the long days when she had remained human; she tried to imagine never slithering along the earth again, feeling so connected with the wild, and the notion frightened her, smothered her. "It's a part of me, a part of who I am. I can't deny myself that side. You were right to end things with me."

"I never ended things between us." He leaned closer so their legs touched.

Skybright gaped at him, speechless.

"I only wanted for you to stay safe," Kai Sen said. "Yet everywhere I turned, you seemed to be there, in serpent form, watching over me."

Skybright hid a small smile. He was right. Like some love-sick maiden from tales of lore, she couldn't stay away from him. "I've always been so practical, with everything. Until I met you."

He raised a hand and ran his fingertips along her left cheek, tracing the scar he had given her. Her heartbeat stuttered. "Your cut healed. I'm sorry."

Freeing one arm from beneath the blanket, she grabbed his wrist and pressed her lips against his palm, rough and calloused from his endless battles. "Stop apologizing."

Kai Sen made a low noise in his throat and circled his arm around her waist, drew her to him until she was reclining on the soft earth and he was propped above her. He leaned down and she caught the glint of his dark eyes before she felt his lips upon her face, kissing his way from her temple, along her scar, until he reached the side of her mouth. "I like you, Skybright, exactly the way you are." He kissed her softly on the lips. "And I promise not to apologize again," he said with a lopsided grin.

Her mind constricted, oblivious to all else except for his mouth marking a slow path across her skin. She had objections. There were things she needed to say. Instead, she wrapped her arms around his neck, tugging him closer for another kiss. Kai Sen slipped his hand underneath the blanket as he kissed her, and paused when he felt her bare skin, his palm cupping the curve of her waist, gliding across her ribs. Her entire body flushed, thrilled from his touch. He drew back and she lifted her head, trying to capture his mouth again.

"Have you seduced anyone then?" he asked in a rough voice. "Some hapless man traveling on a deserted road?"

"Only you," she replied.

He laughed, and she could feel the rumble of it in his chest, before he leaned in to kiss her neck. "Are you sure this is what you want?" he asked. His hand had slid to rest above her heart, and it beat so wildly that for a moment, she felt faint.

"Yes. But is it what you want? You're forsaking everything—"

Kai Sen gently pushed the blanket aside so she lay exposed, naked beneath him. But his eyes never left hers. "I've made no vows, Sky. And even if I had, I would break them for you."

She untied his sash and he shrugged off his tunic, taking in the sight of her now, his gaze causing her whole being to shiver.

"You're cold?" he whispered, lowering himself and

covering her body with his own. His skin felt hot, warmer than the summer night.

She smiled. "Far from it." Skybright pressed a hand to his birthmark, a deep purple in the dim light, then ran her fingers along his collarbones, before skimming down his torso, stopping at the bandage that wrapped around his waist. "Your injury ... "

"I'm fine," he said, and she felt his muscles bunch as he leaned in to bite her shoulder, taste the hollow of her throat. "More than fine."

They took their time exploring each other in a wordless dance that alternated between unhurried and frenzied, until her senses were filled with the salt of his skin, the pressure of his mouth and his hands. She twined her fingers in his hair, her palm cupping his nape, and she felt him smile against her neck before he grazed her collarbone with his lips. Finally, when their bodies joined, she felt as if her soul would overflow with the feeling of him, and tears slid down her cheeks. She glimpsed the moon above, splintered between thick branches, before Kai Sen dipped his head to kiss her deeply. "Skybright," he murmured against her ear, as if her name were a secret or a revelation. Then he pulled back, suddenly tense. "You're crying. I've hurt you."

He had tasted her tears.

"No." She grasped his shoulders with both hands and pushed, until he rolled onto his back and she was above him, her loose hair draped across his chest. He let out a surprised laugh, his eyes filled with her, dark with desire. "Don't stop, Kai," she whispered. "Don't stop."

Kai Sen had fallen asleep almost immediately after, but not before he had laced his fingers through hers and pulled her hand to rest against his chest, so that she could feel his heartbeat. "I'd give up everything for you," he had said with a slow smile, his eyes heavy lidded, reminding her of the orange tabby. "Sing for me?" he asked drowsily.

And she did.

She watched him sleep now in the low lantern light, studying the hard lines of his body to her content. Kai Sen's physique was lean and powerful, yet still elegant. She carefully untangled her fingers from his hand after awhile, and he slept with his fist curled beneath his chin, like a child. Skybright hummed to herself, and gently picked off the pine needles that had stuck in his hair, lips curving as she did so. She didn't know that she could feel so tender yet fevered for someone at the same time.

There had been no pain when their bodies had come together. Nothing that had been warned of repeatedly in *The Book of Making*, had been whispered about in hushed tones between Min and Zhen Ni. Only pleasure. It was what her body was made for. There would be no checking for blood stains on the bed sheet the morning after. Even if she had been chaste, she was never meant to play the role of the virgin. The role of the bride. Heart heavy, she slid off the blanket and folded it over to cover Kai Sen. Husband and wife and toddling children with chubby cheeks. Love and family. A simple life. This was something that she and Kai Sen could never share, even if the Yuan family, if Zhen Ni, were willing to relinquish her from service.

She leaned over to peer at her lover. *Lover.* Kai Sen's face was completely relaxed, the hint of a smile upon his mouth. He took deep, even breaths as he slept, and Skybright's fingers drifted over his shoulder, his cheek, but she didn't touch him. The scent of their love making, their passion for each other, lingered, stirring something deep within her, and she was tempted to wake him so they could do it again. She darted her tongue out to taste the air, and for one brief moment it appeared forked. She jolted back from him in panic, feeling a slow familiar heat threatening to rise, urging her to change. She tamped it down forcefully, and remembered Kai Sen reading to her from that awful book filled with descriptions of monsters and demons: *By then the victim is usually sound asleep after an amorous encounter and is brutally murdered, either poisoned by her bite or strangled by her coil. It is unclear why she kills.*

What had she done?

What if she had been compelled to shift after their love making, and killed him? Without being able to control herself, because that was what serpent demons did? Her scalp crawled at the thought, and she touched her abdomen, just to be certain it was human flesh and not serpent scales covering her torso.

She drew her bare legs to her chest and crushed her arms around her knees, as if this would ensure that she wouldn't change against her own will. Stone had told her how much her own mother had enjoyed it, seducing men then murdering them. How Opal had killed her victims with such *finesse*. She had been selfish to risk Kai Sen's life when she still knew so little of her own true nature.

It should never have happened.

Skybright pulled away, not daring to steal one last kiss, for fear she'd wake him. She quietly gathered her knapsack and Zhen Ni's, but left the blanket and travel lantern for Kai Sen, as she had her mistress's to use. Her limbs felt languid, and if she caved to instinct, she'd nestle against Kai to sleep as well. But it wasn't meant to be.

It had never been meant to be.

She ran noiselessly into the dark forest, shifted when she was far enough and hidden among the trees, ready to shift back if she was suddenly filled with murderous intention. Instead there was nothing but an emptiness in her chest, and the tears that had gathered at the corners of her eyes evaporated as she slithered into the night.

CHAPTER TEN

Skybright pushed Zhen Ni's handkerchief against her nose. The hint of jasmine perfume lingered, and her chest tightened with the faint connection she felt to her mistress. She gripped the handkerchief in one hand as she traveled through the night, determined to save Zhen Ni. Slithering within the forests for two full days, she felt Zhen Ni's presence grow stronger as she slipped between the majestic pines, the scent reminding her of Kai Sen and their time spent together.

She broke through the forest near dusk on her third day without rest. Her mind buzzed with the taste and sensations of wild creatures that scampered in the forest, of the earth thrumming beneath, too full with life. Exhausted, she turned back into a girl, collapsing to the ground, wrung out from the serpent form that demanded so much of her mind and senses.

The dense trees opened onto a landscape of jagged gray rock. Pointed or domed, they towered at various heights, some so tall she couldn't see their tops, others just reaching her chin. They clustered around the magnificent mountain ledge, and Skybright walked to the edge, saw how the stones formed their columns down its side, the gray melding into other colors—tans, pinks, and blues—until they met the border of another forest far below.

She found a mound of soft earth surrounded by domed rocks and slipped through, craving to sleep beneath the open sky. The evening had deepened to a dark indigo, and a sliver moon hung like a thin smile far in the horizon as tiny stars began to shimmer into existence. Skybright devoured a custard bun, licking her fingers after. She had refilled her flask at a creek and now she drank, cool water sliding down her parched throat. Then she gorged on some dried dates. Laying Zhen Ni's travel blanket on the dirt, she curled up to sleep, naked. The summer night was warm, and she didn't want to risk losing the last tunic and trousers she still had in case she needed to shift without warning.

Her eyelids grew heavy as she studied the night sky. And when she finally slept, she imagined Kai Sen was beside her, that she was wrapped within his arms, even if she knew it was foolish to wish it.

It was still night when she awoke, groggy. The moon had faded from her vantage point, and instead, Stone filled her vision, sitting poised on one of the rocks, gazing down on her. Resplendent in his gold and silver armor etched with crimson, he appeared exactly the same as always. His black hair was pulled back in a top knot, emphasizing his widow's peak and the chiseled planes of his face. The immortal's soft glow illuminated her bare skin, and she sat up, not bothering to cover herself. She felt no shyness as she stood, drawing the blanket around her shoulders. For all she knew, Stone could see through clothing if he willed it.

"How long have you been here?" she asked.

"A while." He sat with his chin propped in one hand, and the relaxed posture made him seem almost ordinary. "You appear very vulnerable in sleep. Very mortal."

"As mortal as a half-serpent girl can be?" She wrapped the blanket above her breasts, tucked tight, then began plaiting her hair, binding it against her head. "I sent the undead away the other day. The monks were too outnumbered. And they obeyed me like I commanded them." Skybright patted her hair while studying the immortal beneath lowered lashes. This was their fourth meeting, and no matter how much she forced her voice even, how casually she spoke, she could never tamp down the awe she felt in his presence. Had to fight the urge to fling herself at his feet.

"So I have heard," Stone replied, a hint of a smile on his sensuous mouth. Skybright wanted to seize him by the shoulders and shake hard, rattle everything he knew from him, wipe that aloof impassiveness from his handsome face. The immortal stirred a tumult of warring emotions within her— awe mingled with fear, desire with mistrust. Stone's dark eyebrows lifted, as if he had read her thoughts. "It is because your mother led them in our last Great Battle."

The blood drained from her face. "What do you mean?"

"Opal commanded the undead the last time there was a rift between the mortal realm and the underworld. She led them well. The undead risen this time must have recognized her in you in their collective minds, and turned to you for guidance. What did you have them do?"

"I sent them back to their graves. Or told them to dig a hole and climb into it."

Stone threw his head back and laughed. "That is not a command your mother would ever have issued."

Frustrated and confused, she wrenched her body away from him, resisted the urge to stomp her feet. "Why didn't you tell me?"

"You did not ask."

She would have thought he was mocking her further, but his black eyes were widened in genuine surprise. "Of course I would have wanted to know!" Was he truly that dense? "And why are you laughing that I sent them away? You said when we first met that I should be on your side. Well, I'm not. I fight for the monks." Skybright tilted her chin. She'd like to see Stone laugh at that.

Stone jumped from the rock in one swift motion, landing noiselessly. "I have offended you somehow." He swept his arm in an arc and the circular alcove she had slept in filled with silver light. "You do not get to choose whose side you are on, Skybright." Stone pointed to the ground on her left and tiny, bright images of people emerged from the earth, wearing straw hats and tilling fields, dressed in finery and lighting incense for the gods. Dozens of them, all going about their daily lives, swarming like ants. "You are either human," he nodded to the ground to her right "or not." Other tiny images of bright beings sprang from the earth there: demons who were part human and part beast, beautiful gods taller than the others, their every movement touched with impossible grace.

With a turn of Stone's hand, Skybright was suddenly clothed in a luxurious brocaded dress of deep purple, in a design that was centuries out of style. Gold and jade bracelets adorned her wrists; her fingers seemed to be filled with as many rings. There was no weight to them. Somehow, she knew that this was how her mother had dressed once long ago. "And you are not human, Skybright," Stone said. He flicked his fingers and her serpent length stretched out behind her, the crimson scales covering her torso glittering in the silver light. "You are one of us."

Skybright folded her arms, trying not to show her discomfort, to feel the blanket around her and her bare feet in the dirt, but appear as a serpent from Stone's illusions. "But why aren't you angry that I don't fight for the underworld?"

Stone stepped closer, bringing with him the rich scent of wet earth. The alcove dimmed, and all the illusions he had conjured dissipated. "You say that you fight for the monks. But can you fight *with* them?"

Skybright stood her ground and gritted her teeth. She wanted more than anything to retreat, to increase the distance between herself and the immortal. But she refused to show him any weakness.

"In the end, it does not matter who you kill or who you send to their graves. The Great Battle would have served its purpose, as it always does."

"What's The Great Battle?" she asked.

"Every five centuries or so, the gates between the underworld and the mortal realm are breached. It has happened for as long as I can remember, and my memory is long—an age-old agreement between the gods and mortals."

"But why? No mortal would agree to this."

"Wouldn't they?" A wooden stick materialized in Stone's hand, and he sketched a spiral on the ground that rose like a loosely coiled ribbon. The line shone silver in the dirt. "Human lives are cyclical, as is the rise and fall of civilizations. We exist to remind them of their mortality. Their frailty. The underworld, and the demons and hell lords that dwell there, are a caution for humans to be good, to do good, lest they be harshly judged when it is their turn to stand before the Mirror of Retribution. Mortals are born with many foibles, but their worst are probably their short memories and their tendency toward hubris. After a few hundred years, their prayers become rote, and their belief in the gods, in us, dim within their hearts. Nothing short of catastrophe, such as the breach in the underworld, can set them right again." He followed the glowing spiral with the tip of the stick. "And so entire civilizations rise and fall with the consciousness of its people. As gods we have to discipline them, as a parent would a petulant or willful child."

She stared at the silver loops etched in the ground, trying

to grasp everything that Stone had said. His lecture, spoken in a detached tone, showed no interest in anything except for the facts. She suddenly thought of Zhen Ni's expressive eyes, remembered Kai Sen's unrestrained laugh and was struck by their frailty, by the brevity of human lives. "It seems a poor bargain for the mortals, to be subjugated through fear," Skybright said. "I can't believe that anyone would agree to this."

"It is true, we could do as we please without mortal intervention, but what we have arranged with the monks works well."

"The monks … ?" Her voice trailed off, for her heart had risen into her throat.

Stone scratched away what he had drawn on the dirt. "Only one abbot knows. Our covenant has been passed down from the first abbot to his successor, and then the next, for almost two millennia. The monks are trained and fight valiantly, as they should. The people are warned, and we send enough creatures from the underworld to roam the lands to be seen. Those who are unfortunate die, but it is a necessary consequence, and not a tremendous loss for what is gained. The mortals pray again, with conviction, and give to the gods. They are reminded of how things are—of their place in the world." He leaned closer, and Skybright could feel the heat radiating from him. "So you understand now, how it matters very little what your actions are? Our show was set in place ages ago, and this is just another repeat performance."

Skybright began pacing, if only to put some distance between Stone and herself. She was drawn to him by compulsion. If her feelings for Kai Sen brought to mind a warm embrace, then they were a hard tug with Stone. Her head ached with everything that Stone had told her. What did all this mean, and what was her place within it? She was starving and her limbs were sore, and she cursed her human form for all its demands. Stone tracked her erratic marching the entire time, his gaze like a physical touch.

Finally she paused to stand before him. "Why would my mistress be abducted by a demon then? Was it simply bad luck?"

"Was she wandering alone outside of town?" he asked.

"No. She was with me, in an empty town that had been attacked by the undead. I tried to save her, but the demon disappeared into the air." Skybright bit her lip hard when she heard the rising panic in her voice.

Stone stiffened, standing even taller, if that were possible. "The demon stepped through a portal? Could you glimpse the other side?"

"No. The tear glowed red, but closed before I could see anything." She clenched her fists. "Do you know where she is?" She was beyond caring that she might be indebted to him. Too many days had passed. What horrors was Zhen Ni suffering? "Please, Stone. I have to find her."

He shook his head. "I feel no connection with mortals and would not be able to locate her with ease. I can send my informants to search for her. You are using your tracking abilities?"

So he was aware of that. Skybright wondered what else he knew about serpent demons that she hadn't even discovered herself.

"I found her once that way. But have had no luck this time. I've been wandering for days."

"But you still sense her?" he asked.

"I can."

"She is alive then. Don't lose that connection. Focus and you will find her soon. Few demons have the gift of tracking as serpent demons do." Stone scanned the horizon; the sun was beginning to rise, suffusing the sky in gold and red. "I must go," he said. "I stayed longer than I had intended." He lifted her chin so her head tilted back and she was forced to meet his dark eyes.

She felt the heat of him against her chest, became light-headed from his vibrant earthen scent. "No," she said.

Skybright wanted Stone's kiss, whether because of his sorcery or her own desire, she didn't know. She'd never know. Was this how it was for Kai Sen? She swallowed and hardened her features, clearing her mind.

He smiled, truly amused. "And if I do anyway?"

"You'd force me?" she challenged. "Would you enjoy that?"

"You are the one who takes pleasure from it."

Were immortals incapable of feeling pleasure? What she had felt in her kiss with Stone wasn't sexual, but an unanchoring of herself, both liberating and terrifying.

He leaned in and spoke against her ear, "It is only a kiss, Skybright."

"Then what does it matter?" She somehow managed to keep her words even, although her entire body had tensed when she had felt his breath upon her neck.

Stone straightened and took a step back, but she knew

better than to consider it a victory. He was unpredictable, and so difficult to read.

"It is how I learn more about you," he said. "But I will respect your wishes and go."

She didn't miss what was implied. He was indulging her, like giving a child a sweet.

"I will send word if I learn anything about your mistress," he said, and resting one hand against her shoulder, pressed his lips against her forehead instead.

The heat of the mark stayed upon her skin long after Stone had disappeared, vanishing like a phantom.

Morning dawned cold and clear.

Skybright had washed and dressed after Stone left, then sat on a rock to take in the majestic valley of pines below. The view eased her mind, filled her with a peace that she hadn't felt in weeks, She let her gaze rest on the dark green of pine needles, and her thoughts wandered. What if her mistress had been dragged down to the underworld itself? She realized after some time that she could feel her faint connection to Zhen Ni, even while in human form—still distant, but there. She had nothing left to eat except for a few pieces of dried beef that she had found at the bottom of her knapsack. Slowly chewing on one, she stood to continue her journey. After more than three days of traveling in her serpent form, Skybright wasn't ready to shift again. The idea caused her senses to buzz with anxiety. So she walked instead, on weary legs, glad for the feel of her feet in her slippers, and concentrated on the pull of her mistress at her core.

She walked for two days, downward toward the base of Tian Kuan mountain, foraging in the forest for roots and berries she knew were safe to eat thanks to Nanny Bai's teachings. Her connection with Zhen Ni grew stronger as she continued to descend toward the valley of pines.

Skybright was filling her water flask by a creek when she heard voices; she ran into the trees just in time. She leaned into the giant trunk, making sure she was hidden, before peering from behind it. Six monks had appeared from among the pines, walking along the edge of the water. Skybright recognized Kai Sen's confident lope before she could distinguish his features, and she felt as if she had been knocked flat by the rush of emotions that surged through her. By the *familiarity* of him. She pulled herself back, drawing deep breaths to try and slow her racing heart, before dashing into the forest, away from the monks.

Was Kai Sen using his clairvoyance to follow her? But who were the other five monks accompanying him? She knew she shouldn't linger because she'd give herself away. Kai Sen's gift in sensing her was too acute and she ran, trying to put distance between them, unable to disperse the memories of their love making as she did so. Finally, not seeing where she was going, she stumbled over a twisted root and crashed to her hands and knees, breathing hard. A branch snapped behind her and she whipped around, feeling dread and hope at once, but there was no one behind her.

Slowly, she rose to her feet, centering herself so she could touch that connection with Zhen Ni.

It was growing stronger, the taste bittersweet in the back of her throat. Skybright tugged the knapsacks closer, squaring her shoulders, and continued on her journey.

Skybright was eating wolfberries, her mouth puckered with the sweet tang of the bright red fruit, when she heard voices in the distance again. She had been considering shifting into serpent form after harvesting enough of the berries, but the monks' proximity decided it for her. After tying the wolfberries in a handkerchief and stuffing it into her knapsack, she began to undress so she could shift, only to freeze when Kai Sen pushed his way from between the foliage.

"You need to stop doing that," she croaked, re-clasping the button she had been undoing on her tunic. She hadn't spoken in days, not since seeing Stone. And while she had hummed softly during her journey, she had been too afraid to draw attention to herself by singing.

"Why did you leave without saying goodbye?" Kai Sen asked, his voice low.

It was such a simple question, one that she had no ready answer for. Skybright had not allowed herself to imagine what it would be like to face Kai Sen again, what she would have to say to him. She stood there, mute, and they stared at each other for a long time, the chatter of the other monks drifting to them.

Finally, she said, "Kai, it was a mistake—"

"Don't say that." He tensed, his stance as rigid as an ancient oak.

They had not closed the distance between them, and Skybright refused to take a step forward. "You said yourself that you'd give up everything for me, even your vow of celibacy as a monk if you had taken one. It's because of what I am. You're *compelled* to feel this way about me, don't you see?"

"You believe me to be so weak, so brainless, that I have no choice but to … to love you?" He stalked a tight circle, his frustration palpable.

But she couldn't hear for those few moments, as the blood had roared into her head when he had said *love*. He finally strode to her, stopping near enough that she could rise on her toes and kiss him. But Skybright held still, red-faced.

"You're right. I have no choice, Sky. But it isn't for the reasons that you think. Is it so hard to believe that I could love you simply for you?" He caressed her cheek and his touch was cool against her skin. "For your laugh? And the way you make me laugh? For your bravery and strength and loyalty? For all that I see in your eyes and the way you look back at me? Is that false and contrived?"

He brushed his thumb over her lower lip, leaning in, and it took all of her willpower not to give in to his touch, not to tip her head back and surrender to his kiss. "It meant nothing to me," she forced out, and he froze, so near she smelled his clean scent—lemon soap mingled with camphor wood. Skybright stepped away from him, glaring at the ground strewn with pine needles. What did it matter if their feelings for each other were true? She saw again her forked tongue darting out and the strong urge to turn into a serpent after making love with Kai Sen. There could be no good outcome if he continued to care for her. She needed to end this, even if she had to hurt him to do so. She lifted her chin and looked him in the eyes, before saying with deliberate coldness, "I could make anyone bed me."

The color drained from his tanned face, then surged back again, mottling his cheeks. Kai Sen grabbed Skybright by the wrist and pulled her with him. "I won't let you do this."

She scrambled to keep up, until they crashed through the trees into a small clearing. The other five monks sat in a loose circle, talking quietly; all turned to them in shock.

"Kai Sen, we thought you were only going for a walk, not collecting lost maidens in the woods," one of the monks said, and the others broke into nervous laughter.

"Bao Yu, this is Skybright," Kai Sen said brusquely. "She's pretty, isn't she?"

"Pleased to meet you, Skybright." Bao Yu gave an awkward wave. He appeared to be around twenty years, and was stocky with round eyes set far apart, giving the impression of a surprised calf. Bao Yu kept peering at her face then away, as if embarrassed to look at her fully. Skybright lifted a hand to touch her cheek. Her scar. She must appear like the victim of some tragic accident. "She's very pretty, Kai Sen," he replied, then grinned at her shyly. "You're quite beautiful, mistress."

"Wonderful! We're in agreement then." Kai Sen pushed her forward a little toward Bao Yu. "Would you like to bed her?"

A monk behind her choked on whatever he had been drinking, coughing spastically as Bao Yu's eyes grew even rounder until he looked like the goldfish Zhen Ni kept in a ceramic bowl in her reception hall. "What?" he managed to force out.

Kai Sen waved a hand up and down beside her, as if showcasing an expensive vase. "Beautiful, right? Do you want to bed her?" he asked again with a wink. "I'll give you two privacy."

Skybright's face was so hot her ears felt on fire. Finally breaking from her stunned silence, she slapped Kai Sen on the shoulder. "What're you doing?" she sputtered in a low voice.

Kai Sen ignored her.

Bao Yu gathered himself after an uncomfortable pause and said, "I've taken a vow of celibacy, Kai Sen. You know that. And stop offending the mistress."

"You're saying *no*?" Kai Sen exclaimed in mock surprise. "Skybright, did you hear that? He's refusing you. Go ahead, work your magic." He crossed his arms and nodded at her, thrusting his chin out as if in challenge.

"*I* haven't taken my celibacy vow yet," a voice piped up

from across the clearing.

Kai Sen picked up a small pine cone and threw it. It hit the young monk who had spoken square on his forehead. "No one asked you, Huang."

"Oww!" Huang rubbed his brow, scowling. He was no more than thirteen years.

Huang was so offended that Skybright burst into laughter, and all six monks gawked at her, as if she were in serpent form dangling from a tree limb. "All right." She took Kai Sen by the elbow and drew him away from the clearing. "You've made your point," she said when they were hidden in the thickets again. His arm had been stiff beneath her touch the entire time, his stride halting. "I'm sorry for what I said, Kai."

His body was angled away from her, the cords of his neck taut. "Don't ever do that again, Sky. Belittle what we have between us. As if it were cheap and something to cast aside." He made a frustrated noise and met her eyes, and a knot rose in her throat when she saw the devastation there. She *had* hurt him. And yet he would not let her go—would not let *them* go.

"Oh, Kai," she said. "I just didn't want to hurt you—"

He let out a harsh laugh. She grasped his fingers in hers and he quieted the moment they touched. "I care for you, but there isn't a future for us together. Not when I am what I am. I don't even know my true nature yet—it terrifies me. What if I *do* harm you one day, because I have no control over my demonic side?"

"Why have you dismissed us over what ifs? Over things that you don't even know will come to pass? Why can't you live in the moment and accept this?" He drew her closer and wrapped his arms around her waist. "Why can't you just accept us?

"Because I'm too practical, Kai."

"No. Not when it comes to me, remember?" He grinned. He had changed into a clean tan-colored tunic since she had last seen him, and she pressed her cheek against his chest, breathing in the subtle scent of camphor wood.

"There are no love stories between serpent demons and monks," she murmured. "It's impossible and ridiculous."

"I'll write one, then," he replied, and she laughed, despite herself.

They stood together, holding each other, until Skybright pushed away from him. "Your brother monks must be waiting for you. Why are you traveling in such a small group? It can't be safe."

"We've been sent on a special mission." Kai Sen shifted on his feet, suddenly unsettled—something she had never sensed from him before. "We're closing the breach between the underworld and ours."

She stared at him in disbelief. "With only six monks? And one barely out of puberty? That's suicide!"

"Abbot Wu hand selected the group and gave us a map of where the breach is supposed to be. He said we would be blessed—protected—on this mission."

Should she tell him what Stone had told her? Or let Kai Sen complete the part that was expected of him? How could she even explain what Stone had divulged, when she wasn't certain if she believed it herself—wasn't certain if she could even trust the immortal? "But how can you close it?" she asked.

His expression became unreadable, and he raised his head to stare beyond her, into the dense forest. "I was given clear instructions," he said vaguely.

"Did Han ever tell Abbot Wu about your ... confrontation?"

Kai Sen smiled, but his dark brown eyes remained solemn. "He didn't. I knew he never would—we're too close. But I'm certain someone else told Abbot Wu what happened. It's probably why I was sent off with this small team on an impossible mission."

"Do be careful, Kai. Our world has gone mad." She wanted to go with him, felt an ominous premonition about this task Abbot Wu had given. Still, Zhen Ni was her primary concern, the one in immediate danger. Skybright shuddered, imagining her mistress being held captive somewhere by that ferocious bull demon.

"I wish I could help you find your mistress. But I'm the leader and cannot abandon the group." He leaned in and kissed her softly on the mouth. "Promise you'll keep safe?"

"And you," she whispered. She had wanted to end things between them, but now the fear that they might never see each other again overwhelmed her with foreboding. Backing away with reluctance, Skybright said, "I must go. Goodbye, Kai Sen."

"Farewell, Sky." He held still as a statue, the only movement in his eyes, which followed her progress as she retreated from him. He remained there until she could no longer see him.

CHAPTER ELEVEN

Skybright concentrated on the pull she felt toward her mistress. She undressed and shifted after she had left Kai Sen half a league behind her. The earth beneath her serpent coil sang with life, the strength and depth of it so ancient it was beyond her comprehension. But she understood it on a visceral level, and her serpentine senses stretched, just as Zhen Ni would fling her arms out wide after a particularly good nap. Skybright luxuriated in it, in the rich life that the earth sustained and cradled.

She was certain that she was drawing nearer to her mistress as she snaked her way toward the valley of pine trees she had seen days before, enveloped by the pine needles' crisp, clean scent. They reminded her of Kai Sen, and of the needles she had carefully plucked from his black hair as he slept after their love making. He was being evasive with her about his mission to close the breach to hell and it filled her with unease, as she had never known him not to be completely truthful with her.

Craving sunlight on her skin, Skybright veered toward the mountain's edge, her connection to Zhen Ni pulling ever stronger. It was a blessing her mistress still lived days after her abduction, but Skybright feared what she must have suffered—might still be suffering. She traveled through the night, emerging into the valley of pines before dawn, Zhen Ni's scent blooming in the back of her throat. Squirrels and rats scattered as she slid between gnarled trunks. A fox burrowed deep into its hole, abandoning its hunt for a forest hare that had also dashed into its nest beneath the ground.

She began passing points in the forest that tasted burnt and smoky, exactly like the scent that had lingered after the bull demon escaped with Zhen Ni through the rent in the air. Her pulse raced to recognize it; she must be on the right track.

Just as the sun rose, she slithered to the edge of the forest that opened onto Tian Kuan's base, and the almost floral taste that she associated with Zhen Ni flared, distinct and sharp. Her mistress was close! Skybright remained hidden in the trees, following the tug she felt in her chest, when she spied the opening to a large cavern in the mountain's base. Giant stone torches were lit at either side of the entrance, and a deep red glow filled the cavern's mouth—the same glow she had seen when the demon abducted Zhen Ni.

A flick of her forked tongue, and Skybright knew that her mistress was held captive in that cave. Zhen Ni paced in short steps, as if the space she had were limited. Skybright sensed no one else within, human or monster. She slid to the entrance, glad for the morning mist, and peered inside. A wide crevice ran through the center of the cavern, from which the red glow emanated. Skybright could see a cage set far in the back, and Zhen Ni walking an erratic circle inside. She had to smother a hiss that nearly erupted from the excitement of seeing her mistress again, alive and well. Instead, Skybright quickly shifted back to a girl and tugged her clothes and shoes on, not even caring if her tunic was buttoned correctly.

She withdrew the dagger from Zhen Ni's knapsack and tiptoed into the cave. It was huge, its stone walls a deep gray. She couldn't see the top of the cavern, as the torches anchored to the walls didn't cast enough light. Her serpent senses had never failed her before, but Skybright was unable to believe that she'd found her mistress unguarded. Murmuring a prayer to the fickle God of Luck, she clutched the dagger close as she crept along the narrow path against the wall, keeping a safe distance from the fissure that seethed an acrid heat. Zhen Ni finally saw her when she was halfway through the cavern and cried out. Skybright pressed a finger to her lips then ran quickly to cover the remaining distance between them, reaching between the iron bars to touch her mistress's cheek. Zhen Ni appeared the same, with dark circles beneath her eyes from lack of sleep. She wasn't bloodied or bruised, and her clothes, though dirty, were not ripped. Overwhelming relief filled Skybright, bringing tears to her eyes. A tray of half-eaten rice was set on a low bamboo stool in the corner, with a dirty bedroll made from hay beside it.

Her mistress had reached through the bars and wrapped her hand behind Skybright's neck, pulling Skybright's face close to kiss her frantically twice on the cheek. "How in the goddess's name did you find me, Sky?" Zhen Ni cried.

"Not now, mistress. I'll tell you everything after we're far from here," Skybright whispered. She grabbed one of the iron bars and shook it with dismay. How could she ever break this?

"The key's on a hook behind you," Zhen Ni said. "He had no fear of anyone coming to rescue me—and I had no hope of it, either."

Skybright ran to where Zhen Ni pointed, her light footsteps echoing too loudly through the vast cavern. She sent a prayer of gratitude to the gods as she took the key from the wall, right beneath a blazing torch. "Are there no demons to guard you?" she asked as she tried the lock, her hand shaking with nerves. Skybright laid the dagger on the floor so she could use both hands. Her stomach turned from the reek of sulfur that hung heavy in the air.

"The only guard I've seen is a monk," Zhen Ni said.

Skybright was so shocked she dropped the key. She cursed, picked it up and tried again. "A monk? Are you certain? What of the demon that kidnapped you? He didn't hurt you, mistress?" She willed her voice steady, even as she stiffened her arm so she could work the lock.

"He brought me here and put me in the cage, then disappeared through a hole in the air right outside the cavern." Zhen Ni's knuckles were white from gripping the bars so hard. "And yes, I know a monk when I see one. He's been bringing me my meals and letting me out to relieve myself."

Skybright almost hissed, reciting a quick prayer of gratitude to the Goddess of Mercy. Her mistress had been ill treated, but not tortured or raped. What did it mean, for a monk to be holding Zhen Ni captive? Had Stone been speaking the truth all along? That there was one abbot who knew and orchestrated this breach in the underworld with the gods?

The key finally turned and the iron door swung open. She reached for Zhen Ni's hand as the earth beneath their feet heaved. "Quickly, mistress," Skybright said, and they tried to run toward the cave entrance, even as the crevice split wider, the ground groaning as it did so. The two girls clung to each other as the earth tilted beneath them, and they crouched low, unable to run for fear they'd tumble into the gaping hole.

"Crawl, mistress! I'm right behind you," Skybright shouted above the grinding of stone against stone. "I won't let you fall in."

Zhen Ni did so, navigating on her hands and knees as quickly as she could, with Skybright at her heels, ready to throw herself forward if she needed to protect her mistress. But when they finally made it past the shuddering ground to the cavern's entrance, the forest scene split open in front of them, and Abbot Wu stepped through the portal, blocking their path. He held a dark walnut staff in one hand.

"What is this?" he asked in that resonant voice. "I'd never imagined there would be an attempt to rescue the sacrifice."

Sacrifice?

The abbot was the same height as Zhen Ni, but stout, and

although he wasn't muscular, he carried a powerful presence. He spread his arms and the crimson sleeves of his robe fluttered for a moment; the ground had stilled as soon as he appeared. "Please return to the cage. You also." He pointed his staff at Skybright. "I'm afraid I can't risk you trying to save your friend again." Abbot Wu then took a long look at her, and his eyes narrowed. "I know you." The tone of his voice turned much more menacing with those three words, and Skybright felt her stomach clench. "Into the cage or I'll have the ground open up to swallow both of you in an instant. The gods would have an extra sacrifice this time."

He marched toward them, tall staff raised like a weapon, and Skybright wondered if she could shove him into the glowing fissure. If she shifted, they would have a better chance at escape. But as if reading her mind, the abbot touched his staff against Skybright's bare arm, chanting beneath his breath. There was a shock from the contact, so strong she felt it in her bones. "Don't even consider fighting, girl." The abbot smiled. "I have other plans for you."

Furious, she reached for that unbearable heat to change into her demonic form, but her mind slammed into a wall. The abbot had cut her access to her own magic somehow.

The earth rumbled beneath their feet again, and Zhen Ni clutched her hand so hard, Skybright's knuckles hurt. They had no choice but to retreat, shuffling along the edge of the crevice as the abbot herded them. He kicked Zhen Ni's dagger aside after they entered the cage, the ground still trembling. It stopped as soon as he locked the door and slipped the key into a hidden pocket.

"I was so disappointed to lose you that first time," the abbot said. "What a gift to have you return to me."

Zhen Ni stared at Skybright, her eyes wide with fear and filled with unasked questions. Skybright gripped her mistress's fingers to reassure her, although her own palm was damp with sweat. "I don't know what you mean. I've never seen you before," Skybright lied.

"Perhaps we've never formally met," Abbot Wu said, "but you're the serpent demon we caught when the breach first broke."

Zhen Ni's hand shook in her own, and Skybright released it. "No," Skybright whispered, but without conviction. What would he do to her now that she was trapped within the cage?

"I'd recognize that scar anywhere." The abbot ran a thick finger alongside his own cheek. "It's healed well since that night."

"What's he saying, Sky?"

"Ah," Abbot Wu said. "Your friend doesn't know? But then, why would she? Your demonic nature is something to be hidden, isn't it? Until the time comes to kill your victim." His tone was not unkind, merely conversational, as if they were discussing the taste of a new tea. "The gods do create such fascinating creatures to punish us." He stared at her through the bars, a hawk eyeing its prey. "There is a way I can make certain," the abbot said, speaking to himself. "There are so many questions I want to ask."

Skybright backed away from him, away from Zhen Ni,

until she was pressed against the cold bars at the rear of the cage. Her mind had gone blank, numb with fear. Now that she was captured, could the abbot force her to shift? No. Please no. Not in front of Zhen Ni, not like this.

Abbot Wu closed his eyes and began muttering, as if trying to recall something, before he proceeded to chant in a deep voice. The archaic words pulled at Skybright, tugging her sternum, like something physical dragging her forward. She tried to dig her heels into the dirt, but her feet continued to shuffle, enchanted. A frustrated whimper escaped from her, and she bit down hard on her lip, furious with herself.

"What's happening?" Zhen Ni cried. "What's the matter, Sky?"

Skybright shook her head, unable to look at her mistress. Compelled to go to the abbot, she was at the cage door within moments, extending her forearm between the bars because he willed it. He opened his eyes; they were the color of dark amber. "A demon, as I thought," he said, and stooped to pick up the knife that had spun away from the cage. The abbot seized her by the wrist and started chanting anew, then began carving the inside of her forearm with the tip of the dagger. His grip wasn't tight, as she was frozen, unable to move. Tears slid from the corners of her eyes from the pain, from the frustration of feeling completely impotent against his spell.

Zhen Ni screamed when the abbot sliced the knife into Skybright's skin. "What are you doing? Stop!" She tried to beat at the monk's head with her hands.

Abbot Wu didn't attempt to dodge her punches, but broke

from his chanting long enough to say, "I'll cut her more deeply than I intend if you continue. Would you want that, when I'm cutting so close to her wrist?"

Her mistress was sobbing now, gripping the iron bars with both fists. "Why are you doing this?"

Skybright watched, removed from herself, while the abbot resumed his chanting and carved three characters into her flesh. Blood welled as her skin split open, like sap from a tree. But the sharp pain was nothing compared to the deep ache in her chest to see Zhen Ni crying for her. The monk continued chanting, and a tight sensation gripped her heart, began to writhe into her belly, through her groin. She was being forced to shift. Gasping, Skybright tried to wrench her arm free, to fling herself against the bars until she lost consciousness, yet still she could not move. She wrangled with her inner self, trying as best as she could to fight the change, the familiar feeling of heat blazing through her legs. She tried to douse her mind with coolness.

But she couldn't conquer the insistent drone of Abbot Wu's mantra, and after a long moment that seemed to stretch into forever, her serpent body emerged, and she was released from his enchantment. Skybright fell onto the dirt floor, suppressing the hiss that was about to erupt from her throat. Her forearm was washed in her own blood, and it trickled onto the ground, staining the earth with crimson drops.

"How curious. I've only seen serpent demons described and rendered with the face of a woman and an entirely serpentine body." The abbot studied Skybright as one would a specimen in a jar. "But you, you remain half human on top."

"What did you do to her?" Zhen Ni screamed, and leaped at the abbot again, thrusting an arm out through the bars as far as she could. "Stop what you're doing to her!" Her mistress was horrified and enraged; Skybright could taste it on her tongue.

But Abbot Wu had stepped smoothly out of the way as soon as Skybright had shifted. "I'm not doing anything other than revealing your friend's true nature." He nodded at Skybright, and she couldn't lift her face, only watch as her blood dribbled onto the ground. "See how she lied to you? What she hid from you? *This* is what your friend truly is."

"No!" Zhen Ni cried.

He folded his hands in front of himself. "I don't have the power to turn people into demons. Why would I want to? Tell your friend the truth, Sky."

Skybright flinched to hear him call her that, felt as if he had kicked her in the gut. She finally raised her face, trying to plead with her mistress for forgiveness only using her eyes. But Zhen Ni was crying so profusely now, it was a wonder she could even see. "She'll bleed to death," her mistress stuttered.

"The cuts are superficial," the abbot said in a soothing voice.

But Zhen Ni ignored him, rummaging through her knapsack until she found the cloth that Skybright had wrapped her dagger in. She crouched down beside Skybright and tied the material snug against her forearm. "I'm so sorry, Sky," she said under her breath as she did so. "So sorry," she repeated after she made certain her knot was tight enough, then smoothed the wisps of hair from Skybright's face. "I'll fix this somehow," Zhen Ni whispered against Skybright's ear, trying her best to sound courageous, but terror seeped into her words.

This was something that could never be fixed.

Skybright wanted to throw her head back and howl, to pull her mistress into her arms and cry onto her shoulder, to apologize for lying to her. Instead, she touched the bandage Zhen Ni had made, already seeping red, and gave a nod, feeling as if her heart would break.

Suddenly, the rich scent of earth filled the cavern. Skybright reared up on her serpent coil. Stone stood only a few steps behind Abbot Wu, having appeared from nowhere. "What have you done with the serpent demon?" Stone asked. Skybright had never heard his tone so hard and cold. To her amazement, she was relieved to see the immortal.

Abbot Wu jumped in surprise, and whipped around. "Nothing, master. Only a simple spell to ascertain her true identity. I'm eager to question her."

"She is not yours to question," Stone replied. It was obvious that he and the abbot were no strangers. "Release her."

Abbot Wu masked his shock within a moment, and bowed his head. "Of course, master. I didn't realize she was one of yours."

Stone didn't reply, but stared at the monk, his chiseled features unyielding. The abbot fished the key from his robe and began fumbling with the lock. "Yes, of course," he repeated, "Merely a misunderstanding." He pulled the door open and Zhen Ni slipped her arm around Skybright's shoulder to support her. Skybright shivered. She'd never felt a human's touch as a serpent before, and Zhen Ni's nearness disturbed her. Was her mistress safe while she was enchanted and a demon?

The abbot raised a hand. "Only the serpent leaves the cage."

Zhen Ni froze and Skybright hissed, before slamming the cage door shut again with a swipe of her coil. The bars reverberated with a loud clang. Skybright would never abandon Zhen Ni, would do all that she could to protect her. Her mistress cringed to see her tail move so swiftly, and released Skybright, dropping to the floor and pressing her face into her hands. Skybright wanted more than anything to comfort her mistress, but knew that she was only adding to Zhen Ni's anxiety.

"Who is the girl?" Stone asked.

"Our chosen sacrifice." Abbot Wu had retrieved the walnut staff from the ground, holding it wearily. He kept his distance from Stone. There was no doubt in Skybright's mind that Kai Sen's abbot was the one in alliance with the gods. He alone knew the truth about the breach in hell, and was willing to sacrifice innocent mortal lives as part of the pact. Still, what was Kai Sen's role in closing the breach? She couldn't shake the dread she felt for him, even as she tried to devise a way to somehow save Zhen Ni. Could she appeal to Stone for help?

He was pacing in long strides before the cage.

"The covenant states that we must have a sacrifice to close the breach," the abbot said.

"Do not tell me what I already know, Wu," Stone replied, enunciating each word, casting them like knives. The abbot took a step back. Skybright had never witnessed Stone appear so tense, his immense power wound tight. Where he was silent in his motions during their previous encounters alone, his gleaming armor resounded now with his every step. It was like watching a leopard, and even Zhen Ni had lifted her face to stare at the immortal, his presence was so forceful.

Finally, he stopped in front of the girls, and said to Skybright, "A sacrifice is needed."

Skybright dropped down beside her mistress and wrapped both her arms around Zhen Ni's shoulders. Her throat spasmed, filled with words she couldn't say. No, she mouthed to Stone, and pressed her lips to Zhen Ni's temple. Her mistress grasped Skybright's unwounded arm with both hands, back arched and chin thrust forward. Defiant.

"I can go in her stead," someone said from near the entrance of the cave.

The cavern spun for a long moment when Skybright heard Kai Sen's voice. Her vision blurred as he appeared from behind a small outcropping, and he walked toward them, the outline of his familiar shape limned in light. The five other monks lingered behind, dark shadows beyond the entrance. Skybright collapsed forward, catching herself by her wrists against the dirt floor. Her stomach heaved. No! What was Kai Sen doing here? Then her mind filled with sudden understanding—his mission—and she wanted to dash out and thrust him from this place, would accept never seeing him again to make him vanish.

"In her stead?" Stone lifted one dark brow. "How gallant."

"Kai Sen. You're early," the abbot said, his expression shuttered.

"This is the false monk boy?" Stone's words were like ice.

Kai Sen grimaced. He glanced toward Skybright briefly before he looked Stone square in the face. "I was sent to close the breach. And if a sacrifice is needed, I can take the girl's place."

Abbot Wu thrust his staff into the ground. "Stay out of it, Kai Sen. This was *not* what we discussed."

Skybright slithered away from her mistress, and leaned into the cold bars of the cage. Kai Sen was covered in dust. She had little doubt he had run the entire way here, probably sensing the danger she had been in. He stood with his feet planted apart, a hand on the hilt of his saber. Skybright had never seen him look so young. Although Stone wasn't more than a year older in his physical form than Kai Sen, the disparity between the immortal and boy couldn't have been more pronounced as they faced each other; Stone, as cold and removed as his namesake, and Kai Sen, feigning bravado. He had never appeared more *mortal* to her.

"Why would you give your life for this girl's?" Stone asked with genuine curiosity.

"Because Skybright cares for her," Kai Sen replied. "I—I don't want her to grieve. Her mistress is innocent. It's the right thing to do."

Skybright clenched the bars in her hands until it felt as if she'd dented the iron. She wanted to rattle them like a mad thing for Kai Sen's foolishness.

"As it was the right thing to do to leave Skybright trapped in a cage when your abbot had captured her?" Stone clasped his hands behind his back, the muscles of his jaws flexing. "She'd be dead now if it weren't for my interference, Kai Sen." The immortal spat out the last two words, like something rotten in his mouth.

Skybright's hands flew to her chest. It wasn't true. *Kai* had saved her, unlocked the cage for her so that she could escape. Her eyes sought his, but Kai Sen would not meet them. His fists were clenched at his sides, his face flushed red. In disbelief, she slid away from the bars, her vision beginning to swim.

Instead, Stone was the one who glanced her way; and his full mouth curved. "Ah. I see. You led Skybright to believe that *you* had saved her?" He laughed, the sound remorseless and chilling. "Is that how mortals *care*? You were too moral to free her from slaughter but base enough to bed her?"

Kai Sen unsheathed his saber in one swift motion. "It wasn't like that." His voice trembled, but the tip of his saber pointed unwavering at Stone's throat. "Sky, I couldn't believe it was truly you that night. I didn't know." He spoke so swiftly he choked on his words. "Forgive me." Kai Sen's dark eyes finally met hers, and they were filled with pain and regret. "I love you."

Skybright hung her head, feeling broken. Shattered. He loved her, and she believed him. But despite his assurances, he would never truly accept her demonic side. How could he? He had been trained to kill creatures such as herself since he was a boy.

"Touching," Stone said. "You are convincing me more and

more that you would indeed make an appropriate sacrifice, false monk." Despite his cutting words, Skybright was certain she was the only one who could actually detect the sarcasm in Stone's emotionless voice.

Kai Sen jerked, his body tensing as he shifted his attention back to the immortal. "Why do you speak like you know me?" Then Kai Sen winced and his hand rose to the birthmark at his throat involuntarily.

Stone laughed again and the hairs on Skybright's arms stood on end. "Do not flatter yourself. I only know you because of Skybright."

Kai Sen's sword arm went rigid, its corded muscles tightening in definition.

"You believe you are special because of that birthmark?" Stone smiled. "That the gods in heaven—or underworld—have taken notice of you somehow? You are only an ordinary mortal, one of millions scuttling your blind way on earth like so many ants." Stone raised an arm and Kai Sen twitched, but stood his ground. The immortal swept his hand in the air as if he were holding a calligraphy brush, and Kai Sen's saber clattered to the floor as he lifted both hands to touch his own throat again.

Skybright surged forward, hissing deep.

"How could you *possibly* be special? Now you are no longer even accidently marked. Because do you know how brief human lives are in an immortal's eyes?" Stone made a twisting gesture with his fingers and the air suddenly chilled, suffused with snowflakes. They swirled, so abundant that they blinded Skybright with pristine white. "Like this," Stone snapped his fingers and all the snow fell to the ground at once, melting instantly. "Like this," Stone repeated, and the air crackled until Skybright's hair lifted from her head. Lightning blasted all around them, blazing, so intense and loud that Skybright cowered, covering her ears.

When the air cleared, she was momentarily deaf. She blinked the bright halos from her vision, and saw Zhen Ni curled in fetal position on the ground, sobbing into her knees. Skybright slid to her mistress and slipped her arm around her, trying to comfort her. The scent of burnt hair hung thick in the air.

"So it matters little to me who is sacrificed this time," Stone said. "And you will do very well."

Kai Sen stared at the immortal, his eyes rimmed in white from shock. When Kai Sen finally dropped his hands from his neck, she saw that his birthmark had disappeared, leaving pale skin, stark against his tan.

Skybright lifted high on her coil and hissed again, the sound too loud in her own sensitive ears after the lightning strikes. "Enough," she said, the word grating out like granite. She had covered her own shock by the time Stone turned to gauge her. The immortal's power was so intense, it hummed against her skin. She would show no weakness.

"She speaks," Stone said. "Finally."

She slithered through the unlatched cage door and stopped between Stone and Kai Sen, rising so she was as tall as the immortal. "I'll take Zhen Ni's place," Skybright said. Her voice was deep and rough, completely inhuman. She cringed inside to hear it.

"You?" Stone chuckled, amused. "We need a *human* sacrifice. From someone who has a soul. You are a demon."

"You're wrong." The words rasped, harsh and without inflection. "I have a soul just like any other mortal." Skybright thrust her wounded arm out. "I bleed red like any other mortal. And I'm capable of love, Stone. Unlike you."

Stone's cheekbones colored with two bright spots of anger, but they disappeared so quickly, Skybright wondered if she had imagined it. "So you do," he said.

"Don't do this, Sky," Kai Sen whispered from behind her. "Please."

The ground began to rumble, a violent earthquake beneath their feet.

"Sky! No!" Zhen Ni had run to throw herself against the bars. "Why didn't you tell me?" Her mistress was shaking her head, her face wild with sorrow and terror. "How could you have kept this from me?"

Zhen Ni's last words were tinged with the spirit that Skybright knew so well—and with anger and accusation. Skybright's throat snapped shut, as if large hands were crushing her windpipe. Kai Sen had betrayed her trust, and she had done the same to Zhen Ni. She flicked her tongue out and turned away from them both, unable to consider what she had lost within a matter of moments. "It's better this way," she hissed.

The floor undulated, throwing everyone to the ground, except for Skybright and Stone. Pebbles struck them from above, and dust stirred in plumes beneath. She had forgotten about the abbot, who pressed his brow into the dirt now, his lips moving in constant prayer. The other monks shouted from outside the cavern, and Skybright felt them flinging themselves against an invisible barrier; the entrance had been magically sealed.

"There might be an alternative," Stone said above the roar of shifting rocks.

Steam erupted from the yawning crack in the cavern, suffocating the air with sulfur.

"I won't lose either of them, Stone," Skybright said.

The immortal lifted a hand, palm facing the heavens, and the ground stilled so that her words rang out.

"Let me have you, Skybright, and we can forego the sacrifice."

"No." Kai Sen had leaped back on his feet behind her. Skybright swung her coil so she blocked him completely, afraid he might do something rash.

"I'd rather die than to surrender my soul to you, Stone," she said. "I may be young and half mortal, but don't belittle my intelligence."

Stone laughed, his first genuine one since he appeared in the cavern. "I do not want your soul. You are so much more intriguing with one."

"Then what?" she asked.

"You forsake your mortal life and come with me." He smiled, his countenance entirely different than before, more open than she had ever seen it.

Skybright felt sick. "For how long?"

"As long as I want," Stone replied.

"No," Kai Sen said again. "You don't know what he wants, what it could mean. It could stretch into eternity if he willed it."

"You are smarter than you appear," Stone said to Kai Sen. "The risk is Skybright's to take. But know that if you agree, you will never see your mistress or this false monk again."

"But that is no sacrifice," the abbot interrupted. He had risen to his feet, and pushed the walnut staff into the ground, his stance wide, as if he were certain the earth would begin quaking again any moment. "The covenant says—"

"A sacrifice can be interpreted in multiple ways, Wu," Stone cut in. "This is something Skybright would never give willingly. I should feel more insulted." The immortal stalked toward the abbot. "But if you take issue, I could just throw *you* down the crevice."

"Me? But—but I'm the abbot," he sputtered. "My monks need me."

"You agreed to this, Abbot Wu?" Kai Sen said incredulously. "You knew about the sacrifice of an innocent person all this time?"

Abbot Wu met Kai Sen's shocked gaze. "One does what is necessary, Kai Sen. For the greater good."

Kai Sen recoiled from the abbot, jaw clenched. He bent down to retrieve his saber, appearing as if he were ready to stab someone with it.

"Enough," Stone said. "The Great Battle will end today. Your job is done, Wu. You served well enough, and so would your soul."

Abbot Wu had stood his ground but took several steps back now, until he was pressed against the cavern wall. The staff rattled in his hand, and he clutched it against his body. His ruddy face had gone pale.

"I did not think so." Stone pivoted from the abbot. "Well, Skybright?"

Skybright stared at her hands. As much as she disliked the abbot, she wouldn't sacrifice another person's life for her own freedom. But what could Stone want with her? She knew it wasn't to bed her—he could have that, probably more easily than she was willing to admit. Her physical pull to the immortal was strong, though it was nothing like the love she felt for Kai Sen. But what did her love mean, when it only hurt the two people she cared about most? That was the painful truth. "Agreed, Stone," she finally said, the words as unpleasant to hear as she felt speaking them.

"Agreed." The immortal nodded and the ground rumbled again; the glowing red fissure that had widened began to close. The entire cavern shuddered so violently that Skybright's teeth clacked together. The mortals had thrown themselves to the ground again, but she slithered to the edge of the chasm, peering down. Heat blasted her face, so hot her eyebrows felt singed. Molten red careened endlessly into the earth's depths, but she could glimpse nothing beyond it.

Stone joined her side, one hand casually encircling his wrist behind his back, and watched with her, as the earth ground together, obliterating their view. "It is an interesting place," he said, as the sudden silence rang in her ears. "I will show you."

CHAPTER TWELVE

A moment after the breach had closed and the earth stopped rumbling, Stone slashed a portal in the air and pulled her through it, before Skybright could even throw a backward glance. They had stepped into the center of a circular space surrounded by high walls, with soft earth beneath them. It smelled of moss, and there was the comforting scent of wood.

Skybright winced as Stone unwound the cloth from her arm. Her dried blood had stuck the material against her flesh, and he had to gently ease it from her skin. She held her forked tongue as Stone, head bent, worked at the binding, as patient as the Goddess of Mercy herself. Finally, he was able to pull it free, revealing crusted blood and the three characters Abbot Wu had carved into the inside of her forearm.

"What do they say?" she asked. Skybright loathed the

deep, grating tones of her new voice.

"Show yourself true," Stone replied. His large hand held her wrist lightly, as if afraid he might cause her pain. But despite his soft touch, she still felt the strong heat of him. She imagined that his core was molten lava, just like the view she had glimpsed into the rift of the underworld. "I cannot heal this," Stone said. "It is a spell. But the enchantment will wear off once the wound closes. You will be able to shift back into your human form then." The immortal cursed. "I should have tossed Wu into the breach anyway, for inflicting this upon you."

He was kneeling before her, on one bended knee. A clean cloth soaked in something astringent materialized in his hand, and Stone began cleaning the blood from her cuts. Skybright held herself still, not wanting to show how much it stung. His concern seemed genuine, but it didn't ease her distrust. He could afford to be kind now that he held her captive.

"What was that display back there?" she asked, feeling combative and wishing to get a rise from him.

"Display?" The single word resonated between them.

"You reminded me of a rooster strutting among hens," Skybright grated out.

Stone paused mid-swipe over her tingling skin. One corner of his mouth tilted upwards. "You must remind mortals of their place," he said.

"You don't like Kai Sen very much."

He took his time running the soft material over her cuts, shaking the cloth so that the blood would magically vanish from it and become soaked again with fresh medicine. Whatever Stone was using might have stung her nostrils, but its coolness now soothed her wounds. "I suppose I do not," he finally replied. "He would have let you die in that cage, Skybright. It is unforgiveable. You are a rarity among demon kind."

His words burned more than the cuts, and it took all her willpower not to wrench away from him, to scream in anger and grief. The characters were rising like welts now, after he had cleansed the blood away.

"You must let me follow them," she said.

He laughed under his breath. "You promised to relinquish your mortal life then demand that I let you chase after those humans like an abandoned dog? I warned that you would never see them again, Skybright. They are no longer part of your life."

"I need to make certain that they're safe." A sob threatened to rise, but she swallowed it. She had sacrificed her old life, her ordinary life, to save Zhen Ni and Kai Sen. What was the use in mourning it? Besides, the tears would never come, trapped as she was in demonic form.

"The breach is closed. And your false monk is taking your mistress to her lover. Nothing will harm them." He began applying a salve to the cuts, with as much expertise as Nanny Bai ever did. "You will never again have to be a servile handmaid. It was beneath you."

She barely heard him in her agitation. "I didn't get to say goodbye." The words came out even gruffer than before. "You should have given me that."

"I owe you no favors. Would you really have wanted to speak with your mistress as your demonic self?" Stone stood, and she lifted high on her serpent body, so that their eyes were level. She may be shorter than him as a girl, but never while she was a serpent. "Give your lover another kiss?"

If he were mortal, she would have known he was being cruel. But as in so many instances with Stone, she didn't know for certain his true intent. "He's no longer my lover," she said, her throat constricted over the words.

"Not anymore. No." The immortal spoke with such quiet finality that she turned from him, hiding her burning face.

"Why did you do it?" She rasped through her thick veil of hair. The careful arrangement and pinning of her locks had come loose long ago. "Let me save their lives?"

"Because I knew you would agree to this in exchange," Stone replied.

"But why? What do you want with me?" She began twisting her hair as a distraction, trying to still the tremor in her arms.

Stone handed her hair pins, gold ones bejeweled with rubies and studded with exquisite jade, ornaments he pulled from thin air. "I have a debt to pay," he said.

Skybright jerked her head up.

"Your mother tried to reach me when she became pregnant with you." His expression was as unreadable as ever, but his features were softened by the silver glow that illuminated him. He appeared more human than she had ever seen him. "I was occupied. I did not know the circumstances of her … distress. You were—you are—an impossibility, Skybright. I thought nothing of her request. Time stretches long for an immortal. I believed I could go to her in a few years time, be of aid when I was less busy. I was wrong."

Skybright imagined Opal, a demon centuries old, suddenly with child. *An impossibility.* How confused and frightened she must have been, perhaps for the first time in her life. How desperate.

"Do you know who my father is?" she asked.

"Human, I am certain, by the looks of you. No doubt a victim of your mother's. I never knew Opal to take a lover solely for pleasure."

Her demonic mother dead from giving birth to her. Her mortal father murdered by her own mother after a single tryst. Skybright felt hysterical laughter bubble in her throat, and stabbed her nails into her arms to quell it. "But how? If I'm meant to be an impossibility."

"Our worlds are filled with anomalies," he said. "Perhaps you are what the mortals like to call a miracle—a demonic one. Or perhaps your mother crossed a higher deity, and the immortal wanted to teach her a lesson. I have no answer for you." Stone took a long stride to close the distance between them. "But Opal was a good friend and ally to me through many centuries. You have lived as a mortal for sixteen years, Skybright. I owe it to your mother to show you what it means to be a serpent demon."

Temptress, seductress, and murderer.

Would this be her life now? Would Stone force it upon her? Feeling trapped, she veered from him, unwilling to contemplate her endless future. "Where are we?" she asked. She slithered to the wall and ran her fingertips along it, feeling rough bark. Lifting her chin, she saw that the hollow trunk thrusted high above them, but a small opening at the top revealed the night sky, speckled with stars. There was nobody, god or mortal, within leagues of them.

"At one of my favorite places in your realm," Stone replied. "Nowhere of importance."

Skybright slid along the edge of the entire circle, trailing her hand against the ancient trunk. "One thing I don't understand— if the breach was at the base of Tian Kuan mountain, why did the demon attacks begin near the top?"

"Once the demons emerged from the breach, we were able to send them all across the kingdom through portals. The Great Battle always begins near the monasteries. It was what the monks were trained for, what gives them purpose and glory. The mortal sacrifice is a ritual that only Abbot Wu and his chosen successor would have witnessed, as agreed in the covenant."

Had Abbot Wu groomed Kai Sen to be his successor all these years? As the special one?

No moonlight filtered into the ancient hollow of the tree; the only light came from Stone himself. Skybright studied the immortal, standing tall, arms hanging loose at his sides. Majestic. She knew what he was capable of now, in an instant, with one small twist of his hand. "Thank you, Stone," she said, and touched her injured arm. "For this. And for saving me … from the abbot." Although he seemed to answer all her questions candidly, Skybright was still uncertain of Stone's true motives. It was better to remain in his good graces, to bide her time.

He smiled, and his expression was almost wistful. The feeling dissipated as soon as the curve of his mouth did. "I cannot let you track your mortal friends. But I may be able to offer you something else. It is something I have seen your mother do."

Her heart leaped.

Stone dropped gracefully to his knees and a bronze bowl manifested on the earthen floor. The immortal's silver glow gleamed off its smooth surface. He glanced into the bowl. Curious, Skybright slid closer to him. What did he see? The bowl was filled with water, reflecting nothing but Stone's glimmering face. "You think of what you wish to see, and it will appear for you," he said, moving aside.

Disbelieving, Skybright bent forward, peering into the bowl. She thought of her mistress and Kai Sen, closed her eyes and pictured them in her mind, then swallowed the lump rising in her throat. Skybright opened her eyes but the water reflected nothing back at her, not even her own image—she didn't glow as Stone did. She tried again, holding the image of these two people she loved, but kept her eyes wide open this time.

After a long moment, Stone leaned in, and her senses filled with his vibrant earthen scent. His shoulder pressed against hers, and she was aware of her own nakedness in a way that she hadn't been in a long time. He appeared armored, as he always was, but it wasn't cold metal she felt against her skin; it was the soft fabric of a tunic. Her heart began beating so fast that she felt faint, and she shook her head to dispel it. "It did not work," Stone said, more to himself than as a question directed at her, oblivious of his effect on her. "Opal was fully immortal. It may be your mortal half that is hindering the spell." He stared into the water, so close that if he turned his face, he could kiss her shoulder. Skybright swallowed and didn't move.

"Give me your hand," he finally said, and she extended her uninjured arm. He pricked her index finger, and one drop of her blood fell into the water. "Try again." And he shifted from her. The tension in her chest eased, and she was able to breathe again.

Skybright bent her head over the water, and almost jolted back when she saw Kai Sen and Zhen Ni's image cradled within the bowl.

Kai Sen and Zhen Ni stood in a narrow alley in front of a wooden door set in mud-colored walls. One faded paper door god was plastered on the door, its edges curling with age. They were dressed in the same clothes as when Skybright had last seen them, although both Zhen Ni and Kai Sen must have taken the opportunity to wash up. They seemed weary, but less travel worn.

"You're certain this was the manor where Lan told you she lived?" Kai Sen asked.

Skybright let out a low hiss, leaning in closer to the bronze bowl. She could hear Kai Sen speak as clearly as if she stood beside him.

Her mistress shifted on her feet, wringing her hands, her

impatience so obvious Skybright imagined she could taste it on her tongue. "Yes, I'd memorized it."

Kai Sen nodded then raised his fist to pound on the door. They waited long moments before it was pulled open by Lan's mother, Lady Fei. They truly were much lower in stature than the Yuans, if Lady Fei was answering the outer door herself. It wasn't a task that even Skybright had ever tended to.

"Zhen Ni!" Lady Fei exclaimed. She was dressed in a simple peach tunic and trousers, unadorned with decorations. "What an unexpected surprise." She gave Kai Sen a sidelong glance, and the corners of her rosebud mouth pulled down in a frown. "Is everything all right?'

"Lady Fei, I apologize for not sending notice that I would be visiting." Zhen Ni gripped her hands so, Skybright knew, she could still them. "No one has come from the Yuan manor before me?"

"No," Lady Fei said. "No one."

So the search group led by the head servant, Golden Sparrow, never arrived. Skybright watched her mistress in the reflected water, and felt the same sense of foreboding Zhen Ni did. Nothing good could have come to the group, when they had traveled while the breach to the underworld was still open.

"I see," Zhen Ni replied. Skybright could tell by the way her lips pursed a touch that she was thinking quickly, trying to gather herself. "Kai Sen was sent as my escort on this journey. He's training to be a monk and is a close family friend."

Kai Sen gave a formal bow, but not before Skybright caught the amused expression on his face.

"Welcome, Kai Sen," Lady Fei dipped her chin. "But why are you here, Zhen Ni?"

"I've come to visit Lan!" Zhen Ni's words were pitched too high, and she cleared her throat. "Is Lan here?"

Lady Fei's thin eyebrows lifted in surprise. "She is. Lan was so upset when she was sent back home early. I hope it wasn't over something she did? Your mother gave little in way of explanation."

So Lady Fei didn't know.

"No, not at all," Zhen Ni lied. "I was truly sorry to see her leave, too. I've missed her companionship so."

"Lan will be so pleased—Lan!"

Lan pushed her way from behind Lady Yuan, cheeks flushed pink as a peony. "Zhen Ni," she cried, before throwing her arms around Zhen Ni's neck. Her mistress laughed and hugged the girl back.

"Come in, come in," Lady Fei pulled the narrow door open, waving for Kai Sen and Zhen Ni to enter the modest courtyard. She turned away from the girls and walked down the stone path. "We were just sitting down for our midday meal." Her voice was faint.

In that moment, Zhen Ni leaned forward to kiss Lan full on her lips, and Skybright almost laughed aloud before throwing a hand over her mouth. It was just like her mistress, Skybright thought, to be so bold. Lan melted into Zhen Ni, fingers gripping the dirty collar of her mistress's tunic, kissing fervently, as if she couldn't bear to ever let Zhen Ni go.

Skybright felt her own heart swell for her mistress, and

the pain of losing Kai Sen for the first time. She hadn't let herself think about it, but Zhen Ni and Lan's reunion brought it achingly to the forefront of her mind.

Kai Sen had already vanished down the path, following Lady Fei. Skybright urged the scene to shift to him. Instead, the water within the bowl rippled, as if a pebble had been dropped into it, and the image dissipated, before reforming again.

Zhen Ni and Kai Sen sat in front of a camp fire, surrounded by pine trees towering like wraiths. Her mistress's eyes were red-rimmed, as if she had been crying. Skybright crouched closer to the bowl, wanting to comfort Zhen Ni, even though she didn't know what had upset her.

It was evening, and the fire cast leaping shadows on her mistress's face. Zhen Ni sat clutching a travel blanket around her shoulders—Skybright's own. She buried her face in the material for a moment, taking a deep breath. "This smells of her. Skybright's always smelled like—"

"The forest," Kai Sen said.

Her mistress lifted her face and smiled. "In springtime. When everything's in bloom and fragrant."

He nodded and cleared his throat, then picked up a stick to shift the wood within the fire, just for something to do.

"I didn't notice it. We were together so much—her scent was always there." Zhen Ni rubbed her eyes against the blanket. "I didn't notice until we were separated. Then she found me, and I hugged her and—" She faltered. "It wasn't until then I realized. And it felt like I was home again." Her soft features suddenly tensed. "You don't think Skybright is ... like them?"

Like them, Skybright thought. *Like all the other demons Kai had slain.*

Evil.

Kai Sen's dark eyebrows furrowed, and his hand rose unconsciously to touch where his birthmark had been. "Of course not. You know Skybright better than anyone. She's still the same girl you grew up with."

"Is she?" Zhen Ni spoke so softly that Skybright had to read her lips. The uncertainty in her mistress's face felt as if someone were pounding Skybright's chest with a hard fist. "I don't know what to believe anymore," her mistress finally said. "How do you know?"

"I can feel it." He pressed a hand against his heart. "Here."

Zhen Ni wrapped the blanket tighter around herself, and she and Kai Sen stared at each other until her mistress bowed her head. "I wish I could feel as certain as you do. I think the fact that I did know her better than anyone—was supposed to know her better than anyone—is what makes this hurt the most." She swiped her cheek with one hand, as if she could scrub the thoughts away. "But in the end, it's like I never knew her at all."

"That's not true," Kai Sen said. "I've had longer to accept the idea of Skybright's true nature. That's all."

Her mistress nodded, and Skybright suddenly caught herself. How could Zhen Ni still be her mistress when she was no longer her handmaid? Skybright blinked at the bright image of Kai Sen and Zhen Ni huddled before the fire. It only emphasized how much of an outcast she had become—spying on them from afar through magic, trapped in her demon form. She no longer belonged there, with them.

"Perhaps," Zhen Ni said. "I'm sorry I never got the chance to say goodbye. To hear her explain things to me herself." She rested her chin against her folded arms. "Thank you, for offering to take my place, Kai Sen."

"It was the right thing to do." Embarrassed, he turned away and began rummaging through his knapsack. "I was told by Abbot Wu after the breach closed that he wanted me to be his heir. That this was an honor. I was meant to witness the sacrifice." Kai Sen gave a slight shake of his head, and his hair fell across his brow. Skybright wanted to reach through the water, to brush it back, like she used to. "It didn't seem right. It didn't *feel* right, that he was willing to sacrifice an innocent life because of some age-old covenant. None of the other monks even know the truth." He cleared his throat. "Here, eat something," he said, passing her a wedge of sesame flatbread rolled with slices of stewed beef.

Skybright could smell it.

Zhen Ni smiled and extended her hand to accept the food. "You sound like Skybright." Her mistress took a few bites, and she and Kai Sen ate in silence for a while. "She told you her secret, but not me."

He wiped his hands on a cloth. "I found out by accident. And to think she believes now that I had abandoned her in that cage on purpose." His face hardened. "I swear I never would have if I'd known it was truly her. I'd been fighting monsters every night for weeks, and what kept me going, what kept me alive, was the image of her in my mind. When I first saw her as a serpent demon—when I almost *killed* her—" Kai Sen threw a rock with a swift furious motion into the dark forest—a motion that was entirely different from the young man who had shown Skybright how to skip stones across the water. Who had told her with a grin that he enjoyed jumping as a pastime. "I wasn't able to grasp it, to accept it. Now she may never know how much I love her."

"Oh, Kai Sen," Zhen Ni said, and her voice broke. Her mistress was thinking of her, Skybright knew, but she was also remembering Lan. "She knows."

Kai Sen flashed her mistress a half smile that almost made Skybright knock the bronze bowl over. She stilled, too afraid to disturb the image, to break the enchantment that allowed her this small comfort.

"Thank you for coming with me to see Lan. Skybright knew how much it meant to me. And it was like you were there in her stead." Zhen Ni sighed, a sigh that seemed to tremor through her entire being. So her mistress and Lan had parted ways, probably for the final time. Skybright's chest ached that she wasn't there to console her. Zhen Ni looked small, exposed, in that vast forest, but Skybright knew that her spirit was strong.

"You care for Lan," he said in a quiet voice. "You love her. As I love Skybright."

Zhen Ni's fingers clenched into fists. "How did you know?"

"I have eyes. It was obvious." Kai Sen arranged his knapsack and blanket so he could settle down for the night.

His fingers grazed the pale skin of his neck again, a nervous gesture that was new. It made him appear uncertain and vulnerable. "Love is obvious."

Zhen Ni's smile was tinged with sadness. "Do you think Lady Fei suspected?" She turned a jade bangle on her slender wrist—one that Skybright had seen on Lan. The only jewelry Lan had ever worn; Zhen Ni had gotten her keepsake.

"No. She didn't want to see it."

"And what do you think?" Her mistress posed the question to her feet, nestled beneath the blanket. "That I love another girl?"

"I think ... " Kai Sen lay down and folded his hands behind his head, gazing into the night sky. "I think that we don't choose who we fall in love with. It just happens." He closed his eyes. "Like springtime. Or the phases of the moon."

Zhen Ni lay down as well, shifting on her side, the way she always liked to sleep. They were quiet for some time, each lost in thought. Finally, her mistress said, "Will you return to the monastery now?"

Kai Sen dipped his chin to stare into the flames, and it felt as if he were looking directly at Skybright. "After all I've seen? I'm not certain the monastery is the place for me anymore. But I promised Abbot Wu I'd return to give him my answer, whether I would be his heir."

"I understand," Zhen Ni murmured. "Nothing seems the same anymore, not after everything that's happened ... not now that Skybright's gone."

The cords of Kai Sen's neck drew taut, and he looked away

from the fire. An owl hooted somewhere in the distance, one mournful note. "No," he replied, his response barely audible. "Nothing is the same anymore—"

The image wavered, then dissipated. Skybright was left staring into the still water, her drop of blood dissolving. She gasped, and reared back.

"Did it work?" Stone asked.

"You didn't see?"

"No. Only you are capable of capturing the vision. You peered into the bowl for just a moment." The immortal was lying on his side a short distance from her, his head propped up casually in one hand. Any other time, she would have found the sight absurd; Skybright had never seen him so at ease.

"What I saw lasted much longer than a moment." Skybright glanced into the bowl again. Her blood had vanished, leaving clear water once more. "But was it true, this vision?"

"Yes," he said.

"I want to see them again." She squeezed the finger Stone had pricked over the bowl. But the tiny wound had already closed magically. "Give me something sharp," she demanded, casting her serpent coil about for a jagged rock on the floor.

Stone was a silver streak of motion; he crouched beside her before she could blink. He pulled her away from the bronze bowl, and it pinged a resonant tone before evaporating from sight. "I think you have bled enough for one day."

"No! I need to know that they'll be all right." She pounded her fists against the ground, unwilling to believe that she would never see them again, never laugh with Zhen Ni or feel Kai

Sen's arms wrapped around her. A sharp pang shot through her injured arm and she slammed it down again and again, even more violently than before, savoring the pain. Her heartbeat thundered in her ears. This fury was better than the grief that threatened to overwhelm her. The rage was her own, but the sorrow and loss had been forced upon her.

Stone caught her hand before she could strike a third time and kissed the inside of her wrist. All her senses leaped to that one spot where his lips met her flesh. "They will be safe, Skybright. I promise." He drew her to him, and she leaned in, unable to resist.

"Why should I believe anything you say?" It still shocked her—that she sounded like the monster that she was.

"Because I have never lied to you," Stone replied. "Unlike those mortals you care for so much."

She had been breathing in Stone's deep earthen scent but shoved away from him then. "Yes, people do lie. Because they're imperfect. They feel deeply and they care." She realized a moment too late that she had referred to mortals as something separate from herself. Irritated, she slithered away from him, circling the hollowed trunk with unrestrained fervor. "And you were wrong, Stone." Skybright turned her head to see him gazing intently at her. "Kai Sen *is* special."

The immortal's expression didn't change.

Maybe she shouldn't have said it.

"Your mortal life is of the past, Skybright. Hold on to what memories you have, if it pleases you." Stone shimmered from view and manifested again right in front of her. She glimpsed silver starlight in his fathomless eyes, and the glowing embers of hell. He touched her cheek for the briefest moment, then said, "For you will forget them soon enough. And what you can recall will only feel like a fleeting dream."

Skybright hated him then. Because she knew Stone spoke the truth. Just as he always did.

But she would prove him wrong one day.

She had an eternity to do so.

ACKNOWLEDGEMENTS

When I started *Serpentine*, I knew that the major focus of this novel would be a strong sister friendship. So it isn't surprising that I want to acknowledge many female friendships in my own life, women who have encouraged me, boosted me, cheered me on during the writing and selling of this novel. It has been a long journey and would have been a much lonelier and harder one if not for these friendships.

Heartfelt thanks and fuzzy hugs to Malinda Lo, whom I most definitely consider a sister and best friend. Gratitude for the Mexico Retreat crew, especially Delia Sherman, Sarah Rees Brennan, and Holly Black, who took the time to read *Serpentine* then talk through both this novel and its sequel with me. Hugs to Cassie Clare for inviting me to these fabulous retreats and your support of my novels! You ladies are spectacular and amazing. Thank you to both Emily Kokie and Juliet Grames, who also critiqued this book and gave feedback and encouragement throughout my entire time as a published author.

To Ellen Oh, Marie Lu, Kristin Cashore, Leah Cypess, Shveta Thakrar, Megan Whalen Turner, Cinda Williams Chima, and Kate Elliott, whose stories I love and whose friendships I hold dear. You have all raised my spirits and inspired me more than you can know.

To Megan O'Sullivan (Raddest Fan Ever) of Main Street Books, who never fails to make me laugh in her enthusiasm for reading and boosting authors and spreading the love. To my favorite local indie, Mysterious Galaxy, and all the wonderful folk there, who have always supported me and greeted me with smiles. Eternal gratitude to the multitude of librarians who have encouraged me and supported my books since *Silver Phoenix* published in 2009. I have loved libraries since I was a kid, and I never thought there'd be a day when I'd be an author with books carried in them. Putting more diverse young adult novels onto library shelves is something I'm very passionate about and one of the reasons I keep writing!

Thank you to my old college roommate, Dr. Natalie Grunkemeier, pathologist extraordinaire, who continues to answer my random and grotesque questions on injuries, death, and the human anatomy.

Delicious pastries to my critique group: Kirsten, John, Tudy, Janice and Mark. My novels are so much better for the feedback you give me. Here's to many more years writing and critiquing together!

Many thanks to my agent Bill Contardi, who has been with me from the start. I couldn't have asked for a better Partner in Crime. And to my editor and publisher, Georgia McBride, without whom this book would have had a much different journey. Thank you for your passion, humor, drive and innovation! It's been a true pleasure to work with you and all the fine folk behind Month9Books.

And finally, last but never least, to Sweet Pea and Munchkin, growing faster than I can believe, and every bit as goat headed as their mom. I feel so lucky to have somehow plucked you from the stars to have you in my life. And to M, my goat headed love, who supports me in all my artistic endeavors.

San Diego, CA
November 9, 2014

Photo credit: Jen Kerker

CINDY PON

Cindy Pon is the author of *Silver Phoenix* (Greenwillow, 2009), which was named one of the Top Ten Fantasy and Science Fiction Books for Youth by the American Library Association's *Booklist*, and one of 2009's best Fantasy, Science Fiction and Horror by VOYA. The sequel to *Silver Phoenix*, titled *Fury of the Phoenix*, was released in April 2011. Her first published short story is featured in *Diverse Energies*, a multicultural YA dystopian anthology from Tu Books (October 2012). She is the co-founder of Diversity in YA with Malinda Lo and on the advisory board of We Need Diverse Books. Cindy is also a Chinese brush painting student of over a decade.

Social Links:

Website : http://cindypon.com
Facebook: https://www.facebook.com/pages/Cindy-Pon/44479388541
Twitter: https://twitter.com/cindypon
Tumblr: https://www.tumblr.com/blog/cindypon

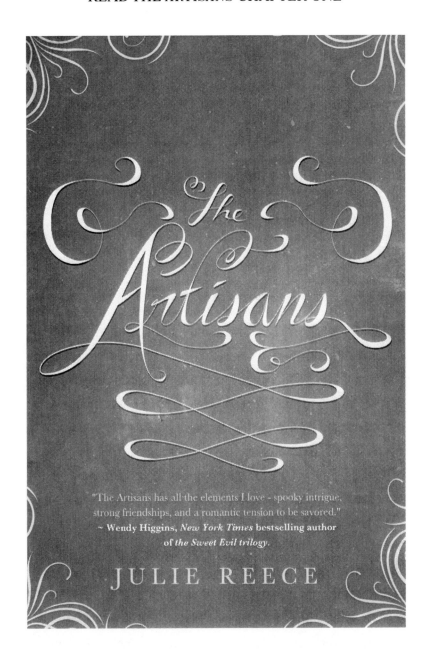

"The Artisans has all the elements I love - spooky intrigue,
strong friendships, and a romantic tension to be savored."
~ Wendy Higgins, *New York Times* **bestselling author**
of *the Sweet Evil trilogy.*

JULIE REECE

The Before

The winter of two thousand nine brought influenza, taking twenty-seven souls from Colleton County, South Carolina. The good people of Sales Hollow deposited their corpses in the ground. The following spring, Hurricane Isaac hit the coast, and the earth gave them back.

Scandal covered the news. It seemed the proprietors of Coffee Funeral Home took money from several grieving families to cremate their loved ones, including my late mother, Ida Elizabeth Weathersby. They buried the bodies in their own backyard. Granted, the Coffee family plantation consisted of sixty acres. Still, the urn filled with pasty white sand was a poor substitute for my mother's actual remains, and the undoing of my stepfather, Ben.

While the sheriff handcuffed Wade, Jerry, and Thomas

Coffee and led them away, the deceased, who had resided up until that point in shallow graves behind the crumbling Coffee family tennis courts, were identified through their dental records.

Some things you never see coming. Like Ben's attempt to smuggle a gun into the courthouse at the Coffee brothers' arraignment, his subsequent arrest, release, and emotional breakdown.

Other things are glaringly obvious. Like the crippling pain of someone you care for. Dreams wither and waste away much the same as an apple core curls under the hot southern sun.

What sacrifice is too great when you love someone?

I decided there was none—the day I gave my freedom away.

The Middle

Chapter One

Sweat drips from my temple as I push a needle through my friend's torn flesh. Years of sewing custom clothing enable me to make tiny sutures in his skin, close the three-inch gash in his shoulder. I hope it won't leave another scar.

Dane sits on the closed toilet seat in my bathroom. The space is too tight, the air between us close and cloying. I toss my head, shaking damp hair away from my eyes. Blood trickles down his bicep as I pierce him again. Today makes the third time I've sewn him up. He doesn't complain about the pain. I don't ask what pissed his father off this time.

Dane Adams introduced himself in my English Literature class a year ago when he first moved to Sales Hollow from Nashville. He missed the drama concerning the Coffee brothers, my mother's corpse, and Ben's trial. After Ben got out of the psyche ward, my name became synonymous with social pariah. People don't look me in the eye anymore. Pity, guilt, fear … whatever the reason, I make them uncomfortable.

Dane doesn't treat me that way.

Angry and incessant buzzing breaks my concentration. I scowl at the window where a fly is trapped between the screen and the world outside. I can't set him free. The windows are painted shut. Refocusing on my task, I complete two more stitches, tie them off, and cut the thread. Not bad. I tape gauze loosely over the angry wound and straighten. He grabs my fingers, giving them a tender squeeze.

Sorrow mixed with gratitude shines from his dark brown eyes. I clear the knot from my throat. "All fixed up, bro."

I take a step back allowing Dane to stand. The guy dwarfs the little space. He leans around me, lifting a white cotton tee from its place on the sink countertop.

"Wait, you'll tear your stitches." I help him stretch the fabric over his head and cover his impressive torso.

When he showed up earlier, he was wearing the new, camel-colored leather jacket I made him. Double lapel over a red button up paired with dark stonewashed jeans and boots. Sharp. He can't afford to pay me for the clothes I make him. I wouldn't take his money if he could. The dumb guy spent ten minutes hanging out, bleeding, until finally admitting he needed stitching up.

I glance at my wrist for the hundredth time. The watch is my own design, fashioned from discarded parts into a silver, steampunk beetle. The wings slide to reveal a clock face. Two forty-five AM.

"How long has he been gone?"

The 'he' referred to is my stepfather Ben. I raise my eyes to find Dane studying me. He lifts an eyebrow, waiting. My shrug is my only answer.

A heavy breath leaks out as my friend leans against the wall. "You should have called me when he went missing."

Hoping to avoid an interrogation, I head out of the bathroom and into the storage area of our leather repair shop. The lease doesn't cover our living here, of course, but since we lost our apartment two months ago, we had no place else to go.

Dane follows and I face him. "It's not your job to protect us all the time. You've got your own problems. I can handle this."

"As if." He snorts. "Don't I always find him? You need me. Besides, I'm scary as hell."

I can't help my smile. He *is* scary as hell. Severe facial bone structure makes him look perpetually pissed off. He's tall and skinny but in a wiry, muscular sort of way. The boy can bend metal pipes with his bare hands. I've seen him.

Our rent is overdue. I glance at the fabric piled on the work counter. Resentment sprouts like weeds in my chest. "I have a clothing order to finish …"

"I know you're broke, but can you sew while you're worried about him?" Dane tosses his long, rust-colored dreads over his shoulder revealing the fresh bruise on his neck.

Anger burns a hole in my gut, but there's nothing I can

do to help him. Or anyone else it seems. "I can't always drop everything and go looking for Ben!" I slink to my sleeping bag on the floor. I don't know why I'm yelling. The people I'm angry at aren't in the room to hear. "Sorry. I'm sorry."

"Don't be sorry, Rae. I get it." He scratches his chin. "Leave him be for one night. He'll turn up."

What I haven't told him is that I've already been looking.

All night long, I searched Ben's usual haunts—the liquor stores, card games, and bars he frequents—with no sign. Jacob, who owns the pawnshop Ben visits, said the hot game in town was one held near the docks at Maddox Industries, a textile warehouse district turned seedy clubs and bars. The name Maddox is like a shadow over our town, drawing a collective shudder. Everyone has heard the rumors: money, crime … bodies in the river.

Surely Ben knows better.

I meet Dane's gaze. "I'm lucky to have you looking out for me."

He grins. "Yes you are. Should we go find Ben?"

"Do you mind if we just chill here for a while first?" The truth is, between school, work, my earlier search, and treating Dane's wound, I'm exhausted.

"Whatever you need."

Gratitude pours out in the form of a sigh. I lean my head back against the concrete block wall to rest. Edgar, my twenty-five pound Maine Coon, climbs around in my lap and lies down. He's too big to fit, but that doesn't stop him from trying.

Shirt and shoes discarded, Dane flops on top of Ben's

sleeping bag a few feet away. His long dreads spill across his brown, tatted shoulders. From this angle, he looks like the monster from the movie *Predator*. The thought makes me smile.

He's snoring in minutes. I've lost count how many nights he's slept over. Though his father owns a physical house, the fact he prefers our storeroom floor says everything about his home life. The unforgiving linoleum digs into my tailbone through my thin sleeping bag, and I shift, exacting a complaint from Edgar, whose weight puts my legs to sleep.

My cat purrs, his whiskers vibrating with the contented sound as I stroke his black fur. I wish I were as unconcerned, but honestly, I'm too keyed up over Ben's prolonged absence to think of much else. Anytime he's missing longer than forty-eight hours, bad things happen. A grueling night of searching turned up nothing, so we wait here. School starts in a few hours, but I won't sleep.

Pounding on the back door sends Edgar scrambling for the corner. Dane's up in seconds, chest heaving, my baseball bat clenched in his hand. I hold up a palm and slowly step to the back door. The one leading to the alley reserved for loading and deliveries. "Who's there?" I ask.

"Jacob. Let me in!"

Fingers tangle as I unbolt the lock and push the door wide. Jacob stands in the sickly orange glow of a buzzing street lamp in a rumpled trench coat. His green Cutlass idles in the background. Hanging limp at his side is Ben. "Come inside," I whisper.

Dane drops the bat and rushes forward. His stitches might rip, but there's no use trying to stop him. He lifts my unconscious stepfather like he's a small child and lays him on the other sleeping bag. His body is too thin, wasting from addiction and despair. His clothes are covered in black smears. A purple bruise blooms like an inkblot across his forehead. His nose and lip are busted.

"Is he okay?" Dane asks what I can't. I rub my forehead where an ache starts, weary of this scene.

Jacob hitches his broad shoulders, stretching his fleshy neck to one side. I feel for him. As my stepfather's oldest friend, I've lost count of the times he's brought Ben home. "Took a beating, but yeah, he'll be okay."

I stare at Ben's listless form on the floor. He stinks of cheap booze and body odor. It's hard to get really clean in the little sink in our half bath, not that he tries.

"Raven?"

My head snaps up. I have no idea how long Jacob has been calling my name. "Sorry, what?"

"There's more." He rubs his neck and stretches again. "I hate to tell you this kiddo, but Ben hawked your mother's wedding ring last night." My chin drops. "Well, you don't think I'd let him pawn it in my shop, do you? Don't you look at me like that!"

"Sorry, I just—"

"I know, sweetie. Lost every dime in a poker game." He shakes his head, stroking a hand down his ample belly. "I never thought he'd give up your momma's ring, never that."

My heart cramps with every word. "He left the casino but showed up again an hour later, begging for a chance to win his money back. When they told him to get out, he went wild, tore the place up. He was so drunk, he ... started a fire. It was an accident, but the place went up like a match. Thousands in damage. I can't see any way out for him this time."

An arm comes around my shoulder, and I lean into it. The next thing I know I'm sitting Indian-style on the floor, staring at Ben. How did I get here? My cheeks are wet. My chest tightens in a vise grip of fear, and I release a sob. I'm so tired. All I want is to curl up and sleep. Forget.

"It's okay, Jacob, I'll stay with her."

Dane? His voice is distorted, as if he's floating somewhere above me. Wouldn't that be nice? All of us floating away together, like puffy clouds on a summer's day.

"Will they arrest him now?" Dane asks.

"These people don't arrest you, boy. They make you disappear, you know that. Best to get him out of town. Oh, Ben had a letter with him ..."

I glance up at Jacob. Our old friend pulls a thin, white envelope from his coat pocket. "Give it to me," I say.

He hesitates, gaze darting from Dane to me and back.

"It's all right, guys. I need to know." Dane nods to Jacob, and the letter finds its way into my hand. I'm not sure how long I sit there. Shoes scuff the dull linoleum. I'm vaguely aware when the door clicks shut behind Jacob as he leaves. Outside, his motor revs, and then fades as he drives away. The letter still waits in my shaking hand.

"Give it here, little Rae." Dane pries the envelope from my tightly clenched fingers. "We'll read it together, want to?"

Edgar curls up next to Ben still crumpled on the floor. I don't speak. I can't.

Mr. Benjamin Edward Weathersby,

This letter is an attempt to collect a debt. Please meet me in my office at 11:00 AM Friday morning on September 21st to discuss my terms for your restitution. The judgment has been recorded and documented in my ledger and needs to be paid.

Come alone. Do not contact the authorities, do not sign the payment arrangement attached to this letter, and do not respond to this communication in any way other than to meet me in person. If you fail to appear, I will take whatever action necessary to collect the debt owed me.

Sincerely,
G. N. Maddox

Blood turns to slush in my veins, thick, barely moving, slowing my ability to hear, or breathe, or think. *The* Mr. G. N. Maddox. Are the rumors true? Crime boss, ruthless killer, an evil beast incapable of compassion or mercy. Of all the people Ben could owe ... I stare at my hands. My fingers quake, but I can't feel them. Everything's gone numb.

Ben. I can't lose him.

"What is today?" I ask. My voice is quiet but hard as an ice pick. Every sacrifice I've made to hold on to what's left of my family seems in vain.

"September 21st. That meeting's four hours away." Dane drops down on my sleeping bag. "There's no way Ben can make it, Raven. Look at him."

"It doesn't matter, bro. Can you check on him after school today? I'm going to skip."

"Why?" He props himself up on his elbows. "I'm almost afraid to ask what you're planning in that stupid, stubborn head of yours."

"Ben's not going to make the meeting at Mr. Maddox's house this morning."

Dane scowls as if he knows what's coming, and I think he does.

"I am."

OTHER MONTH9BOOKS TITLES YOU MIGHT LIKE

HUNTED

VESSEL

MINOTAUR

I HEART ROBOT

Find more awesome Teen books at Month9Books. com

Connect with Month9Books online:

Facebook: www.Facebook.com/Month9Books

Twitter: https://twitter.com/month9books

You Tube: www.youtube.com/user/Month9Books

Blog: www.month9booksblog.com

Request review copies via publicity@month9books.com

THE·SINNERS SERIES

HUNTED

ABI KETNER & MISSY KALICICKI

VESSEL

LISA T. CRESSWELL

SOON THE WORLD WILL KNOW WHAT REALLY
HAPPENED IN THE LABYRINTH.

MINOTAUR

PHILLIP W. SIMPSON

I ♥ ROBOT

SUZANNE VAN ROOYEN

CPSIA information can be obtained at www.ICGtesting.com
Printed in the USA
LVOW07s1737140915

454101LV00005B/374/P